I0683227

Parting Ways

Unwilling to leave...unable to stay

by

Patrick Sipperly

Parting Ways

By Patrick Sipperly

©2011 by Patrick Sipperly

All rights reserved.
This book or parts thereof may not be reproduced in any form, stored in a retrieval system, or transmitted in any form by any means without prior written permission of the authors, except as provided by United States of America copyright law.

Cover design: Patrick Sipperly

Published by: TreasureLine Publishing
www.TreasureLinePublishing.weebly.com

ISBN: 978-1-61752-198-0

www.PatrickSipperly.com
www.TreasureLineBooks.com

The following is a work of fiction. Names, characters, places, and incidents are fictitious or used fictitiously. Any resemblance to real persons, living or dead, to factual events or to businesses is coincidental and unintentional. The views expressed are solely those of the author.

Printed in the United States of America.

Acknowledgments

The number of people I wish to thank for helping me to weave scriptural truths, personal experiences and a little imagination together into this story are almost countless.

I must first thank my wonderfully supportive parents, Jack and Jo Ann Sipperly, who encouraged me to pursue my dreams – whatever they were that week.

To my beautiful wife, Charla, who is living proof that God answers prayer. She never ceases to amaze me.

To the people who encouraged me to write in the first place: Michael Taylor, Cindy Martinez, and Linda Boulanger.

I also owe a huge thank you to my fabulous editors Chris Janzen and Dolly Rix. So much red ink...

Finally, I must thank all the godly people who helped me to know Jesus Christ and to worship him in spirit and in truth over the years. From the small Pentecostal church in Kenai, Alaska, to my Bible school classmates in St. Paul, Minnesota, to the many ministers and families in Portland, Oregon, to friends and neighbors in Colorado, and to the many others I'm getting to know online, I've learned so much from each of you! Your impact on my life will have to wait for eternity to be fully measured.

Thanks to all of you.

Chapter One

Daylene Bishop was a spiritual nomad; a woman of the wind. She embraced a variety of beliefs, faiths and gods which was a laughable contrast to the rest of her family. Her parents who were proud atheists. Charles and Dorothy Bishop were living caricatures of wealthy elites who looked down upon the "little people" of Richmond, Virginia. Their hatred of anything Christian propelled their success as ACLU lawyers, activists in various causes, and anchored their position firmly to the hard-left side of the local Democrat machine. A dream they shared was the end of "Christ" in any public setting or holiday celebration. Faith in God, after all, was a crutch. Who needs crutches?

Daylene was an unexpected surprise to the Bishops. Not only were they in their mid-forties when Dorothy became pregnant, but neither wanted children. Abortions weren't legal in 1953 but they were still attainable with the right connections. In the second month of her pregnancy, Dorothy planned to end her little *inconvenience* thinking it was best for any career-minded woman. She knew of a doctor outside Richmond who'd lost his medical license for performing surgery while drunk. He agreed to assist her privately in the basement of his home.

All that changed the night before her scheduled procedure. At two in the morning, Dorothy awoke from a horrible, suffocating dream. She envisioned herself being strangled from inside her own womb. She struggled in vain for what seemed hours trying to escape the chilling grip of an unknown force. She awoke drenched in sweat, flailing her arms and screaming.

Seven months later, an eight and half pound baby girl joined the Bishop family.

Daylene was a bright, curious child who was fascinated with the world around her. She was spellbound by new colors and sounds. Every day was filled with something to see, noises to hear and smells to absorb. She especially liked the sights others couldn't see.

One afternoon while Dorothy folded laundry, she watched three-year-old Daylene looking at something, smiling and pointing. Dorothy looked to see what was so amusing to her daughter. It was a blank wall. "What baby?" she asked. "What do you see?"

"Him, Mama! He's big," she answered. Then she turned and skipped down the hall, giggling all the way.

Dorothy's eyes ran the entire length of the wall from end to end. There was nothing there.

It wouldn't be the last of such experiences.

Daylene grew into a carefree girl with light blue eyes that sparkled with life, and thick brown hair framing her attractive, freckled face. From high school on, she disagreed with her parents on almost every topic, especially spirits, ghosts, the afterlife and God. She read horoscopes, carried crystals, learned about real witches and once participated in a late night séance. What she saw beyond the dim candlelight was so terrifying, she was too afraid to sleep for two days. She never went to another one.

After graduating from high school, Daylene moved into a five bedroom Victorian with three girlfriends. The house was in desperate need of paint and sundry repairs, but the neighborhood was peaceful and the rent affordable. She worked at an organic bakery within walking distance, much to her parents' chagrin. They did all they could to steer their daughter toward law school, or at least college and a lasting career. Daylene would have none of it. She was a leaf riding the breeze, taking each day as it came.

Daylene loved her new surroundings and being with her friends. They were light-hearted, kindred spirits who called themselves the "house girls." They worked together, shared responsibilities and divided the bills equally.

Every Friday night, the girls threw a party and invited friends and co-workers to celebrate the end of a work week. There was never a shortage of beer or boys and the festivities would frequently roll on to sunrise. Occasionally the police showed up to remind them to keep the noise down, but those visits were rare.

One icy February morning, Daylene was too sick to go to work. After the third day of feeling ill, she went to a nearby clinic where she was informed she was going to be a mother. She started laughing.

Then the tears flowed. She couldn't be sure who the father was so the tears flowed harder.

Her roommates couldn't have been more supportive. They helped Daylene prepare for the new life on its way. Her parents were less than excited. Charles Bishop was puzzled that Daylene didn't want the father of the child involved. Daylene's only response was, "It's my baby. I don't want him to interfere...whoever he is."

Earlier that year, a decision was rendered by the U.S. Supreme Court on a case widely known as Roe V Wade. After January 22, 1973, abortions were legal in America. Though it didn't matter to Daylene, she noticed that her mother never brought up the subject of abortion. Not even once.

He arrived on a humid November morning. Daylene named him Peter. It was a sweet and strong name that she'd always liked. It meant *a rock* or *a stone*.

"Welcome to Earth, Peter Bishop," she said to the tiny form looking up at her with sleepy eyes, "I think you're going to like it here."

Out of the corner of her eye she saw something move next to the nurse who had brought Peter in to her. It was the form of a man. The attentive nurse seemed oblivious to his presence. Daylene's eyes rose slowly up the towering figure with massive shoulders. She fixed upon his translucent face; every hair on her neck stood on end. The hidden man seemed to be looking at the child. Then he looked directly at her.

He was smiling.

Chapter Two

To Daylene, Peter seemed to grow an inch a day. He was healthy, responded to her with rapt attention, and was her constant joy. He loved the affection from the women who were equally thrilled to have a little man running around.

Daylene was able to juggle motherhood and work with the help of the house girls and her mother. Dorothy Bishop was never more than a phone call away and never tired of having Peter with her.

After a Friday evening dinner, Charles watched his wife while she played blocks with Peter in the living room. "You've become quite a grandmother, haven't you?" he remarked.

Dorothy moved some stray hairs out of her eyes as she sat up and smiled. "Yes, I have, haven't I?"

They pondered each other for a moment in silence. Charles noticed a hue of regret in her eyes.

On the mornings Daylene opened the bakery, she took Peter with her. He was bundled tightly in his basket and slept soundly while Daylene kneaded dough and prepared various baked items. Peter would awake to the amazing aromas of fresh sourdough bread, cookies, and muffins. He savored everything Daylene made except carrot cake. It didn't agree with him. Simple bread amply buttered on the other hand, was his absolute favorite. Then came another discovery...coffee.

Daylene was on the phone trying to get a special order filled and accidentally gave Peter her lukewarm, richly creamed cup of coffee. He took the paper cup from his mother and took a tentative sip. When she finally hung up, she looked back to her smiling son, who was holding her empty cup and licking his lips.

"Peter, you drank my coffee."

Peter, obviously very proud of himself, motioned for more. Daylene looked at her beaming boy then grabbed something off the shelf. "Well, if you want more coffee," she said with a wry smile, "you should have your own cup."

The days turned into a blur of years. Two of the house girls got married and moved out. By mid-April it was obvious the house was going to be too expensive for only two meager incomes. Daylene took Peter and moved into a nearby apartment. Long before it seemed possible, that summer was almost over.

While studying her tired eyes in the bathroom one morning, Peter came in, sat down on the toilet and watched her with a thoughtful expression.

"Whatcha thinking about Peter Piper?" she asked.

Peter wrinkled his face. "Am I going to school with the other kids tomorrow?"

"You're six. You're supposed to."

Peter smiled and skipped happily out of the bathroom. Apparently she'd gotten that answer right. Daylene turned back to the mirror when it hit her. "Oh my God! He's six. No wonder I've got wrinkles!"

School was a whole new world of coloring, making new friends and playing ball in a great big yard. Peter regularly came home with stories about what happened in school, who his favorite teacher was that week, and how one of his friends got into trouble for eating glue. He also came home full of questions. "Why do they always pick on me?" or "How old do I have to be to fly a plane?" The tougher questions came later. "All my friends have dads. Where's my dad?" "I like Sandy the best 'cause she shares her candy with me. Can I bring her home?"

Some questions made her laugh, others made her cry, but she welcomed them all. She loved her son completely and Peter adored his mother, even if she didn't know *exactly* how many gallons were in the ocean.

Mother and son shared another connection as well. It was a spiritual sensitivity. Peter couldn't see the invisible world swirling around like his mother could, but he possessed an understanding of it.

They complemented each other. He could feel what she could see, and sometimes knew why something was happening.

One afternoon, Daylene and Peter drove State Route 603 out to the Metro Richmond Zoo. Peter was sound asleep in the passenger seat after a big lunch of burgers and fries. Daylene was singing along to the Romantic's *"What I like About You"* on the radio, when a large sedan sped past them out of nowhere. Her eyes followed the car, and the unforgettable image chasing it. It resembled a dark cape or a black tarp whipping and twisting wildly in the wind. The thick mist caught the vehicle and melted into it. The car instantly accelerated. Daylene eyes remained fixed on the car until it rounded the corner out of view.

"We'll see them again when it's hotter," Peter said.

Daylene looked on. "I don't know. They're going pretty fast." She looked over to her son; Peter was sound asleep and hadn't moved.

Three miles later they drove past the car. It had flipped on its side, and was completely engulfed in flames.

Chapter Three

When Peter was nine, he was invited to go to church with a friend from school. Daylene didn't see any harm and thought some quiet time for a couple of hours might be just what the doctor ordered.

At eight thirty, a big blue bus arrived out front. It was filled with children and had the words, "Come to Sunday School With Me" painted on the side in bright rounded letters. Peter's friend jumped out and ran up to the door to get him. Daylene waved good bye as the bus pulled away. This soon became a regular Sunday event.

After several weeks of attendance, Peter came home after church and announced, "I love God, Mama. I'm going to be a preacher and tell the world about Jesus!"

Daylene rubbed her son's head. "Well, sure you love Jesus, Peter. But he's the only God you know. You need to meet some others before you go tell the world."

Daylene exposed Peter to various churches, read to him about other religions, and even visited meetings where people hummed and burned incense. Nothing interested Peter. After every religious excursion Peter asked to go back to the church where he'd met Jesus. Daylene didn't push. She let Peter return to the Christian church.

The following Sunday, Peter waited at the window for the big blue bus. At 8:45 it still hadn't arrived. At 9:35, Peter knew that church had started and he wouldn't be getting picked up. He was heart-broken. He turned to ask his mother for a ride, but saw that she was sleeping on the sofa and he didn't want to wake her.

At 12:30 in the afternoon, Peter called the church office hoping talk to someone who could make sure he always had a ride. Peter was relieved when one of the pastor's rowdy teenage sons answered the phone. When Peter asked why the bus didn't come and get him, the boy replied, "We don't pick up poor kids anymore." Then he laughed and hung up.

Peter quietly set the receiver down. He avoided his mother and went down the hall to his room. After closing the door softly, he sat on the edge of his bed devastated. Peter didn't know he was poor or why it mattered. He didn't know what had happened or why he wasn't welcome anymore. As hot tears rolled down his red cheeks, he only knew one thing. He was never going back to that church again.

Peter's teenage years were mix of triumphs and tragedies. He did average work in high school, except for drama and speech where he was exceptional. He came alive before a crowd and was reprimanded often for being the attention getting clown of the class.

Girls were becoming young women right before the boys, though they were enigmas and impossible to understand. They'd flirt with Peter one moment, then forget his existence the next. It was maddening. "I can't stand them!" he exclaimed to a friend. "I wish they'd all jump off a cliff!"

One triumph Peter enjoyed was running. He excelled at cross country and track. He added a shelf in his bedroom for his many trophies and medals. Daylene was proud of her speedy boy and made it to every local meet, except one. It was against their cross-town rivals. Peter took second place in the 200-yard dash, bested only by the reigning state champion and by only a split second. Peter so wished his mother could have seen him, but she was sick at home.

When Peter arrived back at the house after the meet, Daylene was sitting on the sofa crying. He dropped everything in his arms and went to her. "Mom, what's wrong? You okay?" he asked.

She pointed to the television. On the screen was a famous televangelist preaching from an enormous stage. She blew her nose and said, "I think I just accepted Jesus, Peter."

He sat down beside his mother. It was a surreal moment. Televangelists were his mother's favorite target. She despised their emotional antics and mocked their dramatic preaching. "They're all crooks!" she'd say. "It's all about the money, Peter. Like God's broke or something." Yet here she was crying and trembling, hanging on every word of the preacher who kept calling for people to come give their hearts to the Lord.

Daylene put her arm around her son and held him close. Peter watched with his mother as crowds of people streamed to the front of the huge auditorium. He remembered when he had walked down a carpeted aisle to an old altar with his friend and gave his heart to the Lord. Afterward he felt so light he thought he could float. He wanted to become a preacher to help everyone feel that way... to feel right with God.

Peter leaned back into the loving embrace of his weeping mother and just smiled.

We don't pick up poor kids anymore.

"Well," he thought, "if we can't make to Jesus, looks like Jesus will make it to us."

Sundays became church via TV for Peter and his mother. They'd flip through the channels watching religious shows. Great Sunday Celebration was their favorite. It featured lively music and different pastors. One morning, the same man that led Daylene to Jesus was back on stage. The text at the bottom of the screen read, "Rev. Jay Hammond Live From St. Louis, MO." Jay Hammond became their favorite preacher. Whenever the sharply dressed, articulate Brother Hammond would preach, Peter listened as much with his heart as with his ears.

Daylene bought a couple of battered King James Bibles from the Thrift Store. She put hers next to the crystals and a brass pyramid by her bed. Peter put his on his trophy shelf. When Great Sunday Celebration came on, they'd race to see who would find the scriptures first as they appeared on the bottom of the screen. The reading was usually over by the time they stumbled their way to the verse. Peter decided to memorize the books of the Bible so he could get to the verses before his mother.

If Daylene was interested in men, Peter was unaware of it. Only twice had a man ever come over for dinner. Neither returned for a second helping.

When Peter was sixteen, he invited a schoolmate from his biology class over to study. Her name was Emily. She was a slender girl with curly blonde hair and pleasant features. She was well developed for her age and the life of the party at school. When Peter introduced

9

Emily to his mother however, she was suddenly stumped for words. Daylene's first question to Peter's friend was, "So, what exactly are you studying in biology?"

Peter had never seen his mother look at anyone the way she looked at Emily. Nor had he seen his friend so nervous and shy. It was the most uncomfortable evening he could remember. He didn't invite girls to his house after that.

Chapter Four

At the beginning of Peter's senior year, he started working after school and on weekends at the neighborhood convenience store. It was owned and operated by a tall, older gentleman named Thomas Greene who wore thick horn-rimmed glasses. Mr. Greene was a meticulous man who almost had a personality. When he wasn't there minding the store, his 33-year-old son Melvin was. Melvin was a complete idiot who wore the same black and gray t-shirt and baseball cap every day. When he wasn't staring out the window with his mouth open, he talked about how he was going to make it big in the world.

"How exactly are you going to do that, Melvin?"

After his customary three second pause to any question, Melvin turned to Peter. "What do you mean?"

Peter hung the broom and dust pan back on the nail behind the front door. "Every day you tell me you're going to live in a mansion and drive a Ferrari. Where are you going get all this money?"

Melvin let go of a slow belch and scanned the ceiling tiles.

"I think you live in fantasy land," Peter said shaking his head.

"Hey!" the older man shot back.

Peter stopped and waited to hear the recipe for wealth.

"I don't live in fantasy land. I live in Richmond."

At that moment, Peter was convinced Mr. Greene had really hired him to keep an eye on Melvin.

What Peter enjoyed most about the job was he regularly worked with coffee. The store offered a free cup with any purchase. As an employee, Peter could have as much as he wanted during his shift.

After Peter finished pricing a case of green beans on a particularly slow and humid Saturday, he took a calculator and a notepad and started making a list. Melvin watched his younger co-worker with suspicion. After adding up the costs of coffee, filters, cups, stir sticks, powdered cream, and sugar, Peter came up with a cost of about six and a half cents per eight-ounce cup of coffee.

Melvin watched Peter finalize his list then asked, "What about the brewer? Can't make no coffee without a brewer."

Peter looked at Melvin and then back to his list. He was right. The most expensive element, the brewer, was not on the list. That would change the per cup cost dramatically.

"And don't get no cheapy one neither. I don't know why dad got this piece of junk," he pointed to the filthy coffee maker near the store entrance. "We've had the repair guy out a couple of times already. No warranty. Gotta pay big bucks to get it fixed."

The pearl of wisdom from Melvin caught Peter by surprise. But it was a mere flash of brilliance. In the next breath, he was the old Melvin again, holding up his magazine so a bare Miss July would unfold before him. "Now that's what I'm talking about!" he said with a crooked grin.

Peter moved away from the X-rated picture show and added the words "quality brewer" to his list.

In a blink, it was the summer of '92 and Peter Bishop was a high school graduate. Like most graduates from Thomas Jefferson High, he wasn't sure what would happen next. His grandparents regularly hinted at the benefits of having a college degree. His mother encouraged him to do whatever he loved doing, college or not.

"I think God has something for me mom," Peter confessed. "But I don't know exactly what it is. I still want to tell the world about Jesus, but I don't want to be poor. Those preachers on Great Sunday Celebration aren't poor."

He watched his mother folding laundry. "Do you think I could do that? Be one of those preachers on television?"

Daylene emptied a full basket of clean clothes onto the bed and smiled. "If God has a slot open Peter, I think you're the first one he'd pick. Until then, you might need to get up to the slot that's open for you now at the store before you're late."

To everyone's surprise, Melvin did make it big. He was a $2.2 Million Virginia lottery winner at another convenience store and struck out on his own two days after cashing in the winning ticket. Peter was promoted to assistant manager and learned more about business, ordering, inventory control, and the expensive realities of shoplifting by some of the most surprising offenders.

With his new schedule, he saw less and less of his mother. He was still asleep when Daylene left for work in the mornings, and she was usually in bed when he got home from the store around midnight. Dinner together was rare, but they still gathered together in front of the TV every Sunday morning to hear the Word preached by Brother Jay Hammond. It was the spiritual highlight of their week. Peter's love for the pure Scriptures grew every day. He would write down the extra study verses given at the end of program and look them up throughout the week. Brother Hammond was electronically sowing the good Word of God into good ground.

Chapter Five

Daylene wiped the flour from her hands and looked up at the clock. She was relieved to see in just fifteen minutes she could call it a day. It had been busy at the bakery all week and they'd been shorthanded. All she could think about was how good a long hot shower was going to feel when she got home.

"I'd know that face anywhere!" The voice came from a well-dressed customer.

Daylene looked up and saw hints of a familiar friend from a dozen years before. His hair was much shorter and the beard was gone, but he was still every bit the charmer. "Oh my God! Michael!" Daylene came out from the counter and hugged the man who used to party with house girls. "What are you doing here?"

"I called around and found out you were still here and had to stop by and say hi." Michael stepped back to really see Daylene. "You haven't changed a bit!"

Daylene rolled her eyes at him. "Not a bit, right!" she pushed his arm. "I'm so glad to see you. How long are you in town for?"

The long hot shower would wait.

Michael visited Daylene every afternoon when she got off work until Friday when he was to fly back out. He took her to different places around town for lunch and spoiled her. They picked up right where they left off so long ago, laughing and telling lies. She hadn't felt so alive in years. Fluttery emotions long covered over by daily, single parent responsibilities welled up inside. She caught herself smiling long after Michael dropped her off in the afternoons. She dreamed silly school girl dreams at night. It was frightening.

Friday came and all too soon Daylene was seeing Michael off at the airport terminal. After a warm embrace and a gentle kiss, Michael disappeared down the corridor for his flight to Phoenix.

Daylene kept the visit a secret from her son.

Chapter Six

Every Thursday evening in March, Peter witnessed a bizarre event at the store. Shortly after the street light hummed itself to life at sunset, squealing tires roared into the parking lot. Then long horn blasts were followed by headlights flashing at the entrance. Peter would just wave out the window above the magazine rack. A moment later the obnoxious driver would enter wearing a different hat, or flashy boots. Once he wore a pair of old fashioned goggles, but the dirty black and gray shirt remained the same.

"Saaaay Pete! How ya doin' man?" he said slapping down a five-dollar bill.

"Good, Melvin. How you doing? Just milk tonight?"

"I'm great, buddy. Yeah, just milk. I got subscriptions to all the magazines now so I don't need none of them. Oh, and you know what?"

Peter closed the register. "What?"

"I *am* in fantasy land! Seeee ya!"

Melvin would collect his change and run out of the store like a bandit. The squealing tires could be heard for blocks.

After Melvin's final Thursday night pit-stop, a couple of friends dropped by to visit. Tommy and Jared Liggins were buddies from high school. Tommy graduated with Peter, and Jared was a junior. Tommy and Peter regularly planned to get out and go see the world but it was all talk. The quieter Jared would just laugh at the two of them in a jealous sort of way.

"So Peter, got anything going on around two tomorrow?" Tommy asked.

"No. What's up?"

"I'm meeting this guy about making some real money. He said to invite you, too."

"Making money doing what?" Peter asked.

"I don't know all the details, but he'll buy us lunch at Barbecue Bobs."

Peter smiled, "If he's buying lunch, I'm there!"

The note was on the dining room table when Peter got up.

We have something to talk about. I'll pick you up after work.

He wondered what there was to talk about. His mom never used notes before.

Peter paced the aisles of the store lost in thought. He'd met Tommy and the clean-cut gentleman for lunch earlier, and the meeting had gone well. Very well, actually. Money and travel might soon be in his future, but the note nagged at him. He couldn't think of any reason he'd be in trouble.

At five after eleven, under a dark sky, Daylene pulled up to the front of the store. Peter locked the front door then threw his 10-speed into the trunk of the dented Oldsmobile. He climbed into the car nervously not knowing what the mysterious talk would be about, or how he was going to bring up what *he* wanted to talk about.

"Is Denny's a good place to go? We could get some pie or something." Her hands were shaking slightly.

"Sure."

The twenty-four-hour restaurant was busy for a mid-week evening. They both had coffee and pie and waited for each other to start the conversation. Daylene knocked her ice water over. Twice.

"Mom, what's wrong with you?" Peter tried to stop the cold water from getting onto the seat. Daylene laughed at herself.

After the table was cleaned again they sat staring at each other.

"What?" Peter asked impatiently.

"I'm getting married, Peter." It came out louder than Daylene realized; she put her hand over her mouth.

A man's voice from another booth replied, "Congratulations."

Peter could only blink in astonishment. He swallowed hard and tried to comprehend his mother being married. *Married!*

Daylene took a sip of water. "Okay, you say something now."

Peter took a deep breath. "I'm joining the Army."

Chapter Seven

The Valley of the Sun opened up beneath the red and white Beech Bonanza A36 as Daylene's fiancée, Michael, and Peter flew from Tucson to Phoenix under a canopy of brilliant blue. Michael talked an enthusiastic Peter through the basics of single-engine flying.

"I could get used to this," Peter said into the headset.

Michael nodded with a big smile. "You know what the hardest part of flying is?"

Peter thought for a few seconds. Then shook his head.

"Taking off," Michael said, "it'll come down by itself."

Michael Rogers had pursued a dream to fly since his early childhood. After getting his pilot's license, he landed a job with a small charter service in Alaska. He'd take hunters away from the city of Anchorage into the bush where the big game could be found. After several years of diligent saving and investing, he had enough to buy his own plane. Within a few years, Rogers Air, Inc. became a well-known flight service throughout south central Alaska. In 1991 he got an offer he couldn't refuse from a larger carrier and sold the company. He occasionally chartered his personal plane out, but spent most of his time managing his investments.

When his first wife died of cancer three years prior, Michael remembered Daylene and wondered how she was getting along. A charter flight brought him to the Richmond area and he decided to look up his long lost friend. He was elated to see her again and even more pleasantly surprised to see that she was single. Reconnecting with Daylene came easy. It was Peter they were both concerned about, but the two men hit it off immediately.

The two fly boys arrived back at Michael's house in Scottsdale where the rest of the family was gathered. The spacious home with its inviting southwest architecture, well-manicured lawns, and decorative pool would make a memorable setting for the wedding.

When Peter entered Michael's home, he had a clear view of his grandparents talking with his other set of future grandparents, Dick and Ellen Rogers. While Michael went in search of Daylene, Peter found a comfortable place at the bar where a fidgety Stephanie, his soon-to-be step-sister was setting chips and nuts out for everyone. Stephanie was two years older than Peter, and the daughter of Michael's first wife. She was a gracious hostess, but Peter sensed she was having a difficult time with her father getting married again.

Of all the new family entering Peter's world, it was little Katie who captured Peter's attention.

The previous evening, Peter thought he was alone in the living room when out of nowhere a short haired black cat jumped onto Peter's lap.

"His name's Cab Sav."

Peter looked up to where the voice came from and saw an adorable, dark-haired girl in a white dress. She smiled brightly watching the cat rub against Peter's hand.

"You must be Katie," Peter said.

She nodded. "I'm Katie Anna Rogers and I'm four years old."

The young lady stepped away for a moment, and returned with a tan and white cat. "This one is Chardonnay," she said while sitting next to him. "Do you like cats?"

"I do like cats" he answered.

Katie's hazel eyes sparkled. "Me too."

It was the beginning of a wonderful relationship between Peter and his new niece.

The following evening while a copper sun melted slowly behind the mountains in the western sky, Michael and Daylene exchanged vows. Family and friends wished the new couple well and stayed late into the night enjoying the festivities.

Peter was grateful for the timing of things and comforted knowing his mother wouldn't be alone when he left to begin a new chapter of his own life. Little Katie, however, didn't understand why Peter was leaving.

"We're family now," she protested. "You're *my* uncle. You stay with me."

Stephanie did her best to explain the realities of life to her teary eyed daughter, but to no avail. The little girl, who rarely ever saw her father, couldn't bear to see her new uncle disappear too.

Seven days later, Peter was at Fort Sill, Oklahoma for Basic Training.

Chapter Eight

In the late 1970s, three major church denominations were facing crisis. Various elders in each group were at odds with their respective leaders over certain doctrines and the use of the King James Version. The divisions were so sharp, that each of the denominations fractured and formed other groups. In 1980, twenty-one elders who walked in agreement formed the Great Assemblies of Christ (GAOC).

The GAOC was the most stable of these new church groups and dramatic growth soon followed. In only eighteen months, the organization boasted a hundred full-time pastors and ownership of over $17 million in properties and assets scattered throughout North America and Canada. In the fall of 1981, the Sunday television ministry, *Great Sunday Celebration* was launched.

Much of the show's success was attributed to its high entertainment value, in the vein of the popular but short-lived Barbara Mandrel Show, not to mention the soul-stirring preaching from gifted orators of faith. A different minister was featured every Sunday as well as a different choir or praise ensemble.

The one hour show quickly found an audience in hospitals and elder care homes. Within the first six months, it became the most watched program in its time slot. Mail from all over the country poured into the church headquarters with prayer requests, donations, and testimonies.

One of the regulars on the preaching schedule was Jay Hammond, a truck driver turned preacher from Flagstaff, Arizona. Ratings always jumped when Jay Hammond appeared. His connection to everyday people and command of the Scriptures was remarkable. People in hotel rooms, lonely apartments, single mothers, or drunks trying to sober up from the night before felt as if he were speaking to them – and only them. After a year of steady growth in viewership, he became the regular face of *Great Sunday Celebration*.

Jay Hammond was soon a household name with the likes of Jimmy Swaggart, Jim Bakker and Rex Humbard. Jay ended his show with his famous benediction: "The Word of God is perfect, my friend.

Don't add to it and don't take away from it, for it'll save us all if we believe and obey it. Until we all meet again down the road of life my friends, let's stay in our lane and keep our eyes on Jesus!"

Great Sunday Celebration dominated Sunday morning television and fueled exponential growth. Over the next decade, several missions organizations were started, and more than five hundred pastors ministered under the authority of the Great Assemblies of Christ.

To keep up with growth and communications with its leadership, bi-annual conventions known as "Gatherings" were held every spring and fall. These were catered events lasting Friday afternoon to Sunday evening. Major issues were discussed and elections for various offices within the leadership were held. The pageantry was nearly as stunning as their expense. Great Assemblies made every event a first class celebration that would rival that of any Fortune 500 Company.

The fall Gathering of 1993 would be well remembered. It had been a year of change; a year of progress.

For the first time the relevance of the blessed King James Version of the Scriptures was being brought into question. One Regional Director asked publicly, "Can it speak to our modern generation as fluently as the New International or the Revised Standard Versions?" What wasn't known publicly, were off the record conversations with publishers and distributors regarding enormous profit potential for the organization if these other versions were marketed.

Other important matters included the removal of two pastors who'd fallen into sin. One had lost thousands of dollars of tithes and offerings on a gambling spree. The other admitted to adultery. The pastors' hometown press hyped up their indiscretions for a month, while at the same time, a popular mayor was caught on security tape in a compromising position with someone other than her husband. Strangely, there was no mention *of that* in the papers. No news crews were sent to the mayor's residence for a statement.

Wishing to distance themselves from any hint of scandal, the GAOC leadership acted swiftly to replace the two church leaders.

As expected, Jay Hammond was the keynote speaker for the final night of the Gathering. Jay was the favorite among even the most eloquent of preachers. He spoke with authority even in casual conversation. His appearance was unremarkable, but his skill in the Word was unassailable. So when the occasional disagreement between the elder board and Jay erupted, it echoed through the pastoral rumor mill faster than the falling walls of Jericho. When he voiced those disagreements on live television to cheering crowds, eyebrows raised and warnings were given. His popularity kept him employed but he lived on a tight leash. Behind closed doors he was considered a threat to GAOC.

Jay walked to the podium that night heavy with the thought of what was happening to the church and of the two pastors and their families who were being forced to leave. The soft music ebbed gently to make way for the preacher.

"It's a truly sad day.... when men *can* find forgiveness from God....but *cannot* seem to find it from this board." Jay looked toward the five men seated at the table on the stage near him. "Which of us is without flaw? Who among us is qualified to cast the first stone?"

He looked out to the expectant faces of friends and members of the body of Christ. His voice slow, measured and careful... "Are we so well-dressed...that we're oblivious to our own nakedness? Are we so wealthy we don't have any need? If our sins are less obvious are they somehow less wicked?" He turned to face the leadership again who sat emotionless. "Are we honestly that comfortable with our hypocrisy?"

Descending at the pace of his words into the minds of all in attendance was a plumb line of the soul. Every receptive heart was confronted with the jagged unevenness of their ways. Every quoted verse from the preacher was a painful reminder of some sin or hidden darkness lurking in the recesses of the conscience.

Jay Hammond paced back and forth across the well-lit risers while the unmistakable presence of the Holy Ghost flooded the room, steeping everyone in conviction. Amidst four-star finery, Christ the Righteous Judge came to his church holding a mirror to his bride. But He was gentle. The weeping began slowly.

Jay read from his Bible as a row of men turned their chairs into altars of repentance. Ladies in form fitting dresses and designer skirts wept uncontrollably, their cheeks stained with a mix of tears and mascara. Others jerked and ran to the darker corners of the large, crowded room trying to escape the heat. The most reserved and staid of elders shook nervously while the chosen vessel of the moment continued his delivery of the Word in power from the stage.

From the beginning of the evening, the dozen neatly uniformed banquet servers thought this would be just another shift to get through. Another day worked, another dollar earned.

Then Christ came to each of them.

Jarred the lead server stopped flirting with a few of the patrons and put his wedding ring back on. Jacklyn and Rachel apologized to each other for being so hateful. Mick was in tears, wondering why he'd backslid so long ago. Steve and Amber became so uncomfortable they turned in their aprons and left the building. David, a giant of a man, walked calmly to the phone in the back office and cried to his pregnant girlfriend. Then he agreed to marry her - finally. The others, Monica, Sam, Juan and Abbey, stood against the back walls watching well-dressed people crumble in front of them. On any other evening, they'd joke and carry on. Not tonight. All they could see were the broken reflections of their own past flashing before their eyes.

The important evening did not go as planned nor did it have a certain end. Tissues littered the floor and people prayed with stammering lips late into the night. Dozens of teary-eyed pastors pleaded with the elder board to reconsider or at least to wait before making any final decisions about their brethren who would spend the rest of their lives trying to repair their reputations. It was truly a Gathering to remember.

On Friday the following week, Jay Hammond was fired.

Chapter Nine

Private Peter Bishop was part of Delta Battery for his entire training cycle at Fort Sill. Eight weeks were devoted to the rigors of Basic Training followed by five more weeks of Advanced Individual Training to become a Fire Support Specialist, otherwise known as a Forward Observer. Using a map, compass, binoculars and a two-way radio, these soldiers would learn to direct various weapon systems to take out enemy targets up to several miles away. Forward Observers were literally the eyes of the artillery. Peter was enticed to this occupational field for its financial incentives, but more importantly, for an opportunity to see Europe.

Under the sweltering Oklahoma sun, Peter's unit learned the necessary common tasks every soldier must master. He qualified as an expert marksman with the M16 rifle and was among the fittest of his platoon.

Right behind meals, mail call was the most important time of day. Care packages sent from loved ones lifted a weary soldier's spirit more than anything else. Whenever Peter received a package, tucked neatly next to homemade brownies were colorful crayon drawings affectionately drawn by Katie. Peter kept every single green bird, brown house and yellow sun.

Peter and Tommy Liggins stayed together right up through graduation in November. Then it was time for a very well-deserved two-week leave.

Peter was still getting used to calling Arizona his new home. Richmond, Virginia was the only home he'd ever known. But it wasn't the place that was on his mind when he flew into Sky Harbor International Airport. He missed his mother terribly, though he'd never admit it to his buddies.

At the airport, Peter could see Michael and Daylene searching the faces of the arriving passengers. When Daylene saw her Peter walking tall and proud in his uniform, she ran toward him and crushed him with a hug only a mother can give. Peter saw Michael walking toward him just as another set of arms wrapped around his waist. Peter looked down to see the cheerful freckled face of his niece, Katie. "You're home now," she said with a dance. "Did you get my pictures? I drew them just for you!"

"I got everyone, Katie," he said lifting her into his arms. "How did you get so big so fast?"

It was like getting a hero's welcome as they all walked and talked down the long corridors to the baggage carousels.

"How are you liking Phoenix?" Peter asked.

Daylene had her arm locked in Peter's. "I'm getting used to it. I think the dry heat is good for my bones."

Peter smiled noticing the first flecks of gray in her. "What's this?"

"Age, my boy. It comes to all of us."

"Beats the alternative," Michael said.

On the ride home, the men planned another flight together as well as other adventures. When they arrived, Daylene insisted on getting some pictures while everyone was dressed up and her son was still in his uniform. As Peter posed in front of the rock wall in the living room Daylene slowly lowered the camera. Peter recognized his mother's familiar stare. "What are you seeing?"

Daylene paused in silence watching flicks of blue and gold light, like bright sparks, dance around her son. They appeared long enough to etch into her memory then evaporated.

She shook her head her head and said, "Nothing," while replacing the lens cap.

It was the second time she'd seen the lights.

Michael poked his head around the corner. "Stephanie will be here from work soon. Should I fire up the grill?"

Daylene saw flame broiled delight in Peter's eyes. "Sounds good, honey. Let's get the fatted calf cooking for our G.I. Joe."

The remaining week was filled with day trips, a buffet of

restaurants and relaxing by the pool. On Sunday, they visited a Great Assemblies Church Daylene had found in Mesa. Peter felt a connection to the church and talked briefly with Lee Smith, the pastor. Pastor Lee arranged for Daylene to get regular VHS copies of *Great Sunday Celebration* so she could mail them to Peter after he was settled at his first duty station.

Peter soaked up every fleeting moment of his two-week leave with his family, but long before he was ready, it was time to go.

At the front door the next morning, Katie leaned against her mother as they both watched Peter climb into the car and pull out of the driveway. "I won't cry this time, Mom," she said.

Stephanie kissed her daughter's head. "That's my strong girl."

Katie looked up, "But I need lots more crayons."

Later Peter said his goodbyes to Daylene and Michael and boarded his plane. Then after a nineteen-hour delay in the St. Louis air terminal, he spent most of the next day en route to Frankfurt. He was assigned to the 1st Armored Division at Warner Barracks, Bamberg, Germany.

He wouldn't see his family again for four years.

Daylene and Michael shared only occasional fellowship with The Great Assemblies Church, preferring to spend Sundays at home. Then in the summer of 1994, they were so intrigued with reports of a revival and "holy laughter" in Toronto, Canada, they traveled there to see it for themselves. Not only did they see the extraordinary, they were caught up with the spiritual outpouring and ended up staying a week longer than planned.

A year and a half later, they visited Florida and the Brownsville outpouring, followed by a brief excursion to a series of prayer meetings outside of Dallas, Texas. Michael and Daylene saw some of the same faces and made friends with several like-minded souls. They were a traveling group of mostly retired folks that were labeled as "Fire Chasers." They just wanted to be where God was doing something new. Sometimes they flew, other times they drove in a caravan of RV's going from one spiritual oasis to another.

When the day was beginning in Arizona, it was nearing its end in Germany where Peter fine-tuned his soldiering. He quickly moved through the ranks from Private, to Private First Class to Specialist, and from Radio Telephone Operator (RTO) to actual Forward Observer. He owed much of his rapid advancement to his section chief, Sergeant John Stiles. SGT Stiles was several years older than Peter, a solid professional, and a man of unquestionable character.

"Bishop," SGT. Stiles said while the two walked to the chow hall, "I learned a secret to making rank fast in this man's Army. You find out what your supervisors want and give it to them over and over. If it's a big deal to your section chief to have pressed uniforms, make sure yours has the sharpest creases. If 1SG wants shiny boots, buff yours into mirrors. Impress them with *your* attention to *their* details. Little things matter."

Peter was one of only three soldiers in his unit who made sergeant in under four years.

Sergeant Bishop learned cover and camouflage techniques and how to quickly bracket targets with artillery rounds. When shells landed close enough, the order was given to "fire for effect," meaning a lethal barrage of explosive fury was on its way. He earned quite a reputation for accurately calling for fire on targets with the first round on training exercises.

Peter did his best to keep his faith intact, though after-daylight hour temptations were plenteous. On one occasion he joined a few buddies who prided themselves as connoisseurs of copious amounts of good German beer. Soon, Peter and his friends were mixing whiskey shots between full steins of brew. It was an expensive night, but Peter had only begun to pay. The blinding hangover lasting the entire next day was almost unbearable.

The most important thing to a solider stationed overseas is mail. Peter was more fortunate than most with all the care packages Daylene sent him. Every two weeks, Peter had a box with cookies or candy, a few colorful drawings from Katie, perhaps some pictures from a road trip and a VHS tape with episodes of *Great Sunday Celebration.* The uplifting shows were a wonderful source of encouragement.

Peter noticed on the tapes that Jay Hammond was no longer the regular host, and when he was on, the show was a rerun. He also noticed that the Bibles used by some of the preachers weren't the King James Version. It was a subtle yet noticeable difference.

As the months went by, Specialist Bishop and his Fire Support section spent many weeks out in the field on training maneuvers in every kind of weather. Peter saw the beauty in the execution of a well-coordinated plan, and the disastrous results if orders weren't followed to down to the last detail.

The Lord gently spoke to Peter while on his final mission at the Hohenfels Training Area, a small installation less than 60 miles from the Czech Republic border. He and his RTO had been on a hill hidden in the brush all night watching and eluding the enemy. As the morning sun spilled into the sloping valley below, they were in a rare position of being able to see both the opposing team and his friendly supporting units. It was God's perspective.

Peter's heart raced watching the two forces engage. His team of mechanized artillery and infantry worked together in harmony like living chess pieces on a game board of dirt and brush. Peter requested fire from a unit of 155mm, self-propelled Howitzers onto an entire battalion of mixed infantry and troop carriers. The simulated assault was quickly followed by M-1 Abrams tanks while Apache helicopters provided close air support. The victory was as stunning as the unfolding spiritual lesson. Through thick dust and hot diesel fumes he could hear his Heavenly Father.

"Remember what you see here," he spoke. *"When I direct my church, the gates of hell shall not prevail against it."*

The military had been good for Peter but he was glad to return to civilian life. He now felt more like a real adult than a kid masquerading as one. He'd grown physically, been challenged mentally, and visited many new places. True to advertising, he had done more before 9:00 AM than most had done all day.

The photo album buried in his worn duffel bag held images of him around the Eiffel Tower, beaches in Spain, Bavarian castles and pictures of friends he would never see again.

It rained the morning he said goodbye to his unit and it was still pouring when he flew out of Frankfurt four hours later. It seemed to rain everywhere except above the clouds.

He slept off and on until the eastern seacoast appeared. He was surprised at his response as he watched the gray-blue sea give way to the green earth miles below. It took everything the returning soldier had to hold back the tears. He'd been away for so long and now just knowing he was over American airspace filled him with unexpected emotions. He'd seen the famous European sights and experienced things most would only read about in magazines and books. But to Peter Bishop, there was no place in the world like the good old USA.

After out-processing from Fort Dix, New Jersey, he was back at the airport waiting to finish the last leg of his journey to Phoenix. Soon he'd be home.

Seated in the terminal cafe near his departing gate, Peter pondered his future over a steaming cup of rich Italian roast. He was at an interesting crossroads. He was young, in the best shape of his life, single and now unemployed.

He took another sip and watched the efficient blonde behind the counter steam a steel pitcher of milk for a latte. She appeared to be enjoying herself and the line of customers waiting for her strong brew kept growing.

Peter thought about a girl he'd met on a three-day pass in France. They talked about nothing over espressos as thick as motor oil. The attractive, brown-haired stranger with dark eyes was light and funny. After a few laughs she said she had to go back to work.

"Back to work?" he asked. "This late at night?"

"I need shoes, darling," she said picking up her handbag. "I have three shows. I take off my clothes, the men pay. Perhaps some of your friends and their fathers will pay for all my new clothes tonight. Ciao."

The young stripper turned on her thick heels and waved from the door. Peter watched her disappear into the night between moving headlights and a misty Paris rain.

The loudspeaker announcing his flight number brought him back from his cobble stone memories. He collected his things and strolled toward the gate noticing that nearly every adult held an espresso drink.

"Coffee," Peter said out loud. "I wonder if there's a future for me in coffee?"

Chapter Ten

Life ahead lay before the returning veteran the way a blank canvas does before a painter; full of possibilities but nothing certain. Peter's first week home was dedicated to unwinding from the rigid rules of military living. He slept in till nearly eight every morning. Then he caught up on television, never imagining that he could have missed commercials. Later, he toured several malls with Daylene. That was Week One.

On Week Two, Peter scouted the city to find an opening into the world of coffee beans and espressos. To his surprise, there were several Starbucks offering wonderfully rich beverages, but no job openings. Peter was actually relieved. Who's going to pay those prices for coffee? He doubted they'd be around long.

Nearing Week Three, Peter was no closer to landing a job than at the beginning. He widened his search to include restaurants and bakeries. Unfortunately, the going wages wouldn't make ends meet and Peter was ready to live under his own roof.

While poring over the classifieds one Tuesday morning, Peter got a call from Michael asking if he'd be interested in construction. Open to anything that paid, Peter took down the name and business address of Michael's golfing buddy and arranged a meeting for the following morning at Barker Construction.

On the steps of the on-site office trailer 30 minutes southwest of Phoenix in Gilbert, Peter went through an informal interview from the passenger side of a Ford F250 with Cliff Barker; a short, loud man with a perpetually red face and jovial laugh. They talked and drove through the nearly completed Persimmon Estates with the AC on full.

"You pretty good with numbers?" Cliff asked.

Peter cringed at the thought of anything involving algebra. "Good with numbers how?"

"What I need more than a framer is a roofing estimator. You sound like you've got a brain in your head and you're good with people. Those qualities are far more important to sell a roofing job than shooting nails. I can pair you up with Scott. He'll show you how to work the calculator and prepare proposals. It's hourly pay plus bonuses the more sales you make."

Peter liked the idea of interacting with people rather than sweating walls into place. "When do I start?"

"Monday."

It wasn't coffee, but Peter was excited to be making a paycheck. He hit the ground running and proved to be quick learner. He studied basic roofing materials and learned about their advantages and disadvantages. He worked closely with Scott Thomas, a skilled salesman who was brilliant with numbers. He knew how to present a proposal to homeowners so they wouldn't have a heart attack. After shadowing Scott for four days, it was Peter's turn. Roofing sales continued upward for Barker Construction.

Three months later, Cliff Barker gave more responsibility to Peter. On Friday afternoons, Peter would take one of the big trucks and pick up needed materials to keep the weekend crews supplied.

On one of the regular Friday runs, Peter was stopped just before leaving. A young office assistant, Traci Wesson, was having car trouble and needed a ride to run errands. Peter had only seen her a couple of times in passing and didn't know her name. He watched her climb up into the cab and was instantly taken by her fresh face and bright smile.

"Thank you," she said, while slamming the door. "I can't believe my car."

Peter admired the bouncy chestnut curls and light blue eyes of his passenger. "No problem." He turned his attention to driving and asked, "Where to first?"

"You got it easy today. Just the bank," she said.

"Sounds good. I've got to go to Home Depot and Wilson's Lumber Yard." Peter noticed how her smile lingered as she listened to him. "I'm Peter, by the way."

"I know," she replied. "I've seen you around. I'm Traci."

They talked shop for the first few miles, then exchanged personal bits of each other's past and present. Traci's sharp wit kept Peter laughing all the way to the bank parking lot. Her feminine curves held his attention to and from the bank lobby door. Faded blue jeans never looked so good.

Traci was wonderful company; a very pleasant and unexpected bonus to this payday Friday.

Peter seemed to be at the right place at the right time to see Traci even more the following week. When Friday afternoon came around, she met him by the truck carrying a small clipboard and the dark blue deposit bag.

"I thought your car was fixed," he said.

"It is, but I think you need the help," she quipped with a playful smile.

Peter laughed. "So you're gonna help me?"

"Only if you *can* be helped."

"Okay, get in."

They made the usual bank run and picked up building materials. Then they stopped by a sub shop for sandwich orders called in earlier. From then on Peter and Traci ran Friday errands together. They began seeing more of each other and a workplace friendship grew into an after-hours romance.

While at the lumber yard waiting for a load of trusses during monsoon season in August, the clouds broke open. Peter and Traci ran through a drenching downpour to the truck. Once inside they quickly rolled up the windows and laughed till they nearly cried. They sat close together and listened to the thick pounding rain on the roof. He was intoxicated by the smell of her hair and the way her eyes gently caressed his face. Her lips found his and they sank into each other's arms hidden behind a watercolor veil of rain.

Peter lived with Michael and Daylene longer than planned, primarily because they were gone so often on trips. He was able to keep an eye on things while they were gone. Then in September, he loaded up his Ford Ranger with all his earthly possessions and moved into a leased condo in Scottsdale.

Peter liked his new place. The rooms were spacious and the

complex was filled with other young adults. Within a few days, he befriended a couple who attended the same Great Assemblies Church in Mesa he'd visited before. They invited Peter to go with them to a Saturday night fellowship geared toward young professionals. Peter accepted the invitation and soon found that he liked the casual atmosphere of the group as well as the interaction between other spiritually minded twenty-somethings. Traci occasionally joined in as well and on the surface appeared to be enjoying herself.

Peter invested more time in the Word and looked forward to Saturday nights with greater anticipation. He listened intently to church leaders as they shared truths from the Scriptures in casual round table discussions. More than once he felt the hot spotlight of conviction shining on his heart. So much of his life was lived off of the narrow way, stuck in the mire and tall grass of sin. The goodness of God always led him to repentance. Most evenings would find him wiping his moist eyes at the end of the closing prayer or with others at the altar. Deep was calling unto deep within Peter. He was awakening.

Friday errand runs hummed along smoothly, but Traci saw a change in Peter that she wasn't entirely comfortable with. He spoke more about spiritual things, while she remained a party girl, firmly fixed in the world. Her ties to anything Christian went only as far as her 14K cross pendant. She flippantly asked Peter in the delivery truck one Friday if he was going to join a monastery.

"I've loved God since I was a boy, Traci. I haven't always lived the life, but I'm trying to now. If that doesn't work for you...well...then maybe we're not right for each other."

The cab of the truck was quiet the rest of the afternoon.

A little after nine that evening, a subdued Traci stepped through the door of Peter's condo. They sat close together in the incandescent glow of living room lights and talked openly on the couch. Traci held Peter's hand and listened to him share his heart. In turn, Peter heard from a girl who didn't know the Lord and wouldn't pretend to know him, but tearfully promised to never stand in the way of his serving God.

When their words were finished, she leaned against him, relieved they'd found a place of agreement. She was comforted by the sound of his heart and his hand gently rubbing her back.

After a few quiet moments, Traci rose, turned off the lights, and came to rest on his lap. The faint beams from a street light danced upon her cheeks as she moved closer. Whatever defenses Peter had quickly fell away to Traci's sensual beauty and the dark, dilated pools of her glossy eyes. She took his face in her hands and kissed him slowly and deeply as her hair cascaded around him.

Awash in warmth, she pulled away and slowly unbuttoned her satin blouse.

Chapter Eleven

Daylene relived a thousand memories from a chair in the back yard. The little boy, who had been her constant companion in diapers, became a teenager on a ten-speed, a handsome soldier, a roofing expert - or something - was now getting married. It all happened in a blink. With Michael on her left and Katie seated to her right, she watched Peter and his new bride exchange vows exactly where she had not that long ago.

In her eyes, Traci was a sweet girl, but Daylene thought their relationship seemed a bit like a whirlwind romance. She brushed her concerns aside. They were a beautiful couple and her baby boy seemed happy. That's what mattered.

They honeymooned in Sedona and were soon back to work together wearing shiny new wedding rings.

A month later, the light tone in their relationship was darkening. True to her word, Traci didn't stand in the way of her husband's devotion to God, but she wasn't always quiet about her feelings either. The quick wit that used to make him laugh, now delivered sharp sarcasm that stung long after the words were spoken.

"You read your Bible so much, maybe you should sleep with it too."

To Traci, God was an intruder, an invisible competitor for her husband's attention. All the while Peter was becoming more free.

The first Saturday evening in February, Joe Ryan, an assistant pastor of the church made an announcement of a new minister's course scheduled to begin in the fall. Peter stayed late to get all the information he could.

"It's a fast-track program for someone who feels called to the ministry," Joe explained. "In eighteen months, you'll come out as an ordained minister with Great Assemblies. You'll be assigned an area to shepherd. Then as the church grows, you'll be eligible for building funds and advertising support to grow even more."

It made sense to Peter. It clicked in his heart and confirmed some feelings he'd had about ministry. He wanted everyone to know Jesus the way he had grown to know him.

He sat in his truck in the parking lot, looking over the brochure and the course application. It was affordable and he could start in the fall, but he wondered how Traci would feel about this new direction.

His eyes followed the red tail lights of a car as it exited the parking lot and accelerated away. After a moment in the shadows and silence, he folded the papers and put them in the glove box.

Spring rolled into another blazing summer in the valley and Barker Construction was having a banner year. New construction was up and Cliff needed more roofing crews in Chandler and Gilbert where more snowbirds and retirees were migrating to.

Like most couples, Peter and Traci worked through their ups and downs and managed to keep home and work separate. Saturday nights, however, became a growing point of contention. Peter found deep fulfillment spending time with fellow believers. He was a natural leader in discussion groups, able to show others rich truths from the Word. His wife, on the other hand, wanted to wine, dine, and hit the clubs.

"It's Saturday, night, baby," she pleaded. "Go to church tomorrow. Come dance with me tonight!"

Sometimes he did, but he always wished he were elsewhere. He longed for Traci to be interested in his Lord as he was. Later, Traci found a couple of girls to party with and that seemed to be a workable solution, for a while at least.

At the end of a long week in early July, Peter waited for Traci in his truck in front of the office. He had a date night planned for just the two of them, starting with dinner reservations at Caruso's Italian Ristorante. She'd been quiet for a few days and he wondered if she felt okay.

He watched his pretty wife walk slowly to his side of the truck. He rolled down his window with a smile and said, "I have a surprise for you."

"A surprise? That makes two us."

"Yeah? Well, my surprise involves a fine dinner and a movie of your choice, even a sappy chick flick," he said.

Traci smiled faintly.

"Okay, what's your surprise?" he asked.

"I want a divorce."

Chapter Twelve

The passenger side of the white work truck was empty again as Peter made his Friday supply run. Every day was a colorless experience filled with a sickening ache in the center of his heart. The feelings of rejection met him in the eerie morning hours and lasted till he came home to the collection of quiet rooms. All of her things were gone. Every graceful feminine touch had been removed, including the plants. He'd gone several days without eating or even feeling hungry. He simply hurt. The life inside him was draining out, replaced with the feelings of failure, disappointment and regret.

One evening after talking himself out of calling his ex-wife again, he knelt by the kitchen table, pleading with God to take the gnawing, hollow pain away. It was his constant prayer.

God remained silent.

Peter took a few days off from work to visit his mother and Michael. Then he climbed into his truck and drove away with no destination in mind. He welcomed even the slightest temporary relief or distraction. He stayed the first night in a cheap out of the way hotel in Flagstaff, then drove up to the Grand Canyon and hiked one of the trails by himself. The next day he drove through historic Glennwood, over the mountain to Jerome, and ended his road trip in Sedona. That afternoon, he purchased an ample amount of Evan Williams Straight Kentucky Whiskey and headed to his room to comfort himself.

As the dark night hours drifted into the early hours of another day, he slurred through another one-sided conversation with his Maker.

"Why didn't you or someone tell me or warn me or...something?"

He refilled the Styrofoam cup and played memories on the screen of his mind until the reel ran out of film.

"I thought we were good together. I'm sorry she didn't love you. I'm sorry. I just -" His thoughts became muddy. "I just don't want to hurt anymore." He rested against the headboard. "Please?"

There was no response from heaven that night either.

The following morning was not kind to the scruffy faced traveler.

With a dry mouth and thick eyes, he checked out of his room and walked carefully to his truck. The mid-morning sun slapped his face while a freight train ran through his head. For the first time in a week something else hurt more than his heart.

Peter had no other places in mind to visit, but didn't want to go back to an empty house.

"Well God, if you're not going to heal this hurt, maybe you could give me some direction. How about that, huh?" Speaking out loud only made the pounding headache worse.

He leaned over the seat and searched for a map in the glove box. When he opened it, the map along with the papers from the ministry course fell to the floorboard. His bloodshot eyes rested on the papers. "Is this a joke?" he asked, holding the palm of his hand to his forehead. "If it is God, you've got a sick sense of humor."

After ordering the largest coffee from an espresso drive-through, Peter pointed his truck south on Highway 179. Since there wouldn't be any more fights about church at home, he was believing the papers were a sign to pursue Bible school until proven otherwise.

A few days later, a fully sober Peter was in service on Sunday morning. If ministry was his direction, then he needed to get anchored into the Sunday morning church template. He also made an appointment with the minister who was in charge of admissions for the ministry course. After the ninety-minute worship service, Peter met with Pastor Joe Ryan in his office.

Joe was an easy going, husky man in his early thirties. He invited Peter back to his white walled office, modestly decorated with mismatched furniture and silk plants. After showing off pictures of his new daughter, they got down to business.

"Well, buddy, I am really glad to see you sign up for this," Pastor Ryan said. "I know you'll do well."

"I think this is the right direction for me at this stage of my life."

"Excellent. Is your wife excited for you?"

Peter winced at the question and looked down. "We're actually getting a divorce."

Pastor Ryan leaned forward. "Oh no, Peter. I'm so sorry. What happened?"

He took a deep breath and shook his head hoping the pastor would just fast forward through this part of the meeting.

Is it really over?" Joe asked. "Have you considered counseling?"

Peter chuckled. "How do you counsel two unequally yoked people who should have never gotten married to begin with?" Peter was caught by his own words that just fell out. It was as though he heard someone else say them.

Joe closed his eyes and leaned back in his dark leatherette chair. An awkward silence fell between the men. "How ya holding up?" Joe asked.

"As well as can be expected, I suppose. I don't think anyone aims to be married and divorced before twenty-five."

"Roofing business going okay?"

"Yeah."

The minister ran his fingers over the application in front of him. "Well, this isn't going to be pleasant news either, Peter."

"What news?"

"Your eligibility," Pastor Ryan said while pointing to a folder. "All divorcees must wait a full year from dissolution of marriage to apply for admission."

If there were any silver linings to the clouds that followed Peter it was good health, a steady paycheck and his precocious niece Katie. She somehow knew just when to call and say hi, talk about a field trip from school, or what she and her friends had planned for the weekend. A timely call came after a demanding work day in November. She invited him to her birthday party. Katie Anna Rogers was going to be ten and she wanted her favorite uncle to be there. And be there he would! It was a perfect reason to escape the sea of loneliness that filled his small living area.

After a secret phone call to Stephanie, Peter was on his way to a strip mall on Val Vista Drive to find Katie the perfect gift. New malls were going up all over Gilbert, filled with the trendiest shops and boutiques. Peter found the Super Palace that would have the roller blades Katie had her heart set on.

The storefronts on both sides of the recreational outlet store had butcher paper covering the windows concealing the work going on inside. Peter watched as two men carried a crate into one of the suites. Shiny stainless steel parts to a large, commercial grade espresso machine appeared above the packing materials. He filed the image away for future reference and went back to his search for inline skates.

Katie had quite a birthday. Her grandparents took her out to a pancake breakfast in the morning. At noon, her uncle Peter brought her a beautifully wrapped box with pink and purple bows, and four of her best friends helped her celebrate in the park with cake, ice cream and water balloons. Peter stayed till the end helping Stephanie take the exhausted and lightly sunburned girls back to the house.

"I can't thank you enough, Peter," Stephanie whispered at the door. "Her dad's been just out of it. He must have forgotten her birthday again. You being here means the world to her."

After many hugs, Peter drove over to have a late dinner with Michael and his mother. Daylene was insistent that Peter start coming over once a week for dinner now that he was single again. He savored the fellowship as much as the home cooked meals. It kept the divorced man from feeling broken and inadequate.

The sun had just fallen below the horizon when he pulled up into the driveway, and saw a late model Dolphin motor home parked out front. A colorful map of the United States with most of the fifty states colored in red was fixed on the side. Company for dinner no doubt. Peter had met some of his mom's and Michael's traveling friends. Interesting people. Interesting conversations.

Peter knocked twice then let himself in. Everyone was out in the covered patio.

"Hey honey!" Daylene called. "Load up a plate and come on out."

Peter waved to his mother, Michael, and the two strangers. They were all seated at the outdoor table enjoying the perfection of a southwestern fall evening.

After loading up his plate with barbeque chicken, potato salad and steamed veggies, he ventured out to the patio and to the remaining open seat.

"Peter, this is Tom and Valarie Warner. We met them in Florida a few years back when we went to Brownsville. They're thinking of moving here."

Peter greeted the couple, guessing they were in their fifties. Tom was a tall, fit man with a gentle demeanor. Valarie was an alluring woman, wearing long, wavy brown hair and haunting, dark brown eyes. She gave Peter a smile that made him feel like he'd known her forever.

The two couples finished a conversation about politics while Peter dove into his full plate. Between portions of hearty meat and asparagus he could sense Valarie studying him. He looked up occasionally and smiled at her. She was a warmly attractive woman. Peter wondered how many hearts she'd broken in her younger days.

"Not many," she said, leaning close to him.

He looked up to her and said, "I'm sorry?"

"Not many hearts."

He was caught. Peter couldn't look away.

Valarie shifted her attention to the ongoing conversation while Peter's stare fell to the dishes on the table. He reeled in any other potentially wayward thoughts.

Tom began sharing stories of their travels and spiritual adventures on the road. He'd been an oil man for twenty years and decided to get out before he was too old to enjoy all he'd saved and invested. He grew up in church and had a solid walk with God, though his wife had other plans when he retired. She divorced him and moved in with a former co-worker.

Valarie was a widow in her forties when she visited her sister who went to the same church Tom attended. It was love at first sight.

Valarie spoke of her first husband, an old fire and brimstone preacher from a restrictive Pentecostal denomination.

"We women felt like second-class citizens, really," she said. "Long dresses even in the summer and God help us if we ever cut our hair. It was down to my knees and all split ends from my neck down. It was a mess." She put her arm on Tom and laughed. "Everyone of us ladies thought of ways to get around the cutting issue like using a candle and singeing our hair. At least it wasn't cut!"

"How could you stand that?" Daylene asked.

Valarie's laughter gave way to a thoughtful expression. "I'd have to say that the precious moving of his Spirit made the difference, Daylene. We'd gather in that small chapel and heaven seemed to fall upon us. We'd go home after evening service, sometimes at midnight almost glowing. Harold would preach and lay hands on the sick. I saw blind eyes open. Drunks were instantly made sober and walked away freed from the shackles of liquor. The town pharmacist had one leg shorter than the other. He was healed. His leg grew to its proper length in a prayer meeting. It was difficult at times for sure, but the power of God was real. I'd say that made all the rules bearable."

"Anyone for dessert?" Daylene asked as she got up.

Valarie collected the empty dinner plates and followed Daylene.

Peter recounted Katie's birthday party when the ladies returned several minutes later with chocolate cake, black walnut ice cream and a carafe of hot coffee.

Valarie filled one cup and handed it to her husband. She looked at Peter, "Coffee?"

"Yes, thank you."

She poured a second cup and handed to him, then another for Daylene.

"Do you believe in the gifts of the Spirit, Peter?"

Peter poured half and half into his cup and watched the black contents become a creamy brown and tan.

"I honestly don't know."

"Prophets and miracles?"

Peter felt on the spot with everyone's attention fixed on him. He caught his mother eyes and said, "I've experienced quite a few things that aren't quite...normal. Including this evening. Not the blind seeing or legs being healed like you have. It's in the Bible. I guess I should believe them. How's that?"

Valarie smiled. "That will do, Peter."

Peter was intrigued with Tom and Valarie as they shared more of their lives. Mind reading wasn't a circus side show. It sounded as though both Tom and Valarie had been used frequently in the gifts of the Spirit and Peter was captivated, even envious of their experiences. This was obviously more than a random encounter.

Valarie tossed her hair back and fixed her attention to Peter again. Leaning over toward Daylene she said, "I see the lights around him too. Like little stars."

Daylene raised her brows and looked to her friend. Peter braced himself for another revealing exchange.

"Churches," Valarie said over the rising steam from her cup. "Thou art Peter. And from you will come many churches."

Chapter Thirteen

Peter slowly made friends with being alone again. His heart was mending from the scars of rejection and he was sleeping more, though he often thought of Traci. In the final hours of any given night, he'd relive some of their better days together, before a tattered curtain of reality blanketed the scene from view. Every morning would bring a renewed determination to walk more wisely than in former days. He'd been forgiven of many mistakes and could only give away to others the mercy he'd received from his Savior. It made him all the more desirous to preach the Gospel of Jesus Christ to as many as he could. Waiting a year to attend the ministry course was just part of the price he'd have to pay.

Peter reflected on Valarie's word of "many churches" from every direction but couldn't grasp it. Many churches? Every church model he'd ever known was building bigger; not many. A single church leader over a single congregation was how every church worked, didn't it?

He was pulled from the edge of sleep one evening with a burning idea; what if many churches means many Great Assemblies Churches? He envisioned himself preaching from the stage on Great Sunday Celebration as the General Superintendent of the GAOC.

His mother's voice echoed back to him from their small apartment long ago.

If God has a slot open Peter, I think you're the first one he'd pick.

He leaned back onto his pillow.

"Pick me, Jesus," he said to the air. "Pick me."

It was a sunny afternoon when he drove past the strip mall where he'd picked up Katie's roller blades and saw a new sign hanging in a storefront that read *Stellar Coffee Company*. A few moments and an illegal U-turn later, Peter walked through the front door looking for the owner or manager. Until he took over Great Assemblies, he'd need to support himself. In his mind God and coffee were best friends.

The coffeehouse wasn't officially open for business. A finish carpenter directed Peter to the back room where the owner could be found to answer his questions. Seated behind an antique oak desk was a robust man in a striped shirt and suspenders. He was ending a phone call when he saw Peter and motioned him back.

Peter entered the office that appeared to be decorated by Norman Rockwell himself. The wainscoted walls were complimented by dark green wall paper, brass light fixtures and calming watercolor paintings.

The man hung up the phone and looked at Peter. "You my coffee guy?"

"Not yet," Peter said holding out his hand. "Peter Bishop."

The man stood and shook Peter's hand with a curious expression. "Brad Stellar. So what can I do for you, Peter Bishop?"

"Do you have an opening for a guy who wants to learn the coffee business?"

Brad looked Peter up and down. "Learn the business, huh?" he said rubbing his close cut beard. He pointed to the chair at Peter's side. "Okay, have a seat."

Stellar Coffee Company was an idea sketched on a dirty napkin inside a sports bar in southern California three years earlier. The artist was a corporate manager who'd just been laid off after seven years of ladder climbing. Brad Stellar and two other displaced buddies were kicking around ideas, making plans, and reinventing the wheel. Of the three, Brad was the optimistic risk taker. He was determined to never be at the mercy of another downsizing. Excessive state and federal regulations had caused his company to go overseas to remain competitive. It was time to throw himself into his own dreams. He would do whatever it took to learn to the workings of an exponentially growing business in America; coffee and espresso. His wife Monica was not as optimistic.

Brad swallowed every ounce of pride and worked two minimum wage jobs at competing coffeehouses several miles apart. He opened at one place and closed at the other and paid attention to every detail. One night his morning employer came to the window of the drive-thru and saw him. With a single look, he was down to one job. Nine days later, two other employees didn't show up for work. The owner fired them and promoted Brad to assistant manager. Six months later, Brad Stellar was the new store manager. Monica started breathing easier at home.

A little more than a year after that, Brad received an unexpected inheritance from the passing of his grandfather. It was enough to start his own coffee place in a state more business friendly than California. Monica's parents had moved to Phoenix and she'd wanted to be closer to them. After several months of planning, the right opportunity presented itself in Gilbert.

Smiling as he recounted the story, Brad opened the desk and showed Peter the folded napkin with faded blue ink that was his business plan. The words *Stellar Coffee Company* were written above a drawing of a cup with wavy lines of steam drifting upward. Peter smiled and handed it back to the proud coffeehouse owner.

After Peter sketched out the loose details of his life and interest in hot beverages, Brad said, "I'll make you a deal, Peter. I'll work you like a dog and pay you next to nothing for three months. You'll work different shifts, different days, and do every single task inside and out. All the while, I'll teach you the basics of the coffee business. Within ninety days you'll either be disgusted and quit and go off in another direction – which you'll thank me for later – or you'll know this is right for you. In return, I'll know if I want you around. If so, on day ninety-one, I'll start paying you what you're worth." With an intense look, he finished with, "Give me any guff, and you're outta here. Got me?"

Peter could only smile. "I got ya. I need to give two weeks where I'm at. Will that work for you?"

Brad looked up to a calendar on the wall while whispering numbers. "The sixteenth is a Friday. You be here at four forty-five in the a.m. Lori, my assistant manager, will probably be opening that day. Lori's a good girl." Brad winked. "I stole her from Starbucks."

The men stood and shook hands. "See you in two weeks, Peter Bishop," Brad said with a smile. "Do not disappoint me."

Peter nodded back to his new employer. "Deal." Then he turned to leave, surveying the new decor of the coffee house with its stylish antique counter, pastry case, and comfortable chairs and tables. He was already feeling at home surrounded by the old world feel of natural oak, brass fixtures and the smell of freshly ground Arabica beans.

"All things new," he whispered. Then he slipped back out into the sunshine.

Chapter Fourteen

The next fourteen days inched along until the early morning hours of the sixteenth. Peter met the five-foot-four Lori Wilson as she was unlocking the front door. The almost perky assistant manager flashed her new trainee a smile.

"Brad was right. You ex-Army guys do show up on time. Glad to see that."

Once inside, the security system was disarmed and the training began.

Peter found an apron, a forest green Polo shirt and a badge with his name on it in the back office. Once in proper uniform, he followed Lori on a short tour of the store. She pushed lighted buttons and flipped switches while familiarizing him with everything behind the counter and in the stock room that doubled as a break area.

Fresh coffee started brewing fifteen minutes before opening as Peter finished arranging the pastry case according to a picture display chart. All the lights were on, music playing and the doors unlocked at exactly five thirty. The first customer, a public transit bus driver, came in a few minutes later. While Lori showed Peter how to pull shots and steam milk for a sixteen ounce extra hot mocha, two well-dressed ladies walked in.

"Good morning, everyone," the assistant manager said brightly over the noise of the steamer. "Training the new guy here," she said rolling her eyes. "You know how that goes."

"Thank you, thank you!" Peter said with a wave and a bow. "I'll be here all week."

"You hope so," chimed the bus driver with a chuckle. "Better get my mocha right."

Lori moved methodically, explaining each step in creating the drink. Within three minutes, every drink was made and paid for at the register. Suddenly it was just the two of them again and the upbeat sounds of jazz coming from the speakers overhead.

"One wave down. How many to go in a morning?"

Lori laughed. "That wasn't a wave. That wasn't even a ripple, Peter, Peter pumpkin eater. We'll get a few here and there till about six-thirty. Then it'll pick up. Joel will be in at six and I'll have you shadow him for a while."

Peter filled out new hire paperwork between customers. At five after six, a short, stocky young man wearing a partial uniform entered. He rubbed his bloodshot eyes and yawned.

"Sorry I'm late, Lori. My car wouldn't start," he said. He looked over to Peter. "Ooohh, the new guy. What's up, Bro? I'm Joel."

Peter shook his coworker's hand. "I'm Peter, the official new guy and your shadow."

After clocking in and talking with Lori, Joel continued on where Lori left off. Peter watched with amazement as Joel skillfully handled the dizzying process of making multiple drinks at once. From ten to seven to almost nine-thirty there was a steady line of business men and women, bikers, mothers and strollers, police, cowboys and ladies in Lycra. Peter was completely overwhelmed.

"Don't worry, buddy," Joel said with a smile. "You'll get the hang of it. Just takes lots of practice. And you'll get plenty of that!"

Peter met two more coffee partners when they started their shifts. They said their hellos and seamlessly blended right into their places. Peter glanced at the clock and couldn't believe it was noon already.

The last few minutes of his shift, Lori showed him how to work the coffee grinder and weigh the proper amounts in white filters for the house brewer. Then it was time for him to clock out.

"So what do you think? Still want to learn business?" Lori asked with a teasing smile.

"Oh yeah!" Peter said.

"Good, cause you're with me all weekend and you better not be late like someone else I know," she said kicking Joel's leg playfully as he sat at the break table. "Brad likes to throw the new guys to the wolves the first day so they can see how everything works. Then we'll focus on drinks, the till, inventory, whatever else I can think of. Saturday mornings are a little slower at first, so I'm going to work one-on-one with you making drinks and you better not screw up."

Peter ordered an iced vanilla latte for the road and headed home. It was an odd feeling to be done with a day's work before one in the afternoon. He hoped he could catch on to all the little details he had to learn. There was a whole lot more to coffee than he originally thought.

One day down. It was a good day.

Lori and Peter remained glued to the espresso making beast for the first two hours of Saturday morning. Peter learned what abbreviations to write on the cups and what and how much flavoring each hot specialty beverage should get. They made extra drinks between customers to keep the training going. What wasn't for a customer was given away to another coworker or turned into samples for people walking by outside. Things were beginning to make sense.

Sunday morning was a repeat of Saturday morning. Lori kept up the pace and Peter learned. After the first break, they turned their attention to ice drinks and a new set of abbreviations, clear cups, flavorings and a blender that would make a man go deaf. The blended ice drinks with chocolate, coconut, and almonds were hot sellers and Peter's favorite.

At the end of his shift, Peter noticed the tired expression of a lingering pain on Lori's face. She was rubbing her forehead. He walked back to the office.

"Is working with me giving you a headache?"

"I wish it were just that. I can fire you. I can't fire this," she said with a heavy sigh.

"Anything I can do?" Peter asked.

"No. Thanks for asking." She leaned back in the leather chair. "You're doing really great, Peter. Keep it up. You'll have all this down lickity split."

"I've got a terrific trainer." Then Peter knelt down close to her. "I just wish you weren't hurting."

"It'll pass. Speaking of which, I'm passing you off to Mr. Brad. The schedule's on the wall there," she said, pointing to a cork board. "And don't whine about your hours. It's Brad's idea, and he's the man."

Peter saw that he would be closing for the next four days with Brad. "Sounds great. I could use a break from you."

"Too much for you, huh? Well, better get used to me, buster. I ain't disappearing anytime soon."

"I'll get used to you," Peter said as he walked down the hall. "See you later."

"Don't let the door hit you on the way out."

Peter thought of another smart remark, but stopped when he looked back.

She sat with her eyes closed slowly rubbing the sides of her head.

Peter was glad to see the Warners at Michael and Daylene's house for dinner again. They were back from their trip to Flagstaff to visit Tom's family. Peter shared some of his adventures in espresso making and listened to more of their stories of the road. What he really wanted to know more about was the many churches Valarie spoke of. Later in the kitchen, Peter started to ask again, but stopped when he noticed her furrowed brow and the faint shaking of her head. It wasn't time. Peter didn't bring it up again.

The evening ended with a few a capella songs of harmonized praise on the back patio. The presence of the Lord descended sweetly upon them like a soft blanket, while the stars peered down from the dark velvet heavens, jealous.

Working with Brad Stellar was a kick. He was somehow all business and all comedy, both intense and extremely funny. His motto was, *"If you're not having fun, you're doing it wrong."* Brad lived his motto and did his best to run his coffee house with a strict mix of business and pleasure.

Over the next four evenings, Peter learned the cash register, made drinks and memorized the closing procedures. Evenings were much slower paced, but shrewdly staffed to handle a sudden rush of business and prepare for a busy next day. Brad made sure Peter understood why he wanted things done the way he wanted them done. In most cases, it was about saving money on the single biggest expense of nearly any business: labor. Peter was getting a master's level course on being an entrepreneur from the University of Real Life.

Peter kept a six-day, forty to forty-four-hour work week for just over minimum wage the first month. He received a dollar an hour raise at the beginning of the second month. The tips made up the difference for a small paycheck and kept gas in his truck.

As Peter became more comfortable working the front of the store, and Brad was more comfortable with Peter, he got to see the behind the scenes nuts and bolts of running a successful coffeehouse. According to the books, Stellar Coffee Company was doing better than projected. But Brad was always quick to point out to Peter, "Never rest on your laurels, my friend. All it takes is one nearby competitor, doing things just a hint better, to steal enough business to shut your doors."

In addition to Brad's practical business wisdom, Peter got a free education in politics as well from the most popular voice in talk radio, Rush Limbaugh. During some late morning shifts, either on break or helping with inventory in the back office, Peter listened with Brad as the entertaining commentator explained the virtues of conservatism. It was another bond the two coffee men shared.

He was nearing the end of his ninety-day probation when Peter experienced the darkest day of his new career.

It started at nine-thirty when he missed a mandatory staff meeting. Peter was still in bed sound asleep. When he showed up on time for his shift, Lori let him have it with both barrels. Two hours later, the lid to a large iced mocha came off as he handed it to a customer. The man in a newly pressed, blue pin-striped shirt and tie was headed to a funeral. He vowed to never come back. The evening ended for Peter with his till coming up $9.32 short. The coffeehouse owner was not his chipper self but said nothing about the discrepancy.

Peter set the alarm and the two men headed for the door at the end of the difficult day.

Out on the sidewalk, Peter apologized profusely for his string of errors. Brad threw his apron over his shoulder listening, though disconnected.

"You like Brenda's here in the mall?" Brad asked. "Great omelets."

"Never been." Peter said.

"We'll, let's grab breakfast in the morning. Nine work for you?

"It does."

"Okay. See you then."

Peter sped his way under the streetlights and recounted his many errors of the day. While putting seven dollars' worth of gas in his truck at a Circle K, all he could think about was the angry and embarrassed face of the man he'd drenched earlier. The pump stopped and he replaced the hose with Lori's stern rebuke still ringing in his ears. As he rolled forward from the pumps, another car pulled in front of him. Both of the occupants glanced his way. The man in the passenger seat looked back again. The driver smiled back toward Peter before pulling out into traffic.

It was Traci.

Inside the country-themed breakfast and lunch restaurant, Peter worked on a lightly creamed cup of bland coffee while going over the menu. Brad arrived soon after, wearing comfortable burgundy red sweats. He looked strikingly different out of uniform. Peter watched his employer greet the staff and the owner with his infectious smile and engaging demeanor.

Brad arrived at the table with a cup of coffee and a large steaming cinnamon roll cut in half. "Just came out of the oven," he said. "Is that timing or what?" He handed Peter a fork and sat down.

The butter melted with the icing and dripped down the side of the roll. The rich cinnamon aroma called out to Peter. He licked his lips and said, "This will do wonders for my figure."

Brad laughed. "You and me both." He cut a section off of his half and devoured it with an ear to ear grin. "Speaking of figures, Lori says you were off on your fives. You were only short $4.32, not $9.32. She says you can live."

"Thank God," Peter replied. He was equally relieved that Brad was back to his normal self.

The two men joked through the rest of the cinnamon roll and coffee. Then each ordered something more substantial off the menu. Peter changed his mind from chicken fried steak and eggs to a breakfast B.L.T and hash browns. Brad opted for the sausage and Swiss cheese omelet with jalapeno peppers and onions. They dined sumptuously for the next forty minutes.

"So let's talk shop," Brad said as he pushed his empty plate away and rested his leg up on booth seat. "You've had three months behind the counter. Are you still serious about coffee or do you just want to keep playing at it?"

Peter swallowed his last bite. "Still serious."

"How serious? I mean, how far do you want to go with it?"

Peter slid his plate away. "In the fall, I start training for the ministry. But if I can do it, I'd like my own coffee place someday."

"Sounds good," Brad replied while running his eyes over the cowboy paintings and horseshoe art on the wall.

"I'd like to stay on through Bible school."

"How long is this Bible school?"

"One year of two nights per week and Sundays, followed by six months assisting a local church. If all goes well, then I'll be ordained. After that I'll go start a church somewhere."

Brad listened and calculated. "So you'll be with us for eighteen months?"

"I'd like to be."

"I think we can work something out, so long as you don't have too many days like yesterday."

"Peter groaned. "Yeah, sorry about all that."

"No one else is interested in going further at the shop. In fact, we'll be losing a few when school starts back up. But that's expected." Then Brad became somber. "Then there's Lori."

Peter leaned in closer. "What about Lori?"

Brad sighed, choosing his words carefully. "Between family situations and health issues that I don't know all about, she's going to be leaving soon. We were both hoping for at least a year, but she can't do it anymore. Keep that to yourself, please. I'm telling you because if I can count on you for the next year and half, then let's start training you to become assistant manager."

Peter heard more bitter than sweet in the news of a promotion. Lori had been a good trainer and friend. The place wouldn't be the same without her. Finally, Peter said, "I'm game. Let's do it."

Lori trained Peter on back office tasks until he was proficient. Then he became the regular opener, allowing for her to work a shorter, mid-morning to mid-afternoon shift. Three weeks later, Lori was down to two days a week. Then she was done.

On her last day, the staff gathered around Lori. Brad handed her a large bouquet of flowers while others handed her cards. After a round of hugs from everyone, a teary-eyed Lori pinned a new assistant manager badge on Peter. There were no dry eyes.

"Quit crying you big baby," she said, giving Peter a hug. "Don't not let me down or don't tell anyone I trained you."

Lori came into the coffeehouse the following week for her favorite chai latte. Peter never saw her again after that.

Business growth and staff changes over the remaining days of summer made Joel and Peter the old-timers. In six months, Stellar Coffee Company had become the favorite haunt for many locals and sales steadily grew every month. Brad and Peter worked together on clever ways to promote the coffeehouse. They were active in the Chamber of Commerce, offered coupons, gave discounts to veterans, and offered samples of something every day.

At the end of every evening, any food items left over picked up or delivered to the local women's shelter. Brad made sure of it. Peter was grateful to be working for a man with such integrity and generosity.

Chapter Fifteen

Sunday, September 7th arrived on time and with much anticipation for thirty-one would be pastors. Peter sat in the front row of the Mesa church sanctuary, blending in with the other energized young men around him. The well-orchestrated kick-off event starting the new academic year was in the famous Great Assemblies first class tradition. Ernest Blake, the most visible personality from The Great Sunday Celebration Show, as well as Evan Seager, the Senior Pastor in charge of Pastoral Training were headlining the evening.

Peter looked around at the large, open auditorium. The Mesa church building was chosen for the Bible school for its size. The GAOC purchased the property after the former department store went bankrupt. Worshipers now gathered where racks of clothing and housewares used to be. Attendance for a typical Sunday morning was about three hundred with a good number of empty seats. Tonight was a capacity crowd with several rows of extra chairs brought in to handle the people still coming through the doors. The air was charged with excitement and anticipation.

At 7:05 the lights dimmed and the audience quickly hushed. Those still standing scurried to their seats while a river of melody cascaded majestically from the musicians behind a woman in the ethereal glow of a spotlight. She sang in the key of honey. Her words fell like warm oil upon the ear. Never was *"How Great Thou Art"* more eloquently sung.

After a well-deserved standing ovation followed by applause and shouts of praise to the King of Kings and Lord of Lords, Senior Pastor Evan Seager addressed the crowd.

"Tonight we begin the second year of accelerated training for ministers to go out into the field that is already white unto harvest. Thirty-one men have accepted the challenge to learn from those who have gone before them to reach the lost. Last year was our first year to offer such an intensive course that would, in eighteen months, prepare a diligent individual for the ministry. I can say with a grateful heart that there are a dozen new assistant pastors who have completed the academic portion of their education, and are now in the apprentice phase, being mentored by veteran pastors in churches all over these United States as a direct result of our efforts last year."

Applause broke out across the sea of attendees. Peter and the young men next to him clapped vigorously, expecting to be among the new assistant pastors only a year from now.

"Last year was, admittedly, a year of trial and error. Many of our plans needed to be fine-tuned and adjusted as we went on. This year, we'll build on a more sure foundation, with a new identity. May I present to you The Great Faith College of Ministry."

A large, circular logo of glistening gold and purple instantly projected onto the large screen behind the assembled presbytery on stage. More applause and shouts encouraged the senior pastor on as he outlined the direction for the coming year.

The course of the evening was inspiring for all in attendance. Peter was captivated by the glitter and challenged by the lofty preaching of Brother Ernest Blake.

At the conclusion of the preaching, each new student received a beautifully embossed binder with course materials, a laminated schedule for the year, and the prayers of hundreds of well-wishing strangers. Three television cameras captured the night in vivid color for airing the following weekend on Great Sunday Celebration. Looking over the schedule, Peter confirmed that the first class would begin Tuesday evening, and took note of the special instructions highlighted in yellow to wear work clothes. A fellow student with Stephen on his name badge joked, "Maybe we're to dress for urban spiritual warfare. No ties so we'll blend into a crowd, find our victim, then blammo! Hit 'em with the Word!"

Peter finished his shift at the coffeehouse and arrived a few minutes to six on Tuesday evening. He joined the familiar faces of the others in the large, well-appointed classroom. At the front of the room near the podium, was the instructor, Pastor Jared Daniels. Pastor Daniels was a tall, thin man in his mid-forties with a full head of hair, but in desperate need of a tan. Peter introduced himself, then took his seat in the third row.

The instructor began by going over the schedule and the various blocks of instruction. "Your learning is going to be part heaven and part earth," Daniels began. "Tuesday will be devoted to the Word and preaching while Thursdays will be focused on structure, organization and management and adherence to laws governing non-profit organizations. Let's face it gentlemen, if we get fire, let it come from the Holy Ghost and not from the IRS."

After an hour of instruction, Pastor Daniels led the class to the sanctuary where they had met just a few evenings before. The students stood around the altar that wrapped around the platform, while the instructor wheeled a large crate down the aisle. In the moment of quiet waiting for instructions, Peter thought about the many visits to this very altar where he'd poured out his grief, confessed his sins, and prayed for others. The dark wood, polished with many tears, was a welcome sight. How often had sinners and saints come to a place of repentance at such a place? Sometimes church didn't seem complete unless he'd made his way here and bent his knees to his Maker. Peter was grateful to be learning how to lead others to the saving knowledge of Christ and how they too could unload their burdens as he had done so often.

Daniels asked everyone to take part in clearing off the platform. "We are fast approaching a new millennium," he said as the men worked together. "The ways in which men will reach souls for the Kingdom of God are changing, and we must change with them. Today's highways and byways are more electronic then they are concrete and asphalt. Great Faith College of Ministry will be on the cutting edge of communications and media, on television, radio and soon on the internet. That takes change. And change starts right here by enlarging our platform to preach from."

Pastor Daniels reached into the crate for something. "Everyone grab a hammer. We're ripping out the altar."

Peter's classmates were an eclectic mix of American males

ranging in age from eighteen to thirty-nine. Seven were preacher's kids. Two were former drug addicts. One was a surfer dude and another guy could have been a model on the cover of GQ Magazine. Most were single. Peter was one of four who were divorced. The rest were scattered somewhere between country and city, north and south.

John Thomas Petersen or J.T. to his friends, a local Phoenix dweller and movie aficionado, became Peter's closest friend. He was recently married and had a baby on the way. Next was Daryl Bernard, an easy going ski bum from Park City, Utah. He spoke often of a ministry to other snow lovers. These three became a tight circle of friends and spent many hours together studying, debating scripture, or sharing popcorn in front of the latest DVD release.

The coffeehouse became a regular place for many of the Bible students to hang out. Peter worked out a buy nine get the tenth drink free punch card deal for the students. Every little bit of savings helped.

The Tuesday – Thursday "heaven and earth" schedule went well. Pastor Daniels was a skilled teacher and the course curriculum was clearly laid out and easy to process, though the sounds of construction in the sanctuary were distracting for the first two weeks.

Daniels led the class through the first quarter of the year, then other pastors and teachers took over. On Sundays, the students were divided up and rotated between several churches in Chandler, Gilbert, Tempe, Mesa and Phoenix. They participated in services, and served the pastors and congregations as needed. Serving meant anything from cleaning toilets to passing out songbooks, taking up the collection plates or ushering.

By Thanksgiving, the sanctuary had been transformed into a theater style auditorium. The stage was a full four feet high with cables and wires running underneath. The once level floor for the audience now ascended like a stadium with fold down, theater style seating. State of the art audio and video booths were built in under the highest rows.

The students were trained in the Great Assemblies method of crafting a sermon using a key scripture, an opening illustration, three main points with supporting scriptures, a summary and even a complementary song to close with. They were also taught the history of the GAOC and the backgrounds of the original twenty-one founders.

December was a month devoted to "filthy lucre" with a new pastoral teacher. He was a financial genius and former stock broker. "Wise financial stewardship," he taught, "is as important as anything else. Luke tells us that if we cannot handle unrighteous mammon properly, who will commit to us the true riches?"

Every student was to prepare a sermon about the importance of tithing, giving offerings and managing money. Peter was amazed at how little he really knew about handling money, the miracle of compounding interest, and the perils of debt. It was the last month he ever paid only the minimum on his credit cards.

It didn't seem possible but stores in the malls were beginning to decorate with oversized bunnies and Easter baskets full of colored eggs. Between the coffeehouse and college there wasn't much room anything else. Fortunately, he was doing well at both, though at times he thought he'd lost his personality somewhere along the way.

On a Friday in late April, his only full day off in the week, he decided to go for a hike alone around the base of Superstition Mountain. Along the way, he stopped for an iced beverage at a competing coffee shop off Highway 60. He was in line waiting to order when two young men in camouflage pants and dark sunglasses got in line behind him. He chuckled at their Rambo wannabe appearance and tough guy talk about military tactics. Dime Store Soldiers. They knew nothing about being a soldier. He paid for his drink and snickered all the way to his truck.

Peter parked near the entrance to the trail head system leading up to where many had searched for the legendary Lost Dutchman Mine. The tall green saguaro cactus, like protective sentries, dotted the hills against the dramatic backdrop of jagged, rust colored mountain. He climbed upward for nearly an hour before resting on a rocky ledge near a pool of cool water. Spread out beneath him under a thin layer of late morning haze was the eastern edge of the greater Phoenix area. The warm sun rested gently on his face and shoulders as he considered the view of the sprawling valley of five million souls below.

A light breeze ran up his back and with it came a disconcerting thought. Peter heard voices of other hikers and decided to head back down the rocky trail.

A real minister of God or a dime store preacher?

Peter drove back into the city recounting biblical and present day heroes of faith. Men and women who found the approval of God and inherited promises. They seemed so very different then the man he saw in his own mirror. He thought about the college and what he was learning: basic Old and New Testament, sermon development, enlisting and managing volunteers, loyalty to Great Assemblies, disbursement of tithes and offerings, organizing events, and soon how to install and use the latest multimedia gadgetry. Interesting and helpful subjects all, but he still wondered.

Army Basic Training was eight weeks of learning very specific tasks until they were second nature. He knew his weapons inside and out and how to engage the enemy. At the coffeehouse, Lori had taken him by the hand and showed him how to pull shots of espresso, steam milk, and add flavors to make the perfect drink. Brad led by example how to run a business, practically transplanting his own heart for coffee and customer care into Peter's chest.

By contrast, no one ever led Peter into effectual, fervent prayer. He'd heard about the gospel, but couldn't comfortably explain it to someone else. The moving of the Spirit was a complete mystery, and miracles were always referred to in the past tense. He wondered why there weren't classes on these subjects. "Maybe I'm the only one who doesn't know these things," he thought, though his buddies didn't seem to know any more than he did.

He shook himself and turned on the radio. "Getting too serious in here," he yelled. "Lighten up, man! It's my day off for crying out loud!"

Chapter Sixteen

She sat by herself watching people come in and out of the coffeehouse as she ate whipped cream and caramel drizzle on her drink. She studied the customers; what they wore, how they ordered their drinks, and how they walked out. She watched with hidden jealousy as young girls flirted with him. "That's not okay," she whispered to herself. "How could he even like those girls?"

Then it would calm down again and he would come back to her table in the corner. She watched him walk out to be with her and her alone.

"How's my Katie-Girl?" he asked.

"I'm good. Who were *those* girls?"

"Just customers," he said, while pulling up a chair to sit close. "I don't know their names. I just know I have a job because of them."

The critical shadow lifted and a smile returned to the adoring face of his niece.

"I'll find you a wife, Uncle Peter. And she'll be really nice and won't leave you, okay?"

He hugged the sweetest girl in the whole world. "You do that, Katie. I'm sure you'll find the right one for me."

She nodded confidently. "I will. And I'll come and visit all the time and I can work in your coffeehouse."

"That's right. And have all the whipped cream and nuts you could ever want."

"You'd have to pay me too."

Peter chuckled. "Got that money thing figured out already, huh?

She moved the straw from her lips. "Heck yeah!"

Sundays were as educational as any Tuesday or Thursday evening. One Sunday in particular forever altered Peter's perspective about the relationship between a full-time minister and the congregation.

A meeting was called after worship service for all the men of the 500-member Chandler church. Steve Riggins, the men's ministry pastor, was on a personal mission to involve more men in the activities of the church. Pastor Riggins was an intelligent, gregarious man full of charm, but with a directness that made many uncomfortable around him.

Peter and five other student ministers joined approximately thirty men into the media room just off the sanctuary. Most were casually dressed with calloused hands and weary face from back breaking, outdoor work. From their somber appearance, church attendance was more about placating their wives and children then worshiping God.

"Thanks guys, this will only take a moment," Pastor Riggins began. "At the beginning of the month, we started a Saturday morning men's breakfast fellowship. I was hoping we could break bread together for hour or two and challenge each other to a closer walk with God. But the last two Saturdays, there were only three of us." The polished pastor looked around the room. "If the word didn't get out, then consider this my attempt at fixing that. Is there a way I can get a commitment from each man here to become a regular participant on Saturday fellowships?"

Peter watched some of the men look around at each other for a moment. A retired gentleman with white hair in the corner said, "I'll be there Pastor Steve. How about it, men?" A few others mumbled words of agreement and nodded. Steve looked at a couple of brawny men seated in the front. "Will that work for you, Gary and Robert?"

The two men didn't respond right away and the tension in the air grew quickly. Gary looked at Robert, then up to the younger minister.

"I don't mean any disrespect, Pastor Steve, but what exactly do all day? What's your work week like?"

Steve appeared puzzled and fidgeted with his tie. "I'm part of a full time ministry staff, Gary. I serve the church as needed."

"I know that," Gary said thoughtfully. "But what does that look like on Monday?

"Well, most of the staff takes Mondays off."

A ripple of chuckles came from around the room. Gary smiled. "Okay, Tuesday through Friday then."

Pastor Steven Riggins sighed a bit defensively. "I'm in my office by nine. Usually there are several messages to respond to or perhaps something more urgent. We have staff meetings on Tuesdays and Fridays. I meet with couples, pray and study the word, assist with preparation for Sunday services and coordinate activities till about four or four-thirty."

Gary looked at Robert, then around the room at a few of the other men. He cleared his throat and replied, "Steve, uh, most everyone here will be working Mondays. I'll be on the job site around six running two crews of semi-skilled, semi-sober laborers outside with heavy equipment. If nothing breaks down and we stay on schedule, we'll call it a day around six. If not, we'll be moving tons of equipment by hand between vehicles in the heat without air, and I'll pull into my driveway at home around eight. If we can keep up the pace, we'll keep our jobs. I'll bet most of these guys here have similar schedules."

Robert nodded in quiet agreement while rubbing his cracked thumb over the back of his massive hands. His friend continued.

"My wife already complains that I'm not home enough. I end up missing most of my kids' school events but sometimes I can't help it. We're here pretty regular on Sundays so that only leaves one day for us. So I hope you and God will understand if I decide to stay in bed with my wife as long as I can, make blueberry pancakes for my kids when I get up, and spend as much time with my family on the only day of the week I don't have to be somewhere."

Pastor Riggins thanked everyone for coming and dismissed the meeting.

There were no finals for the ministry students. Instead there were essays and interviews. The essays would gauge comprehension of materials. The interview would reveal loyalty to Great Assemblies and adherence to doctrines and standards. It would also determine where a student would be placed for the remaining six months of their hands on ministerial training.

During Peter's interview, he was asked why he still used the King James Version. "It's what I grew up on, and what has fed my soul the most. The other versions seem to be missing something. Some are missing entire verses."

The college instructor lowered his glasses. "You do realize that Great Assemblies is phasing out the King James in favor of the New International Version?"

Peter stared back unsettled. "No, I didn't know that."

"Is that going to be a problem?"

Memories of watching Jay Hammond preach with nothing but his King James Bible on Great Sunday Celebration, memorizing verses with his mother and reading in the barracks in Germany all collided in his mind. Peter remembered listening to old timers of faith point out the differences in the versions. The changes didn't make it easier to read, but actually added to and subtracted from the Word of God. Changing versions was an issue that had troubled many within the ranks of Great Assemblies. After reading from both the King James and the N.I.V., Peter felt the difference was like comparing steak to jello.

The news was like hearing of a death family. He didn't answer the question.

The interviewer made a note in Peter's file.

Chapter Seventeen

At the end of the last Sunday service in August, the student ministers were honored before the congregation for completing the academic year. The official ordination ceremony would be held in February after their work in the field. They were given their local church assignments in a decorative parchment bound by a thin scarlet ribbon. Peter opened the ceremonial scroll and discovered that he was assigned to Pastor Gregory Barnes in Apache Junction, approximately thirty-five miles east of downtown Phoenix, at the edge of the valley. Gregory was to be Peter's spiritual mentor and evaluator for the next six months. To a large degree, Peter's future with Great Assemblies rested in the hands of Pastor Barnes.

Waves of heat rose from the sunbaked asphalt as Peter drove into the parking lot of the church facilities a mile north of Highway 60 in Apache Junction. Peter was met by a brisk walking man in a faded blue Polo shirt.

"You Peter Bishop?" the man asked, hoping for a quick response.

"I am. You must be Pastor Barnes"

"I am today, but please call me Greg. "Hey you" works too. Can you walk and talk?"

"I've done it before," Peter joked while picking up the pace to keep up.

Greg wiped his brow. "If it's not one thing it's another around here. The AC guy is about to leave and I have to give him the warranty info so he won't bill us directly. It might take weeks to straighten out."

After several minutes in the 112-degree heat with the technician, the two men walked back to Pastor Barnes' office.

Greg was younger than Peter expected and unremarkable at first glance. He was average in height, weight and appearance; a man with light brown hair and gray-green eyes. Nothing about him stood out except a comforting genuineness. Peter felt comfortable with him immediately. They shared ice teas while getting to know one another in his quiet, brick walled office. A small indoor fountain offered the calming sounds of water spilling over rocks from the corner behind the desk.

Greg looked over the papers Peter brought with him then asked with a smile, "So what'd you do wrong to get assigned here?"

"What do you mean by that?"

"This isn't a new church start up. It's more of a stop the bleeding operation. About two months ago, the senior pastor died. Almost as soon as the funeral was over, his wife moved back east where the rest of her family lives. The two assistant pastors squabbled and fought over leadership, splitting the church before I was asked to come up from Tucson to help out. Quite a mess. I was surprised to hear they were sending a minister in training out here with all this going on."

"Maybe to experience the tough stuff first?"

"That's one way to look at it I suppose."

"They brought you up from Tucson? Aren't there other pastors here to take things over?"

"I grew up Great Assemblies and have been an assistant pastor for about three years while working with my dad in his print shop. This was a promotion of sorts, I guess," he said, rolling his eyes and shaking his head. "Makes me wonder if I did something wrong."

Greg shuffled papers looking around for something on his desk. "Regular attendance here used to be around three hundred-ish. Four hundred on holidays. Last Sunday, with a few kids, we had about forty."

Peter listened with a sinking heart. "So what's the plan to stop the bleeding?"

"That's the $3,900 a month question," Greg replied. "We're in the red big time for the lease on this property. And forget utilities or something for the staff." Greg sipped on his muddy iced tea. "Staff. What staff? I'm the staff. And you too if you decide to stick around. Probably won't matter for long. From what I'm hearing through the grapevine the property is being looked at by other churches for an outright purchase. Great Assemblies doesn't want to buy it. Stopping the bleeding will be part amputation, and part helping the faithful few find other churches to join."

"What about expanding or turning it into a new church operation?"

"It could turn out that way. My wife and I agreed to fill the gap until something definite was determined. Then we'll be back in Tucson. That's our home and where God has led us to serve. Maybe you'll be the new pastor here, although I understand that's not usually the case."

Greg adjusted in his chair and folded his hands on the desk. "The most unfortunate part of all this is how the new babes in Christ get shaken. They see God's people, church leaders in this case, arguing and fighting and acting just like the world and they lose their faith. It's like so many Christians don't get a proper upbringing. You see kids today with no manners and you wonder about their parents, right? Same thing spiritually. No manners. No decency or respect to those new in their walk with God, you know?"

Peter never heard spiritual responsibility explained in such a common sense way before. The circumstances of the church were far from ideal, but teaming up with the practical minister before him seemed like a divine pairing. "Well, I'm here to learn, Greg. So let me know what kind of schedule you have in mind, and I'll adjust my coffeehouse schedule around it."

"Oooohhh that's right. You're Mr. Coffee," Greg said with a brightened expression. "I'm sure some of your training will have to involve something cold, dark and sweet, with whipped cream. I'm sure there's scripture on the benefits of such things."

Peter laughed. "There must be."

"I'll prepare a Sunday message on it."

"And I'll bring the visual aids."

"You'll have to bring enough for everyone."

"Forty people, you say?"

"About that."

"I'll see what I can do."

"Excellent, we're off to a great start. Now as I understand the plan, I'm supposed to mentor you for the next six months. I'm a pretty straight forward guy, Peter. I'm not into heavenly knowledge that can't translate into any earthly good."

"That makes two of us."

"Sunday Service starts at ten. Can you be here at nine and we'll have some prayer time together and go over things?"

"Nine works for me."

"And I heard something about coffee..."

"I'll bring the coffee."

Peter coordinated with Brad about a mobile coffee cart set up with air pots, creamer, sugar, stir sticks and cups for the following Sunday. Brad handed his assistant manager a stack of Half Off coupons with the words, "Let 'em know where they can come get more."

Peter set up the cart in the lobby just outside of the sanctuary. At nine, he entered the sanctuary to meet Pastor Greg in front of the stained, dark wood pulpit. He passed several rows of pews with brown colored padding. The morning light poured through a mix of stained and plain translucent windows along the top and sides of the walls. Peter handed Greg cup of fresh coffee.

"You are the man, Peter. Thank you." Greg savored the rich Sumatra blend for a moment. "You'll soon discover that I'm not a typical preacher. I like discussion and participation. To me, Jesus asked questions as much as he preached messages. He drew things out of people as much as he planted into them." Greg turned to the empty pews. "Involving people gives everyone a chance to participate, and gives me a chance to hear other perspectives. Sometimes I teach; sometimes I learn."

Peter looked out to the pews imagining them full of families, when a young Hispanic woman with long black hair in a rose-red dress came into the sanctuary.

"Peter this is my wife, Nona. Honey, this is Peter Bishop my temporary assistant from Great Faith College."

Nona smiled brightly, "How are you Peter?"

"Excellent. Nice to meet you, Nona."

Greg whispered aside to Peter, "She's the smart one in the family. Has a degree in everything."

"Stop, husband of mine. Should I put the music on?"

"Yes, please," Greg said as he watched his wife walk toward the sound room in the back. "Can you play an organ or piano, Peter?"

"I play CDs and the radio."

"Our organ player left a few weeks ago. So we've been singing with just our voices. But this is nice for prayer and to open with."

Instrumental praise music fell from the speakers over head as Nona rejoined the men at the front. Peter watched Greg and Nona turn and face the front. Greg closed his eyes and raised his hands in worship. Nona walked softly moving her hands about her whispering the name of Jesus.

When Peter prayed with others, it was usually with a bowed head in agreement with someone else praying. This was different. He closed his eyes, but opened them frequently to watch them. He saw Tom and Valarie pray like this at times. Where do people learn this? He felt like a child in knee deep water wishing he could go play with the others in the deep end of the pool.

Nona walked softly behind Peter. He heard her speak, but didn't understand her. He thought she was praying in Spanish. She stepped away again, her hands moved and swayed in an invisible current. Greg appeared lost in heavenly conversation. Tears streamed down his face as he lifted his voice up in praise to God.

Peter could feel a comforting presence around him, then moving into him. He closed his eyes again and spoke out praise like Greg was. "I praise you, God. I magnify you, Lord." It was awkward at first. It sounded so personal and intimate coming from Greg and Nona. Then Greg stopped and was quiet. Peter looked over to his mentor. He appeared to be listening to something, even nodding. Nona moved gingerly around the platform whispering her prayers.

Peter suddenly felt embarrassed even naked. "Oh my God!" he thought. "I can't even pray right. What if Greg finds out I can't pray?" A small trickle of sweat ran down the center of his back. "What if he calls the college and tells them I can't pray? What would he say? Hey, you sent me a defective minister! He can't even pray!"

Peter was jarred out of his thoughts by an arm around his

shoulders. "I'll introduce you as my new assistant pastor to everyone this morning," Greg said. "Why don't you stand with me and greet people? They're starting to arrive."

The first couple was dressed comfortably for the heat of the day. They appeared quite interested to know there was an assistant pastor joining the staff.

More cars and minivans pulled into the parking lot. Each person and family, some wealthy, some not, all brought their own sense of style and character as they entered the front doors.

He didn't see them pull in, but Michael, his mother, Tom and Valarie, all colorfully dressed and wearing dark sunglasses appeared at the door.

"Well, who's this guy?" Tom said loudly with a cheesy smile.

Michael followed up with, "Where's the food? We heard it was all you can eat."

Valarie rolled her eyes. "Should have left you two in the car."

Peter hugged everyone and made introductions with Greg and Nona. Peter found himself watching Valarie assess the people and surroundings, always wanting to know what she saw or sensed.

At five past ten, Greg invited everyone into the sanctuary. The service began with a song Peter never heard before, but he followed the words on the overhead projector placed by Nona. Pastor Greg opened with prayer and led another couple of songs.

Then came a muffled, repetitious voice from the parking lot. A woman calling out and a loud thud at the door. Sounds of outdoor noise flooded the building. "Timothy, wait for mom! Come here, Timothy! Timothy!"

Nearly every head turned to see the single mother and her defiant four-and-a-half-year-old make their entrance. The little man made a growling noise that was followed by the sound of a dozen paper coffee cups hitting the tile floor. "Timothy, no!"

Peter excused himself quickly to help with the cleanup. He passed into the lobby in time to see a young woman picking up the cups and a young Timothy flicking sugar into the air with a plastic spoon.

"You must be Timothy," Peter said, taking the spoon away and kneeling at eye level to the boy. "Let's help mom pick up these cups, huh?" To Peter's surprise, Timothy turned, picked up a cup and handed it to his mother.

The woman in a blue dress collected the last cup and placed them on the cart. "Thank God he listens to somebody," she said fixing her hair. "You must be new. I'm Brianna."

Peter shook her hand and introduced himself, then he moved the coffee cart to a safer location. He could feel her eyes on him as he slipped back into the sanctuary and sat next to Michael near the aisle. "The joys of parenting," he whispered.

Michael leaned over, "And a strong case for abstinence."

Brianna escorted her son into the pew directly behind Peter. Then she unzipped her bag stuffed with plastic distractions to keep Timothy quietly occupied.

Pastor Greg looked out to the congregation with a disarming smile and asked, "What is a Christian to you?"

The church was quiet as he walked slowly up the aisle. "Anyone? What is a Christian to you?"

An older woman with salt and pepper hair seated next to her grown daughter responded with, "I think a Christian is someone who doesn't cut you off when you're driving."

"Oh for Pete's sake Etta," snorted a man from the opposite side of the aisle. "I didn't cut you off!"

"Like hell you didn't!"

"Mama, you can't say hell in church."

"Hush Lilly!" she said to her daughter. Then turning back to her highway nemesis, she said, "Brother Arnold, I guarantee you Jesus wouldn't cut someone off like that."

"Jesus would drive the speed limit, Etta! You're a road hazard!"

"Safe driving is always wise," Greg said steering the discussion in another direction. "But, consider this for a moment, according to Acts 11, long before cars and DMV, the disciples of Christ were first called Christians in a place called Antioch. The term 'Christian' was brand new. What would cause people to call other people Christians?"

The responses this time were more constructive and insightful.

Pastor Greg then led people into the word and eventually the timeless characteristics of the fruit of the Spirit. After the closing prayer, the two who had disagreed about driving etiquette acted more Christ-like and apologized to each other.

As much as Peter loved bold, dynamic preaching, he appreciated Pastor Greg Barnes' simple teaching style. It was easy to grasp, simple to apply and allowed for something he hadn't seen before in a church setting; participation.

After service, Peter put his mobile coffee stand away and joined Greg in his office. They talked about the lesson, the outbursts, and the young mother and her son, while Greg counted the tithes and offerings.

Nona came into the office and sat down on the brown sofa. "We had thirty-six today," she said without expression. "Minus your family and friends, we're at thirty-two."

Greg listened and pressed buttons on his calculator. "One hundred, fourteen dollars and fifty-one cents," he said looking at his wife.

"Are you doing anything after this, Peter?" Nona asked. "If not come over and have lunch with us."

"You should do it, Peter," Greg said with a twinkle in his eye. "Nona made a ham the other night that was better than great, and perfect for sandwiches. Add some chips, coleslaw and a gallon of ice tea and you'll whistle a tune!"

"How can I refuse?" Peter said.

"You can't. I'll tell the college board you're being insubordinate and you'll be done. So, just follow us home."

Nona pointed her finger at Peter and smirked. "And don't cut us off. That's not Christian."

"Right."

Peter enjoyed the afternoon with Greg and Nona at their small, two-bedroom apartment. The ham was every bit as good as Greg's claims and he ate his fill. He listened to the story of how they met, and how they'd been trying to have children without any success. Peter came to love this godly couple and relished every moment with them.

Greg and Peter continued their conversation close to the oscillating fan in the living room. "We stopped having Wednesday night services after it became obvious that Nona and I were going to be the only ones showing up. We have some prayer time together here, but I was thinking, if you're up to it, we could have Bible studies here on Wednesdays. It would do us both good to get into the Word together outside of Sunday mornings. Having a simple home Bible study with someone is probably one of the most effective ways to evangelize I've ever found. It's how our family came to know the Lord."

"Sounds great," Peter said. "I can get Wednesdays off without too much trouble. What time do you want me to show up?"

"Come over for dinner about five-thirty. We'll study the scriptures afterward." Greg finished his half-full glass of iced tea. "I asked the congregation what a Christian was to them this morning. You heard the responses. All over the place, right?"

Peter nodded.

"It's how most of us look at doctrine and any important topic really. It's what *we think* about it rather than what the *Bible says*. So few of us Christians really know the Word well enough to explain things from a book, chapter, and verse perspective. Anyway, I was going through some old files in the office and found some old Bible studies. Just scriptures – no commentary. I know I've read those verses before, but grouped together as a topical study the way they were was like reading them for the first time. Those studies are what I had in mind for us to go through."

Peter remembered the young men in fatigues and the conversation in his heart on his hike down Superstition Mountain. The thought of real, one-on-one time in the Word was exactly what he'd wanted. With a smile, he raised his glass to his mentor, "To Wednesday then."

Greg tapped Peter's glass with his own. "Wednesday it is."

Chapter Eighteen

To get Wednesday nights off from the coffeehouse, Peter had to close Tuesday night and open Wednesday morning. When he walked through the door of Greg and Nona's apartment, Peter was physically drained, but perked up when he saw a large bucket of Kentucky Fried Chicken on the table. KFC was a method of bribery Daylene used with young Peter to get him to do something he didn't want to do. It worked without fail.

Greg and Peter took over the kitchen table after dinner while Nona disappeared into the bedroom-turned-office. Greg pulled out a file folder from his briefcase and showed Peter several one-page studies laid out in two columns. On the right column, were several verses listed. On the left was a sentence highlighting each verse, or a question about the passage.

"Each study appears to stand alone," Greg started. "I figured we could go to each verse together, then take turns reading. Sound fair?"

Peter grabbed his Bible from the counter. "Yep."

Greg opened his KJV Bible and after a prayer for enlightenment and guidance, they began the first study on "The Importance of the Word." Greg read the first reading which was Deuteronomy 4:1-2. The highlighted points were, "Obey the Word and live" and "Don't add to or take away from the Word."

"Pretty straight forward," Peter said.

Greg nodded. "You read the next one."

They both turned to Deuteronomy 12:32, and Peter read the verse out loud, then the highlighted point which was, "Observe to do his commandments."

The ministers took turns reading down through the rest of the page. Each verse seemed to stack onto the one before giving depth and definition. They were through the study in about forty minutes.

"Wow!" Peter exclaimed. "I don't see how anyone can look at the Bible as just some nice book of stories after reading those verses."

Greg agreed. "What I was struck with going through this a week ago, was the recurring theme of *don't add to the scriptures and don't take away from the scriptures.* We'd better be careful about what we're teaching."

Peter saw it too, along with the severe warnings from God himself to anyone who tampered with His Word.

"What do you think? How did you like that study?"

Peter took in a deep breath. "I think that was more meaty than anything I've learned in the last year."

There were ten one page lessons in the folder and they agreed to take a lesson a week. One of Peter's responsibilities was to keep a journal of the activities, events and insights he was learning during his six months with a local pastor. The entry into his journal that night before bed was, "Started weekly Bible study with Pastor Greg at his apartment. Obey God's Word and live. Don't add to it and don't take away from it."

The following Wednesday the lesson was entitled, "What Is Believing?" Greg and Peter went through the scriptures in forty-five minutes, then spent another hour discussing the connection between believing and obedience. Peter's late night journal entry read, "Believing is demonstrated by obeying the Word of God just as faith is demonstrated by works according to the Word of God."

After dinner on the third Wednesday, Greg said, "I haven't gone through this one yet. So this will be new for both of us."

The title was "The Gospel," and took over an hour to get through. Peter felt like he was entering a new level of spiritual learning. The bulk of the scriptures were from the book of Acts, and were completely different from anything he'd heard preached before.

Unlike the other times together in the scriptures, Greg was uncomfortably quiet. He appeared troubled and stopped before finishing the list of scriptures. "Peter, I'd like to have some time to go over this a little more. Let's call it an evening if you don't mind."

There was no journal entry that night.

"When are we putting up decorations, Brad?" asked the young girl following him down the hallway.

"They're coming, they're coming. Then you girls can have at it."

The assistant manager was looking over the holiday schedule when Brad came into the back office after a restroom break. "I thought those peppers were hot going in!" he said putting his apron back on.

"Brenda's 4-alarm jalapeno omelet again?"

"You got it. You find a good thing you stick with it." Brad leaned against the office door. "Speaking of sticking with it, when's this ministry thing done for you?"

Peter set the schedule aside. "February 15th."

"Then what?"

"Then, I'll submit a plan for where I'd like to start a church. Once Great Assemblies approves, then we go there and get to work."

Brad listened thoughtfully. "Do they pay you to move and start a church?"

"Not with this fast-track program. We get things started on our own, then once the church reaches a place of growth and financial stability, Great Assemblies will assist with financing for a building and advertising. I'll be tent making till the church is stable."

"Tents?" Brad asked with quizzical look. "What's with making tents?"

Peter chuckled. "It's a church phrase meaning to support yourself. Paul the apostle was a tent maker by trade. That's how he supported himself when he went out to start new churches. My 'tent making' will be coffee."

"Oh. Do you know where yet?"

Peter shook his head. "Not yet. Maybe some place a little cooler. Still praying about it."

Sounds of female chatter bounced into the office along with the voice of Brad's wife. Brad looked at Peter with holly jolly sarcasm. "Christmas decorations are here. Oh boy!"

Peter was given more responsibilities with the church even though attendance continued to dwindle. He was regularly opening services and working the overhead projector. When Greg asked him to preach one Sunday, he spent at least an hour every day structuring his sermon according to the outline he'd learned in Bible school. Then when it came time to deliver, he was so nervous he could hardly speak to the nineteen in attendance. He downed an entire glass of water before finishing the first scripture reading. The supportive faces of his mother and Valarie helped him stumble through. His message on faith lasted thirty-eight minuets when he practiced in his living room. Before the live congregation, it was over in twelve minutes.

Nona smiled and nodded to the perspiring assistant pastor as he sat down on the front pew.

Brother Piles in the third pew whispered to his wife of forty-one years and said, "I like him. He's short."

Greg leaned over to Peter, "Good job, Brother. Next Sunday will be a little easier for you."

"Next Sunday?" he asked with amazement.

"Oh yeah," Greg said, getting up to finish up the service, "You can't pray your way better. Gotta do it."

Chapter Nineteen

The coffeehouse was slow on this cooler Saturday, two weeks before Christmas. Stephanie and Katie had stopped in for a visit and a hot chocolate before grocery shopping. Katie was missing her dad, a man she hardly knew. A ghost really. Stephanie too realized she hardly knew her ex-husband. He'd always been distant, but she hoped with Katie's birth he would've found something to stay for. She was wrong. He was even more distant and Stephanie's threat of divorce was his ticket out. Peter was more of a father to her than anyone, and she wanted to be with him as often as she could be.

Peter poured himself a small cup of house blend and stepped out from behind the counter to join the two. Stephanie added to her shopping list while Katie flipped through the colorful pictures of an Arizona magazine for tourists.

Katie looked up at Peter, "We should go here, Uncle Peter."

"Go where?" Peter looked down at the photo of a snowy town adorned with Christmas lights. "That's pretty," he said sitting next to her. "Where is that?"

Katie flipped a page back to the beginning of the magazine article and slid it toward Peter. The top of the page read, "Glennwood; Christmas In Arizona."

"Glennwood. You get up that way, Steph?"

Stephanie stayed focused on her list. "You know me. 'Go nowhere Stephanie.' I don't have the time or energy."

Katie watched her mother scribble on her paper trying to get the pen to work. She turned to Peter. "We should go."

He looked down at the cheery holiday photos. They were inviting. "What do you think, mom?" Shall we go to Glennwood?"

Stephanie shook her head. "I've got too much to do, Peter. But if you want to take her, that's fine with me. She could use some male influence about now."

Peter looked at his joyous niece. "Today or next Saturday?"

"Uh, like today," she replied in her best Valley Girl.

She was chatty Katie for the two-hour trip, singing songs with the radio and trying to remember punchlines from jokes she heard in school.

Peter parked on Whiskey Ridge Road where Katie pointed to the Court House Plaza she had remembered from the magazine. They found a place that served waffle cones and ate them while walking around the historic town center. A swirling breeze carried an early dusting of snow along the sidewalks and against a nativity scene.

"Mom says she's glad you don't push about God and church and stuff," Katie said trying to eat her cone without it breaking apart in her hands.

"Oh yeah?"

"Yeah. And she likes how you care for me. I take care of you too, don't I?"

Peter couldn't keep a straight face. "Of course you do. We're each other's only; only uncle, only niece. We have to look out for each other."

Katie nodded in agreement.

Peter stopped a local cowboy and his wife and asked about what they should see before they left town. They pointed out a few places of interest on a colorful map, including The Gingerbread Village and The Circle of Lights around the Lake. They saw everything and didn't care about the time.

The late afternoon light only made the holiday decorations stand out more brilliantly beneath a cloudy sky. It was a magical visit.

The two out-of-towners stopped at a rustic western themed cafe for dinner. At a table near an enormous window frosted for the holidays they shared onion rings and a steak burger that was as big as a plate. It was the most flavorful meal either had eaten in recent memory.

Katie slumped back into her chair. "That was sooo good. We hardly ever go out for burgers," she said, wiping her hands with a cloth napkin. "We should do this more often."

"Think so? Who's gonna pay for it?"

"You," she said laughing. "What? You gonna spend your money on your *other* niece?"

"No, I guess not."

They sat quietly at their table in a medium-rare afterglow, neither quite ready to get back on the road. Peter looked at his niece, who watched people walk by the window with heavy, after dinner eyes.

"So what about my Katie Girl? How does *she* feel about God and church and stuff?"

Katie followed the plaid pattern of a skirt on a passing customer then she looked over the empty plates between them. His question hung in the air along with the country sounds of an acoustic guitar coming from an old jukebox. She surveyed the well-worn oak table before finally lifting her eyes back to dinner partner.

"Don't push, Uncle Peter."

They left Glennwood just as light snow flakes filled the air again. The inviting Christmas lights reflected off the aptly named Mirror Lake the town was built around. Peter was drawn to take the main road through old down town once more. At a stop light, a small red and white For Sale sign caught Peter's attention. Between the wiper blades he saw what appeared to be a small drive-through building on the corner. He drove across street and into the parking lot where the building stood.

"Whatcha doing?" his sleepy passenger asked.

"I'm looking at something," he said, opening the door.

Peter walked around the shack that he guessed to be about nine feet wide by eighteen feet long. He walked up the steps to the back entrance and looked into the windows. It was dark but he could see the basic set up of a coffee stand.

"What is it, Uncle Peter?"

"I think it's an old drive-through espresso place, Katie."

Peter walked all the way around the small building again before getting back in the truck. He found a notepad and a pen and wrote the number down.

"Gonna buy it?"

"I don't know. How do you like Glennwood?"

"I like it. It's got snow." She smiled at him as he looked around. "How do you like it?"

Peter set the notepad in the glove box and leaned against the wheel. Scenes from the day, the Christmas lights, the nice couple who helped them find things to see, and the pleasant feel to the area all came together in his mind as he looked at the little building beside the truck.

"I think I like it too."

Peter preached three Sundays in a row but Greg was preaching this morning. Peter was trying to focus on the message but couldn't get the Glennwood trip or the coffee stand out of his mind. He conversed with everyone after service while putting his coffee cart away. Little Timothy was not helping. After knocking the glass carafe off the cart, he kicked the largest broken pieces across the tile in different directions. Brianna seemed clueless about what to do.

Hiding his frustration, Peter quickly rolled the cart to his truck then swept up the mess. Brianna followed him around talking about how much her young son needed a positive male role model in his life. After declining an invitation to lunch back at her house, Peter finished up everything with Greg and Nona. Eighteen in service again. $31.00 in the offering plate.

Peter raced home to call about the espresso stand. An older man answered the phone and gave Peter the specifics of the building and the arrangement with the owners of the property on which it sat. Twenty minutes later he was at the coffeehouse talking with Brad.

"What else should I check out?"

Brad looked over the Peter's notes. "You've got the basics here. Easy access on and off the street?"

"From what I could see in the dark."

He took a deep breath. "You want me to go up there with you and look things over?"

"You're reading my mind."

"Tell me this. Let's say all this checks out, do you have the four grand and the monthly lease for the property covered?"

Peter leaned against the door. "I have a thousand in savings now, and I think I have some options to borrow the rest."

Brad nodded, then called down the hall, "Sharie Lee,"

A sparky blonde appeared at the door. "Brad-lee."

"Peter and I both need to be out of the store for most of tomorrow. Can you handle it from about ten till six?"

"Of course. I'll do better than you two clowns." She nudged Peter. "I give you both permission to be gone the whole day and I'll close. I need the hours."

The older gentleman moved with a slight shaking in his hands as he unlocked the back entrance to the small building. "As I told you on the phone, this was my son's business. I don't know much about it."

He stepped out of the way to allow Brad and Peter entrance. Brad opened every cabinet door, looked for leaks and checked the water lines. Once satisfied, the two men removed part of the skirting around the base and checked underneath. Brad pointed to the axles. "Those are good to have if you ever need to move it."

Brad asked the old-timer about traffic, past business and what he'd settle for on a price. They went into the convenience store to talk with the owner about the existing lease. Peter listened to the many questions Brad asked the man, impressed with his negotiating skills.

They drove around Glennwood for about an hour and picked up local area information from the Visitor's Center before heading south. Brad asked Peter about every detail of a potential relocation. By the end of their all day journey, Peter was relieved to hear Brad's approving comments about his plan.

At eleven that night, Peter was too excited to sleep. He was reading up on Glennwood, Arizona. Population 21,396. Elevation: 5500 ft. Mild, four-season climate. He scanned the pictures of the Mirror Lake, historic buildings and other non-vital statistics. Starting a coffee business and a church in Glennwood was sounding sweeter all the time.

Peter opened the coffeehouse early the following morning and was surprised to see Brad in at ten instead of noon. When it slowed down shortly before eleven, Brad opened the back office door and said to Peter, "Let's talk."

Peter closed the door behind him and pulled up a chair next to his boss.

Brad leaned back comfortably in his leather chair. "Are you still feeling good about Glennwood?"

Peter nodded enthusiastically. "Yep."

"All righty. I think you've got what it takes to make it and I'd like to help. So, I've got a proposition for you." Brad opened a binder with several pages of notes and calculations. "I'm willing to back you in this endeavor. Get you all set up. All the equipment, coffee, supplies, everything. We'll agree on a startup loan amount which you'll pay back interest free. In return, this is what I want: one year after you pay the loan back in full, I get five percent of the net profits and I call the shots, just like I do here, up through that one-year mark. After that, it's all yours free and clear."

Peter listened and looked over the numbers neatly written on the page in front of him.

"You keep your tips. I'll help you work out a schedule and hire people. I'll bet one or two of the girls here would even come up and work for you occasionally."

"What about the name?"

"I don't care. You name it. I might have some suggestions, but I want as much of you in this as possible for consistency. It looks more stable if the name stays the same year after year anyway."

Peter was outwardly calm but inwardly leaping with excitement. "Mind if I take your notes here and think about it for a day or so?"

"Go ahead. Just don't take too long. I might buy that place for myself."

Chapter Twenty

Peter visited with Michael and Daylene about his possible business venture and move to Glennwood. Michael had met Brad before and liked the hardworking man. The business plan outlined on paper looked exceptional and appeared to give Peter every incentive and advantage to succeed. Daylene was glad to know that her boy wasn't looking to move any further away than the two-hour drive north.

After Sunday service in Apache Junction, Peter shared his plans with Greg and Nona. Nona listened while finishing her coffee on the sofa. "Glennwood's probably a safe distance."

"A safe distance from what?" Peter asked.

"From Brianna. Every Sunday for the last month her blouses have been more revealing."

Peter chuckled. "Hadn't noticed."

"Uh huh. I'll bet." She shot him her patented "give me a break" look. "I had a talk with her this morning."

"Thank you for doing that, hon. She was becoming a walking "Cleavage 'R' Us" advertisement."

"Just looking out for one of our new pastors," she said with a big sister's affection.

"I'm sure Glennwood could use another preacher, brother. Oh, and I sent in your evaluation to the college. Friday the thirteenth is the celebration banquet. Sunday is your official ordination. Your Ordained Minister's License fee is $100.00. Do you have that covered?"

"In the bank."

"Then you'll be serving Great Assemblies and the city of Glennwood in no time, brother," Greg said looking over to his wife.

Nona only smiled faintly in return.

A blown head gasket wasn't the news Peter wanted to hear from the mechanic, especially during the same week rent was due. J.T. Petersen from the college was Peter's transportation until his truck was fixed.

"You think trucks are expensive, wait till you have kids," J.T. said. "Our little bundle of joy is costing us a fortune. Sandy and I used to eat out all the time. Now, Hamburger Helper is splurging."

J.T. was Peter's closest friend; A brother he could share most anything with, even the cruder details of life.

"I think I'm going to skip the whole kid thing," Peter said, thinking of little Timothy.

"Aw, don't let that hellion from church sour you completely. What am I saying? Someday, some cute thing is going to bat her eyes at you and you won't resist. You'll cave like the rest of us guys who weren't going to have kids."

Peter's truck was fixed and ready for pick up the following afternoon in time for the Friday celebration dinner at 6:00 PM.

Elegant music from a baby grand piano and dozens of balloons and flower arrangements welcomed the guests into the lecture room. Several round tables covered with crimson table cloths and candles now stood where classroom chairs had been. The event was catered by DeLon's of Phoenix, featuring hand cut prime rib, Swedish meatballs drowning in a creamy gravy that could bring a person to tears, assorted pastas, mixed salad, a baked vegetable medley, and several desserts.

Peter wore a dark sport jacket and colorful tie and was immensely grateful the dressy event was in February instead of August. He mingled amongst the students, their guests, and ministry staff, hoping no one would notice his socks didn't match.

After getting a long stemmed glass of sparkling cider, he went to the table at the back of the room where students verified all their information for the Sunday commencement ceremony and paid for their minister's license. Peter wrote out a check for a hundred dollars even, and collected a receipt that read, *Valid For One Year*. He slipped the folded receipt into his jacket pocket and saw J.T. talking with Senior Pastor Evan Seager. It looked like a serious discussion. Then J.T.'s wife, Sandy, joined them and the two men appeared to lighten up. Peter was glad the young couple could enjoy a night out together.

"Boy J.T.," Peter said, "You clean up pretty good."

"Thanks to his wife," Sandy said, taking J.T.'s arm. "You look very nice too, Peter. A much needed change from the t-shirt and shorts you usually wear."

"Comfort, my dear," Peter said. "It's all about comfort."

Sandy looked at Peter's drink. "Where'd you get that?"

Peter pointed over to the far end of the buffet tables.

"You want one too?" she asked her husband. He nodded and she was off.

Peter studied his usually buoyant friend. "You and Brother Seager looked like you were having a doctrinal debate. I'd hate to be on the wrong side of that discussion."

J.T. looked around the room, irritated. "I won't be graduating on Sunday with you."

"What? What do you mean?"

"I don't have the hundred bucks for my license." J.T.'s face reddened. "Do you believe that?" He folded his arms and leaned against the wall. "I had it up until about a week ago. Then Savanna needed medicine and the AC went out in the house. You know how long a nursing mother's gonna go without AC?"

Peter nodded.

"My tank's been on E all week and the babysitter's gonna get an I.O.U. for tonight."

Peter sifted through the words of frustration. "So, because you don't have a $100.00 license fee..."

"Yeah."

"You aren't graduating."

"Right."

"Which means you aren't a recognized pastor?"

J.T. thought for a moment. "That's how it sounded to me. Hey, don't say anything to my wife. I'm still trying to figure something out."

Sandy appeared with two glasses. "Figure out what? "Have you seen the spread over there? Wow, it looks so good and I'm so hungry." She handed a glass to her husband along with a kiss. "Did you bring a guest, Peter?"

"I couldn't make up my mind, Sandy. So many to choose from."

The high-pitched sound of a fork against a glass signaled everyone to be seated. Peter sat next to J.T. and Sandy. Five others joined the table just before a prayer of thanks was offered for the meal.

Peter savored every mouthwatering bite of the meal, but his mind was on helping his friend. He couldn't help J.T. with his own checkbook in its current condition, and he knew money was tight with all of his fellow students. He looked at his watch.

He had just enough time if he moved now.

He excused himself from the table and exited the back door. He escaped to his truck and drove to the coffeehouse. Behind the counter, Brad was making an Americano for a customer.

"All dressed up and nowhere to go?"

"Can a talk to you for a minute?"

Brad nodded. "Nikki, you got the front."

A slender red head with stylish glasses closed the freezer door. She looked Peter up and down. "Peter! You should dress up more often."

The two coffee men went to the back office. Brad sat down. "Ugh, my feet are killing me. What's up?"

Peter remained standing. "May I please get a $100 advance until payday?"

Brad took a deep breath and strummed his fingers on his desk. He looked down at the safe briefly, then stood up and pulled out his wallet. "I don't believe it. I hardly ever carry money with me. When I get it, poof! It's gone." He laid two fifty dollar bills onto the desk. "Between my wife and now you..."

Peter picked up the money and headed for the door. "Thanks Brad. I'll explain later."

Most of the guests were finishing dessert when Peter slipped into the back of the room where he found a staff member. The soft sounds of the piano trailed off as Peter came up behind J.T.'s chair. "Here you go, buddy. You're walking with us now." He handed J.T. his receipt.

J.T. looked at the paper, then to Peter, who returned to his chair.

"You were gone quite a while," Sandy joked.

"Had to take care of something."

"Must have been important for a man to miss dessert."

"No way. I'm hanging around till the end to get what's left over."

J.T. conveyed a hundred thank you's in his stunned eyes.

Senior Pastor Evan Seager walked to the podium with professional elegance. He was a measured man; respected as much as feared. Never a hair out of place, rarely a word misspoken. Peter noticed one more trait...he never smiled.

"The church is growing, Pastors. And we must grow with it. Our burden is structure for the body of Christ. We must *be* that much needed structure to facilitate proper growth. Upon our shoulders, Christ will reveal his Kingdom."

Peter listened to the well prepared words while watching the reactions of his classmates. Many nodded. Some smiled. The address was without scripture reference. No Bible rested on the podium.

"The time of the apostle is passed. Prophets have fulfilled their purpose. Teachers ushered in the previous century. Evangelists set up their tents and captivated the masses when some of us were small children. The gifts of the Spirit of yesterday are now giving way to the day of the pastor. I sense a soon coming *Priesthood of Pastors*. They will be the new foundation of the church. Some of you here this evening will be a part of that new foundation. You will carry the authority of the called, chosen, and faithful. By your dedication to the Great Assemblies of Christ, and to the priesthood, God will exalt you and bring others to himself!"

The college staff and their families rose and applauded. The students quickly joined in. Peter didn't exactly grasp all that he heard, but found himself caught up in the excitement. Suddenly J.T. appeared at his side clapping wildly.

"I can't thank you enough, Bro.," J.T. shouted over the noise. He gave Peter a hug. "I'll pay you back as soon as I can."

"No problem, buddy."

J.T. beamed in the excitement. "Think of that, Peter! A priesthood of pastors. Brother Seager has such a grasp of the deep things of God. I wish I knew half of what he knows."

The excitement died down again and Brother Seager honored the young men who had studied and worked so hard for the last year and half. He spoke words of encouragement to the future ministers and their families who would take the gospel to the outer reaches of the world. Then he introduced four other men who would be Regional Pastors. They would be ongoing mentors offering counsel and accountability through monthly visits to each of the ministers. Matthew Struthers was Peter's Regional Pastor. Matthew was a distinguished looking man with clean cut features and big brown eyes. He led a congregation of about three thousand with a staff of eleven assistant pastors. As Peter listened to Pastor Struthers say a few words, he felt he could learn a lot under his care, but would greatly miss Greg and Nona.

The evening's festivities came to a pleasant conclusion with raised glasses and a final prayer. Peter visited most everyone while keeping an eye on Pastor Seager. He hoped to have a word with the seasoned elder. Finally, when the room was cleared of most of the guests and the pastor had finished a conversation with a small group at the piano, Peter intercepted him as he was leaving.

They entered an office adjacent to the decorated classroom. Peter cleared his throat nervously. "Thank you, Pastor Seager," he began. "I wanted to ask about the license fees."

Pastor Seager appeared impatient. "Questions about fees can be answered by administration. They'll be in the office on Monday."

"No sir, I'm wondering how it is that a fee would prevent someone from being a pastor. How someone could go through the schooling and months of hands on training, but because they don't have a hundred bucks they can't be a pastor. How can that be?"

Evan studied the young man before him. "Ah, this must be about J.T.," he said as he rested on the edge of a desk. "There's a bit more to this than what you might understand. Licensing fees not only pay to keep ministry records up to date within Great Assemblies of Christ but are an accepted way of separating ministers from laity. A way, shall I say, to separate the serious from those who aren't."

"A walk with God and eighteen months of preparation doesn't prove that someone is serious?"

"Everyone, including J.T., knew about the costs associated with ordination. This is common practice in most denominations and professions. In many ways, how one prioritizes their lives and keeps their finances in order is an indication of how they will keep other weightier matters in order."

"But life happens, Pastor Seager. They just had a baby and a series of other expenses that came up recently."

"I appreciate your zeal for your friend. It's admirable, really. But, if J.T. is serious about the ministry, he'll search and scrape and come up with it much like the woman in the parable of the lost coin. And when he does, when it's important enough to him, he'll receive his ordination and carry on."

"He'll be ordained on Sunday because I paid his fee."

"Then he should be grateful to have a caring brother like you," Evan said, while getting up to leave.

Peter's anger rose. "Sir, can you show me one scripture where a license fee is a requirement to minister? Because this seems closer to what the money changers were doing in the temple when Jesus drove them out with a whip."

Senior Pastor Seager stopped and looked directly at the younger minister. "Careful Peter."

"I'm sorry sir," the younger man said in softer tones. "I mean no disrespect."

"Apology accepted." Evan put his hand on Peter's shoulder. "I truly wish every pastor had your heart and zeal for his brethren. You're at the beginning of your journey, Peter. You'll soon understand why some things are done the way they are. It really is for the best even if it doesn't appear that way now."

Peter nodded in submission to his elder.

"Having this exchange is fortuitous. I wanted to include one of our new pastors in Sundays ordination ceremony. Have a few words prepared, won't you?

He brightened.

"I will, Pastor."

Chapter Twenty-One

Through the curtains on the right side of the stage Peter could see Michael, Daylene, Stephanie, Katie, Greg, Nona and even Tom and Valarie surrounded by hundreds of others in the packed auditorium. Peter would share some of his highlights from the last year and a half right after a praise team and special signing for the deaf was over. Peter looked down at his notes once more hoping he wouldn't need them at the podium. He was startled by a hand on his shoulder.

"Brother Bishop, if I'm not back before you finish, would you take up the offering please." The assistant pastor of the Mesa church appeared to be in pain. He started walking toward the hallway. "Real simple Peter, just take up the offering, the ushers know what to do. Then Sister Grace has a song and you're done."

Peter watched the perspiring man disappear down the hall. One more thing to remember.

"Okay, Peter you're next up," came the order from a short man with a headset. "You doing the offering too if Pastor Bennet doesn't make it?"

"I guess so."

"I told him not to eat those chilies. Nobody listens to me."

"I'm listening to you," Peter said.

"Okay, go! You're up. And don't forget the offering."

Peter stepped to the brightly lit pulpit centered between elders, staff and students behind him, and a multitude before him. A peace washed over him when he saw the familiar faces of his family through the haze of lights.

His words flowed with a calm that came from inside. He spoke of his friendships, the deeper understanding of the word, and the valuable lessons learned from Pastor Greg and his wife Nona. He didn't look at his notes once.

He ended by thanking the leadership for having such a Bible school where one could quickly learn to minister to souls in the field.

Peter glanced to the man with the headset again. He was shaking his head and pointing back at him.

Without skipping a beat, Peter asked the ushers to come forward.

"I don't know how you came to know the Lord. But God used a big blue bus and a sweet Sunday School teacher to reach me. Later, a TV preacher asked my mom to repent of her sins and begin new. Buses aren't cheap and neither are the inner workings of television. But I'm glad someone gave from what they had so someone like me could be here tonight. Would you consider giving to the work here so others can keep preaching the word? They will be blessed and so will you."

The sincerity of his spirit had people opening their wallets before he was finished speaking. Grace, the choir leader and gifted soloist had to sing the third verse twice to allow for the lengthy offering.

Thirty-one men became ordained ministers with the Great Assemblies of Christ Church the following afternoon. After prayers, pictures and farewells, Peter and his guests met at Stanford's Steakhouse for dinner.

Peter looked around the long table of happy faces and basked in the sounds of laughter. He was overcome with gratitude and relished the love of family and friends and a sense of accomplishment. The world was perfect.

After dinner, Greg asked Peter if he would come by the church office around ten the next morning before he and Nona left. Stephanie and Katie were next to leave. Soon after everyone had gone their separate ways and he was back at his condo alone.

He poured himself a glass of cold water from the refrigerator and looked around the kitchen and living room. In a few weeks he'd be packing for Glennwood.

"Pastor Bishop," he said out loud. "Or Pastor Peter." He repeated both titles then thought of Greg's easy going style. He wanted to be an approachable leader like Greg.

"Just Peter?" he asked himself. "Yeah, that sounds just fine."

He walked into the church office just before ten with two large mochas.

"Blessed are those who bear chocolate; for they shall not want for friends," Greg said with an appreciative smile. Then with an uppity British accent, "Thank you and congratulations Pastor Bishop."

"The pleasure is all mine, Pastor Barnes."

"Yes, yes then. Win the world today shall we?"

"We shall, I say, we shall!"

They sat and talked of the evening, the church and the future. "Thanks for coming out Peter," Greg started. "I have something to share with you and then an interesting request of you later."

Peter nodded. "Okay."

"Do you remember the Wednesday night we went over the Gospel Bible study?"

"The one we didn't finish? I remember that."

Greg smiled, "No we didn't finish."

"I wondered if we'd ever talk about it."

"Let's talk about it now," Greg said, setting his Bible in front of him. "If someone came up to us today and asked us how to be saved, what's our standard response? What does Great Assemblies teach?"

The new pastor replied, "To accept Jesus Christ as your personal savior, confess that he is your Lord and turn your life over to him."

"It's the same thing I've told people for years. But, is that what we read that night? Is that what the apostles preached in the Book of Acts?"

Peter sat silently not knowing how to respond.

"The short answer is no. That's not what they preached. Do you remember the *first* study we did and what you wrote in your journal afterward?"

Peter could see the journal page in his mind by the side of his bed. "Obey the Word. Don't add to it or take away from it."

"Exactly. But what Christ commanded the apostles to preach, and what I've been preaching all these years are two very different messages, Peter. That was the start of some uncomfortable nights as I went back through those verses, and through my own notes. I've been repeating phrases and lines I learned years ago from other well-known preachers and teachers. But that's not the same as scripture."

96

Peter listened intently to his mentor

"The more I look at the Book of Acts, the more I'm baffled that it's not regularly taught. Did you get much of it in the college?"

"No, not really."

"One of the biggest complaints I've heard from sinners is how every church preaches something different. Get saved this way here, another way over there, the guy on the radio says something else. They laugh at us Christians and I don't blame them! Why don't we all teach the same thing? I don't know. Peter, Philip, Paul, they all preached the same message over and over and got the same results. They preached the death, burial and resurrection of Jesus Christ and people repented from their sins, were baptized in Jesus' name, and received the Holy Ghost. Peter preached it in the first half of Acts, and Paul preached the same thing in the second half. Same message. We preachers have no excuse for preaching something different."

Greg lifted his eyes and stared up through the ceiling. "I was convicted, Peter. Then it hit me: those scriptures weren't only eye opening; they're career ending."

"Why career ending?"

"Because Great Assemblies doesn't tolerate teaching that is contrary to accepted core doctrine." Greg laughed and shook his head. "I didn't realize it until I went through more church files, but the pastor here who died recently was the last surviving member of the original twenty-one elders who started Great Assemblies of Christ. Those Bible studies were his. After I went through those scriptures again, I showed them to Nona. You know Nona, sweet, gentle, Nona, right? Well, let me tell you, sparks flew between us and we had some heated exchanges. But in the end, she had to agree because it's right there. That's what Jesus and the apostles preached. Later I met with the senior pastor in Tucson and after about fifteen minutes he ended our discussion by putting me on probation."

"Probation? You're kidding me! How can they do that?"

Greg laughed again. "Oh Peter, you have no idea about the layered inner workings of church and politics. Incidentally, the most vulnerable position in a denomination is a pastor without a church.

No backing and no place to go. It's a tough place to be to have to start all over after putting years in."

The water spilling over the rocks from the corner was the only sound as the men sat in quiet thought. Peter sank into confusion. Only hours ago he was celebrating his ordination. Now his bright future was dimming.

"What happens next?" Peter asked.

"Nona dropped me off here about eight this morning on her way to an appointment. I've been seeking God for some direction, some sign of life or something to let me know I'm on the right path. I felt impressed to come here and just wait on the Lord for a while. So, I waited and prayed. Then around eight thirty I got a call from Pastor Rowe letting me know that a Baptist church has purchased this property and will take possession on the first."

A car pulled into the lot. Greg looked out the window and sat back down. "Twenty minutes later, my dad called. And in his roundabout way he asked me to take over the print shop in Tucson."

"Wow. Sounds like direction for you."

"Sure does, doesn't it?"

Nona appeared at the door. "Hello pastors," she said leaning against the door looking at Greg.

"How'd your appointment go, honey?" Greg asked.

"Fine," she said with a smile. "I'm in training for a new position."

Greg paused waiting for more. "New position for..."

"Mother."

In an instant, Greg and Nona were in a joyous embrace. Peter was moved watching the couple hold each other as tears streamed down their faces. "Direction and a sign of life," Peter thought with eyes closed. "It doesn't get more real than this."

"Hug me!" Nona said kicking Peter. "I'm going to be a mama!"

Peter rose and hugged both Nona and Greg who were now giggling uncontrollably. Several tissues later they regained their composure.

"Not to change the subject," Peter said, "But didn't you say you had a favor you wanted."

Greg wiped his eyes. "Yeah, there is. It would be easier at the house. Do you have time to come over?"

"I have today off, so whatever you need, you've got it."

Peter waded back through the conversation in the office as he followed Greg and Nona back to their place Once inside the apartment, the three of them sat at the familiar kitchen table and carefully went back through the scriptures of the Gospel that sparked such controversy. This time Peter was aware of the stark contrast between what he'd been taught and what was written in black and white.

After the last verse on the page, Greg looked over to Peter. "Now, what would you tell someone if they asked you how to be saved?"

Peter looked down at the scriptures and flipped to Acts chapter two. "This seems to put it all together. Repent, be baptized in the name of Jesus Christ, and receive the Holy Ghost."

"Do you really believe that?" Greg asked.

Peter sat blinking. "That's what it says. I can't add to it or take away from it. I have to believe it."

"We've both repented. Nona received the Spirit years ago, I haven't yet, but neither of us has been baptized in Jesus' name. As your first official act as a new pastor," Greg said taking Nona's hand, "Will you baptize us in Jesus name?"

Peter nodded. "Yeah."

"We've got a pool here. I'll go get us something to change into."

Nona watched Peter's face turn ashen as Greg left the table and disappeared down the hall.

"Are you all right with this, Peter?"

He looked into Nona's caring eyes. "I can't believe this is happening."

Nona rubbed Peter's shoulder. "I'm sure Greg told you that I didn't like what I was hearing at first either. That's putting it mildly. You want to know what my biggest concern was? Security. I knew this would cost Greg his position in the church. A note for future reference; you men have your issues, we women have ours, and security is at the top of our list."

"But you believe this change in doctrine now, right?"

"Oh yes. I've heard it before from old Pentecostal friends. But when you've been taught something for so long, and your church family all believes the same thing, you just keep on with what you know. In the end though, it's not Great Assemblies or our church family that makes us free. It's the truth that makes us free." She looked out the window. "And look at how God has addressed my fears. Greg's taking over his dad's print shop. He'll be making more full time there than with the church."

Nona looked down with a glowing smile, "And on a more personal note, God answered a deep longing of my heart. After I saw the truth of what Greg was trying to show me, and I let go of my fear and anger, we made up and that night I conceived." She blushed and gave Peter a devilish glance. "There's something special about make up sex."

They both laughed in agreement. Nona's glow dissipated as she let out a deep breath, "We'll be shunned for this. That won't be pleasant. Baptism in general is hardly taught anymore, but when it is, it's word for word Matthew twenty-eight, Father, Son and Holy Ghost only. Jesus' name baptism is absolutely off limits. Not even up for discussion."

"So my first act as a new pastor is something that will get me kicked out of the church?"

Nona gave Peter a thoughtful smile. "Tough decision isn't it? Just a taste of what any Jew believing on Jesus Christ has gone through. And this is just the beginning, Peter. Greg and I are going back to the foundation of everything we've been taught. You'll need to do the same thing too.

Greg stepped into the kitchen wearing a t-shirt and swimsuit. "Want to borrow a suit?"

After Peter and Nona changed, the three of them walked out through the recreational room and to the swimming area. A few small brown leaves floated on the surface of the uncovered pool. After Greg led them in a short prayer, he and his wife entered the chilly aqua-blue water. Peter read over Acts 2:38 a few times trying to memorize the words before stepping into the water himself.

"According to the word of God," Peter said holding on to Greg, "I now baptize you in the name of Jesus Christ, for the remission of your sins."

Using similar wording, Greg baptized his wife.

Once the water was cleared from their eyes, Greg and Nona started for the steps.

"Hold up," Peter said. "What about me?"

Greg stepped back into the water. "I wanted it to come from you and not just because we were doing it."

"How can I say I believe it, if I don't follow through myself?"

Greg took hold of Peter's arm. Peter closed his eyes and held his nose shut. He heard the name of Jesus slip into his ears just as the cold water wrapped around his shoulders and face. The young minister was placed into a watery grave, then was brought to the surface again.

Peter stayed and visited with Greg and Nona a few hours longer. Greg shared some advice and gave Peter a folder with copies of the Bible studies they had gone through. After a farewell prayer Peter left for home.

He slept peacefully all night with an open Bible on his chest.

Chapter Twenty-Two

The following days were packed with activity. Brad and Peter were inseparable except for when Peter made a trip to Glennwood to secure an apartment close to the coffee stand. The two worked feverishly to be open for business as soon as possible.

Brad located a sturdy, refurbished espresso machine for half the price of a new one, and ordered coupons from a local printer. Peter took care of all the paperwork to go into business legally in the state of Arizona. He was relieved when all electrical connections and water lines passed code the first inspection. After all the coffee making equipment was installed and working and the shelves stocked with supplies, a fresh coat of paint was all that was needed to bring the small building to life.

The coffee stand was located near a four-way intersection. Brad suggested putting small A-frame signs at each corner seven days out from opening day. Each day the signs would be changed to indicate the number of days till opening day. It was a great plan in theory, until a few local kids smashed them on their way to the bus stop.

Nineteen days after becoming an ordained minister, Peter flipped the switch to the neon sign, letting the world know *Bishop's Coffee* was open for business.

The first forty-five minutes were quiet. Then at six-fifteen Peter watched a light blue Toyota slam on the brakes on the road facing the drive-through window. Then it backed up, and entered the parking lot and stopped at the window.

"Welcome to Bishop's Coffee. What can I get for you this morning?"

"Thank God you're open," came the articulate voice of a professional looking young woman. "Please tell me you have great coffee. Not good coffee. *Great* coffee."

"Ma'am, if you don't like it, it's on me."

She smiled and looked over the top of her glasses to Peter. "I'm far too young to be a ma'am, sir. But I like your offer. Let's do a medium cinnamon mocha."

Peter went to work making her spicy chocolate beverage while entranced by the calm, sultry tone of her voice.

"How's your business been this morning?"

"You're my first."

The woman smiled. "Glad to be somebody's first. Oh, and no whip, please."

Peter closed the lid and handed her a hot, sixteen-ounce cup. "Give this a shot."

She took a sip and closed her eyes in apparent early morning euphoria. Then, she looked back up to Peter and said, "I hate it. I want three more."

Peter quickly put together three more cinnamon mochas and set them firmly in a cardboard drink carrier.

"Are you the Bishop of Bishop's Coffee?" she asked handing him a twenty-dollar bill.

Peter set the drinks in her hands. "I am. Peter Bishop."

"I'm Audrey. Nice doing business with you, Peter."

"Likewise, Audrey."

Peter watched her drive away, unable to get her voice out of his head. Another car drove up to the window. An order for regular coffee with extra cream.

It was the last customer for the rest of the day.

At two in the afternoon, Peter turned off the sign and equipment. After cleaning the few dishes that were used, he tallied the sales numbers and called them into Brad.

"Don't worry, buddy. It's the first day and you'll probably have a few more like this one."

Peter locked up the shop then hung several coupons on the doors of nearby houses. He stopped at several offices and handed out "Buy One Get One Half Off" cards to entice the locals to visit.

The first customers arrived fifteen minutes after opening the next day. A caramel latte and a large black coffee.

At ten after six, the light blue Corolla slammed on the brakes again, backed up and drove up to the window.

Peter looked down at the driver. "You've got that maneuver down like a pro."

Audrey rolled her eyes. "I'm not all there in the morning, you know? Got too many things going on."

"Cinnamon mocha?" Peter asked.

"Yeah, but don't get used to me ordering just that. I can switch on a dime. Am I your first again today?"

Peter finished making her drink. "Not this morning. Someone beat you by half an hour."

Audrey saw a car in her rear view mirror and handed him a five. "Keep it. See you tomorrow."

Peter waved goodbye to his first regular, then turned his attention to the driver of an old Chevy half ton truck. He lifted an enormous, dirty travel mug. "How much for this size?"

"Regular coffee? Two bucks," Peter answered.

"Fill it."

The next customer came five minutes later, then another five minutes after that. By the end of the second day, *Bishop's Coffee* made eight sales totaling $27.50 with $2.05 in the tip jar. Peter closed out the day by driving through a different area of Glennwood to pass out coupons.

Sharie Lee drove up from Phoenix to help Peter the next morning. Peter was relieved to see her at the back door.

"Before we do anything, where are the bathrooms?" she asked with a slight caffeine jitter.

Peter pointed to the convenience store. "In there, far back right."

"Be right back," she said walking briskly toward the store.

Sharie Lee was an intelligent woman with warm sense of humor. She was fun to work with and took Peter's place as assistant manager. Peter hoped to have her come up on the weekend, but her schedule prevented that. He would have to take a day off whenever he could get one.

Peter stayed for an hour until Sharie Lee was comfortable with everything. He'd be back at two to close and call in the numbers to

Brad. Next time she could do it all herself.

Peter called his Regional Pastor, Matthew Struthers, to update him with his new address, phone numbers and basic work schedule. They set a meeting for the following week to outline a plan to build a Great Assemblies church in Glennwood.

After he hung up, he wondered how the subject of the Book of Acts version of the gospel was going to play out. Nona's words echoed through the halls of his heart.

We'll be shunned for this.... It won't be pleasant.

Valarie's vision many churches seemed very far away.

Sales at *Bishop's Coffee* increased every day, and Peter was getting used to his early morning to two in the afternoon schedule. Every day he didn't spill a pitcher of hot milk on the floor, that is.

Peter received a few calls from the help wanted sign and from the ad in the local paper. He scheduled interviews when Brad could make it up to help.

The second Saturday after opening was a chilly but sunny day. Peter was surprised at how busy he was up till about nine-thirty, then it slowed to a trickle. A car here. A truck there.

A little after ten, Peter watched a dark haired woman in a wool coat and sunglasses cross the street toward the stand. She seemed familiar to Peter. A thin smile cut across her face as she approached.

"You don't recognize me in the daylight do you?"

"I'd know that voice anywhere," Peter said. "What can I get you?"

She rested her arms on the outside ledge. "I don't know," she said, trying to look inside the stand. "Are there too many secrets in there or can you let a girl inside?"

"Come on in."

Peter unlocked the door as Audrey removed her sunglasses and pushed a strand of hair over her ear before stepping inside. She looked around the utilitarian layout of painted wood, stainless steel, and plastic. She nodded her approval. "It's bigger than it looks from the outside."

Peter showed her around and then walked through the steps of making her favorite cinnamon mocha. He enjoyed watching her take the first sip. Her eyes were closed, head slowly tilting rhythmically from side to side as though listening to a symphony of spices.

"There's just something about cinnamon and chocolate. Gets me every time." She took another sip. "And you have the best I've had so far."

Peter moved his bar stool over to her and cleaned out the used espresso grounds. "So now you know my secrets. What's Audrey's? Why is she out and about at all hours of the morning?"

Audrey moved to the stool. "I'm the office manager for Merrit Brothers. One brother handles investments, the other is in real estate. I have to be in early for the investment brother because the stock market is open on the east coast before the roosters crow here."

A car pulled up to the window and Peter was back to work. He glanced over to Audrey a few times while making drinks, but kept his focus on his customers. Just as he was returning change to a driver, another vehicle pulled in line.

"I'll let you go, Peter," Audrey said, opening the door. She pointed to money on the counter. "Thanks for sharing secrets and my mocha."

He saw the five-dollar bill held down by a cup. "Hey, that's on me," he protested.

"No, Peter, don't start that," she said, opening the door. "Your drinks are worth it. Get this place profitable, then you can treat me every once in a while. I'll see around."

Peter's thoughts went with the young woman as he ground espresso beans. She'd never make the cover of a magazine, but she was clever and comfortable like a favorite sweatshirt that goes with everything.

"My new friend Audrey," Peter thought. "My only friend so far in Glennwood."

Chapter Twenty-Three

Matthew Struthers was all business the afternoon when he and Peter met at a restaurant near the center of Glennwood.

"The fast-track program you are a part of, Peter, is a well-crafted church planting program to promote Christ in our communities and Great Assemblies nationally. The church leaders created materials to help you put your learning into practice."

Pastor Struthers handed Peter a binder entitled, *Doctrines of the Great Assemblies of Christ*. "This will be an important reference for you should you or any of your congregation have questions. It's in binder form for easy, single page updating."

Peter opened the binder and glanced at the first few pages and contents. He noticed the beginning of the last section began on page 306. Hopefully there wouldn't be a test.

"Next up is our weekly teaching plan." Matthew laid it open on the table facing Peter. "We went with a magazine layout for a more modern appearance. We know how difficult it can be for new ministers to come up with fresh sermons and messages every week, so some of our more senior and successful pastors have created weekly lessons to follow. If we all stay on the same schedule, a church member can get the same message no matter where they are, even if they're traveling or on vacation. It's genius really."

Peter took the magazine, *Purpose & Meaning*, and looked over the colorful pages. He saw the familiar message structure and smiled. A key verse, supporting verses and illustrations. Every verse was from the *New International Version*.

"Finally, here's the latest Pastoral Directory. These come out every six months and all of our fast-track graduates are in there as well. Information on any pastor and their family, location, and church name can be found both alphabetically and by state and city.

Matthew finished his ice water and set his glass down. "I understand you had some questions about the purpose of license fees."

Peter set the magazine aside and looked at Pastor Struthers. "I did, but maybe it's not important."

"Part of the fees go to creating these materials which I'm sure you'll find very helpful. I don't know if I'd say that the fees indicate a person's seriousness or not. It's more about the cost of doing business, which I'm sure you understand. Church and ministry are as much business as they are spiritual, Peter. It's just the way it is. The more you can run the church like a business, the more at peace you'll be with some of the necessary – even unpleasant – aspects of overseeing a flock."

Peter admired his elder's practical view of church as much as his colorful dress shirt.

"Does that make sense?"

Peter nodded without expression. "What if we have questions about certain doctrines?"

"I'd suggest going through the doctrinal handbook, read the associated scriptures and the church's position. That should clear up most misunderstandings. If not, then give me a call, preferably not on weekends or Mondays. You can send an email too. The address is on my card."

Peter nodded, deciding not to pursue anything more.

"I'd like to have you come up to Flagstaff this Sunday and share a few words in our two morning services. Will that work for you?"

"Sure. I'd love to."

The elder pastor closed his leather briefcase. "Great. We can visit more then. I need to get back on the road. Got another fast-tracker to visit over in Payson.

Peter followed Pastor Struthers out to his burgundy SUV where he received a church brochure with a simple map to its location before they parted company.

"You're early this morning," Peter said to his only friend in Glennwood.

"I hope that's not a complaint."

"Never. What would you like this morning?"

"Mmmm. Someone else to go into work for me," she said with sleepy eyes.

"How about something minty? That'll perk you up a bit."

"Okay. You talked me into it."

Peter returned to the window a moment later with an extra hot chocolate mint mocha. "I think we should grab lunch sometime."

"I can do lunch."

Peter looked at the calendar just left of the window. "I have this Thursday off. Does that work for you?"

"It can."

"You're not a sprouts and tofu babe are you?"

"God no," she said setting her mocha in the cup holder. "But I won't run from a salad bar. There's a few good places to eat close to my office. I'm usually the last to take a lunch." She handed him another five-dollar bill. "One o'clock works best for me. Is that alright?"

"One will be just fine," Peter said, handing her back her change.

Audrey rolled up her window and waved good bye.

Peter watched her leave, then remembered the six applications he had to go through. Brad was coming the next day to help Peter interview. Most of the applications were legible and complete except for two. Another was filled out with hot pink ink.

Suddenly it occurred to him, that in a matter of days, a total stranger would be running his stand while he was gone. Some unknown person would represent *Bishop's Coffee Company* while he was taking a day off. Peter looked around at the largest investment of his life and his thoughts twisted into a panic. "Some sick creep, cleverly disguised as a nice person, is going to get hired. They're going to poison my customers, wreck the equipment, steal my money and burn it all down..."

A car pulled up to the window in time to keep the stand from spinning around Peter.

"Can I get a small vanilla latte?"

"Sure," Peter said."

"Oh, and an application too, please?"

Brad and Peter interviewed four applicants right after closing the next afternoon. The two who rose to the top were Nell, a stay at home mom and Stephen an avid skateboarder. After sketching out a tentative schedule, Brad helped Peter get up to speed on sales tracking software and insisted that he get a cell phone.

Just after one o'clock on Thursday, Peter and Audrey ventured into Francisco's Mexican Restaurant, about half a mile from Merrit Brother's. Audrey spoke highly of the service and their taco salads.

They were quickly seated at a booth complete with warm tortilla chips and homemade red and green chili salsas. Peter saw an irresistible lunch combination, while his lunch date chose the taco salad.

"So the Army guy does God and coffee?" How's all that all working for you?" Audrey asked while sipping a diet Coke.

"It's working well, I think," Peter replied. "Business at the stand is picking up every day. I just hired two part-timers. I'm working out a plan for the church building process starting with Bible studies. I learned about relationship building from my mentors, Greg and Nona, during the hands on phase at the college. Now it's time to put everything into practice." Peter tumbled the ice around in his glass with a straw. "Do you go to church anywhere?"

"I'm a good Catholic girl," Audrey said. "Well, almost good. I go to mass a couple times a month. Usually when my conscience gets the better of me and I force myself."

Peter smiled at her honesty. "And how did you come to settle in Glennwood?"

"I've lived in Arizona all my life. Born in Flag Staff, spent a few years in Lake Havasu City then Glennwood. Went to Arizona State. After I got my Bachelor's in Business Administration, I came back to Glennwood to escape the heat. I've known the Merrit brothers since I was a teen and when they heard I was back they offered me a job. Been there almost six years. Can't believe it's been that long already, and I still haven't seen the Pacific Ocean."

"Is that a big deal for you? Seeing the ocean?"

"Yeah it is," she said, while picking out another chip for a salsa bath. "I really want to see the whole Pacific Coast. The water, the sun on the waves and the beaches. There's so much I haven't done yet that I should have already, you know?"

They talked up until Peter dropped her back off at work again. As she stepped out of the truck Peter asked, "Would you be open to having a Bible study with me sometime?"

Audrey fumbled with the latch on her small purse. "I could be, though I may not be your best candidate. I'm pretty comfortable with where I'm at with God right now. Not really looking for anything more. But I wouldn't mind seeing what you're doing. Thanks for lunch, Peter. I owe you one."

Nell was a quick learner. She could make drinks and multitask flawlessly. Peter diligently trained her two hours every day for the rest of the week. Sunday would be her first day alone while Peter drove to Flagstaff to speak.

Great Assemblies of Flagstaff was an enormous facility off of the I-40 Business Loop near Northern Arizona University. Peter sat in the front row near Pastor Struthers and his wife Susanna.

At the end of the high energy praise session, Matthew turned to Peter.

"Brother, why don't you take up the offering afterward like you did there at the graduation?"

Peter nodded. Then he watched the Senior Pastor climb the steps to the stage where he picked up a wireless microphone and greeted the congregation. He raised his hands and encouraged the church to shout to the Lord. After the praise subsided, Peter stepped up to the platform. He met Pastor Struthers at the podium and shared the same words from his heart that he did at graduation. He was calm and his delivery was clear. The offering was slow in being collected.

The second service was a larger mirror image of the first. Peter joined the Struthers and a group of other ministers for lunch before leaving Flagstaff. Matthew handed Peter an envelope and thanked him for driving up.

Ninety minutes later Peter was back at the coffee stand to check on Nell. She was mopping up the floor where a latte had fallen to its death, but the rest of the day had gone well. He looked at the numbers from the till and felt a sigh of relief. He'd hired a good worker and the stand wasn't burned down.

Peter resisted looking into the envelope until he'd had a shower. Then he stepped over and around several still full moving boxes on his way to the kitchen to get his Bible. Inside the envelope was a thank you note on embossed Great Assemblies of Flagstaff stationary and a check for a hundred dollars.

Peter wondered if he'd be leading a church like Flagstaff in Glennwood someday.

At a quarter to ten that evening, the phone in Matthew Struthers' study rang. It was a second line with an unlisted number.

"So how was our young minister today?"

"He was a charmer. The people loved him."

"Good numbers?"

"No," Matthew said with a chuckle before sitting in his chair. "They were phenomenal numbers. In both services. I felt myself reaching for my wallet."

Struthers listened to his senior friend pondering.

"Why don't you take him around for a few Sundays? I'll make arrangements and email you a schedule. A gift like this shouldn't go to waste."

Nell would work weekends, while Stephen, who needed much more supervision, would work Tuesdays and Thursdays between his college classes. On Friday, three months and two days after he officially opened for business, Peter gave a set of keys to each of his two employees.

He didn't sleep a wink that night.

Peter was locking up Wednesday afternoon when Matthew and Susanna drove up to the stand. They were a stylish couple with all the trappings of a comfortable level of success. Matthew lowered his window with a touch of a button.

"You can't be closed already. We drove all this way for mochas."

"Not only can I be closed already," Peter said with a weary smile. "I'm out of milk so I have to go shopping. Fortunately, my last few customers wanted iced coffees and iced tea. What are you two doing down this way?"

"As Regional Pastor, I'm going to be visiting the churches over northern and central Arizona the next few Sundays and wanted to take you with me. I think you'll bring some needed encouragement to the churches."

"Sounds good," Peter said. "Thank you for the invitation."

Susanna leaned toward the window. "Be careful, Peter. You just might find yourself a pretty girl on your travels."

"I don't have time for that just yet, Sister Struthers. I have a business to run and a church to start."

Matthew handed Peter a handwritten schedule for the next three Sundays.

"This first Sunday we'll be in Prescott Valley at Pastor Smith's church. I can pick you up around nine and we'll be there a half hour before service."

"Sounds like a plan."

On Sunday, Peter shared his heart before a crowd of two hundred and asked everyone to consider giving from their hearts to the college and the kingdom of God. In this service, baskets were placed at the front and the people came forward to give. The baskets were emptied twice before the last nickel was given by a smiling little boy barely old enough to walk.

Pastor Struthers and Pastor Bishop were in Sedona the following Sunday. In addition to an $80,000 offering total, two fully restored muscle cars were donated to the college.

Seven days later, the two pastors were in historic Prescott where a wide eyed Pastor Mills privately handed Matthew a check for over a hundred thousand dollars from the fifteen-hundred-member congregation.

"Very generous people," Peter said once the two men were back on the road.

Struthers looked over to his gifted friend. "Generous indeed, brother."

Peter showed Matthew the rec room facilities at his apartment complex. The open room with big windows would make a comfortable place for a church to meet initially. Matthew seemed only politely interested.

"I have my first Bible study with one of my regular coffee customers."

"Really? Are you using the outlines in *Purpose & Meaning*?"

"Actually, they're from Pastor Barnes and the church in Apache Junction."

Matthew's smile dissipated. "I'd advise sticking with the approved materials from Great Assemblies, Peter. As I understand it, Greg is no longer with us."

Chapter Twenty-Four

"I've got to find a cheaper habit," Audrey said, handing Peter a crisp five-dollar bill.

"Well, don't find anything too soon. Are we still on for Saturday?"

"Sure we are. But we should get out of here. Maybe drive up to Jerome and have lunch with this Bible study."

"That would make it a missions trip."

"And I'll bet you could write it all off! See you tomorrow morning, mocha man."

The rest of the business day was profitable. Then just before Peter turned off the open sign, the familiar SUV pulled up to the window.

"Gotcha before you closed this time."

"With minutes to spare," Peter said with surprise. "Hello Pastor Struthers and Pastor Seager. What do I owe the honor to?"

Pastor Seager moved closer to be heard. "Besides a good iced latte, how about we talk about your future."

At six-thirty, Peter followed a host dressed in black and white to a large leather booth within the mahogany interior of the exclusive The Lariat Restaurant. Pastor Struthers stepped out to allow Peter to sit in the middle.

Evan shook Peter's hand. "What can we get for you, Peter?"

Peter studied the half empty signature tumblers in on the table.

"I'm working on Scotch," Evan said. "He's finishing brandy."

"Whiskey then, please."

Evan nodded to the host who quietly slipped away toward the bar.

For the first time, Peter felt somewhat comfortable around Senior Pastor Seager. The contents of his glass may have induced his congenial warmth. However, it arrived, it was a welcome change. A moment later, Peter's dirty gold beverage on ice arrived.

"So as your ministry grows, Peter, what do you see happening with the coffee stand?"

"I need to get it paid off first," he started. "Then, I'd like to keep it going. Maybe open another one. I like having a vocational connection to the community."

Evan listened and nodded.

"Pastor Struthers tells me that the churches responded enthusiastically to your testimony. The body of Christ can't get enough encouragement these days Peter." The seasoned minister looked away with concern. "It's so important when souls hang in the balance. It just takes the right vessel sharing the right word at the right time that will be that spark of hope that ignites faith. Lives turn away from the brink like that." Evan snapped his fingers for emphasis. "What I'm hearing from the pastors of the churches you've visited, you have a ministry beyond that of a single church pastor."

Electricity shot through Peter at those words. "What do you mean, Pastor Seager?"

Evan leaned over the table. "Perhaps to properly serve the churches, you need to visit more of them - and not just Arizona, but beyond. Texas, California, New Mexico, Nevada." he waved his hands as if to signal the ends of the known world.

Peter's mind raced to catch up to the rapid beating of his heart.

"But what about pastoring a church here in Glennwood? Don't I have to establish myself as a local pastor before taking on anything else?"

Even shook his head. "There are many pastors over many areas of responsibility. Being the pastor of a church is only one of those areas. Think beyond that. Think *Priesthood of Pastors*, Peter. There are ministers *within* a church, and minsters *over* a church. Great Assemblies needs anointed ministers like you to elevate the spirit of churches. That comes from outside of the church. It's a higher calling."

The young pastor's mouth went dry with a nervous excitement.

"All of your expenses will be taken care of Peter. You'll travel properly and continue doing what you've done with Pastor Struthers. Tell your story about the college and ask the body to consider supporting the ministries of Great Assemblies. And since the worker deserves his wages, you'll receive a percentage of the offerings. Which reminds me," Evan said, pointing to Matthew.

Peter watched Pastor Sturthers reach into his brown leather binder.

"This is for your labors thus far," he said, sliding a check in front of Peter so he could clearly see the amount of $2,500.00. "There's more in a building fund I'll manage for you should you still want to establish a church in Glennwood."

Peter's mind was spinning. A higher calling, and a much higher wage as well as a building fund? With this one check his coffee stand was more than half way paid off.

"Earth to Peter," Matthew said.

"Sorry, Pastor. I wasn't expecting this."

Senior Pastor Seager put his hand on Peter's arm. "No one was expecting any of this. But isn't God good?"

"He is *very* good. When is all this traveling supposed to start?"

"Let's enjoy a nice dinner, shall we," Evan said looking confidently to the other pastor, "then we'll talk more about it."

Three days later, Peter and Audrey drove the winding road to the top of Cleopatra Hill and to historic Jerome. They parked just off the road overlooking the Verde Valley, and wandered their way up and down the steep sidewalks. The old copper mining camp was once known as the wickedest town in the west.

After investigating several pottery boutiques and quaint antique stores, they stopped at the Jerome Grill for lunch, located in the Clinkscales building. The two-story, red brick inn and cafe had been in continuous operation since its construction in 1899.

Peter took the last bite of his club sandwich and chips just as Audrey pushed her nearly empty bowl of southwest chili to the side of the table.

"It sounds like we won't get to do this very often if you're going to be traveling every weekend."

The young pastor leaned back in his chair. "What can I say? I'm in demand."

"Oh brother," Audrey said with a roll of her eyes. "Sounds exciting, but I'm a little confused. Will you still be a pastor if you're not actually building a church in Glennwood? I always thought preachers who traveled were evangelists."

"How did Senior Pastor Seager put it? Peter said. "There are different types of pastors in Great Assemblies. This is a higher calling."

"Kind of like being a corporate manager instead of a store manager?"

"I suppose that's one way to put it. I'll do this till the Lord opens up another door and I'll walk through that one."

"Just as long as you're still around to make my cinnamon mochas during the week, buddy."

"Oh, I'll be there. And you still owe me a Bible study. Just because I'll be traveling doesn't mean you're off the hook."

"You're the one who didn't bring it."

"Only because I was asked to not use the one I had. I'll get things together. Then we'll do it."

Chapter Twenty-Five

Peter sat in the front row with Senior Pastor Seager at the church in Chandler on Sunday morning. He waved to a few familiar faces at the start of the service. Soft music played as he stepped to the pulpit. Once again his honest sincerity captivated the multitude before him. The Chandler church gave a $219,722.16, half of which would go to the Great Faith College of Ministry.

Peter declined a lunch invitation after service in favor of visiting Brad and the coffeehouse. He greeted the baristas behind the counter then led himself to the back office where Brad worked on a crossword puzzle.

"I thought you had to be smart to figure those things out," Peter said over Brad's shoulder."

"Wow, look what the cat dragged in," Brad said, standing to give Peter a bear hug. "All dressed up and nowhere to go, huh?"

"I was speaking at a church nearby."

"Sure you were. You can say it. You missed me."

"That too."

Peter updated Brad on his new church schedule and how the coffee stand was doing. Then he gave him a check for two thousand dollars against his loan. "I hope to have you paid back within two months."

"About time. I could use the money."

Peter detected a quiet seriousness about his former employer hidden in the extended pauses of their conversation. He watched Brad turn and pick up the newspaper from his desk.

"Got this in yesterday."

Peter took the folded paper. His eyes stopped over the text circled in blue ink.

Lori Wilson, 1969 – 1998.

Peter went through the steps of opening the stand without feeling early the next morning. Then the voice he needed to hear rescued him from his sadness.

"Mocha, mocha, mocha," she demanded from the other side of the window.

Audrey stopped when her sober faced friend appeared.

"What's wrong, Peter?"

She watched him search for a response. Then she pulled her car ahead and parked next to his truck. Audrey ran inside the stand where Peter nearly fell into her arms and cried.

Audrey led him to the bar stool and turned off the open sign and closed the window. Then she listened patiently as Peter sobbed his way through the story of his mentor and friend. "I've never lost anyone close before. Lori and I were close."

After wiping her eyes and calling her office, she gave him a comforting embrace.

"One of my friend's relatives had a brain tumor and it was a very difficult time for the whole family. They were able to get it in time, barely. I'm so sorry, Peter." She watched him compose himself. "Are going to be okay working here today?"

Peter blinked away the last tear and nodded. "Yeah. I'm sorry I made you late, but thanks for staying."

"Don't be sorry for a second. I'm always here for you."

Peter stood and wrapped his arms around the five-foot-six comforter in heels before him.

"Let me at least make you a mocha. Sounded like you really needed one when you drove up."

Audrey came by the stand every morning to check on her friend. By Friday, when they met for a casual dinner and a stroll around the lake, Peter had returned to himself. He beamed with affection toward the sweet young woman who cared for him during a week of sorrow.

"I'm going to Phoenix tomorrow. Where will you be here this Sunday?"

Peter had to think. "I'm going to be home, actually. But tomorrow I'll be in Sedona...for a planning meeting with Pastor Seager. It sounds like he's got some week-long tour planned soon. I may have to hire another person just to have someone on call."

Nearing the end of their walk he almost reached for her hand, but thought better of it. At that precise moment she folded her arms to keep warm, none the wiser. He was glad he waited.

Chapter Twenty-Six

Senior Pastor Evan Seager sat across from Peter in a large bakery and deli overlooking Arizona Highway 89A. Peter had never seen Evan wearing bifocals. More surprising was what Peter saw when his elder looked up from the maps and notes covering the table. Evan was smiling. He was on hold while talking to Peter.

"Ever heard of A.J. Jorgan from Baton Rouge, Louisiana?"

Peter shook his head. "Can't say that I have."

Pastor Seager flipped through a few photos. The first showed a man addressing a large crowd in a National Guard Armory. "This is A.J. In Huntsville last year. Over twelve hundred came out to hear him preach on a rainy Thursday night. This next one was in Missouri with twenty-one hundred. And here he is preaching to over three thousand. None of these were regular Sunday services."

Peter nodded and listened to Evan while he spoke to him and someone on the cell. Then he hung up and turned his full attention to Peter.

"A. J. recently joined our ranks and is now a Great Assemblies Pastor of Evangelism."

"Fantastic."

"It really is."

Senior Pastor Seager organized the papers and photos back into his binder and set it down on the empty chair next to them, leaving a clean table before them.

"I see a great opening here, Peter. A. J. is ready and available to spread the Great Assemblies message and there are a number of churches ready to have him come and preach. If you and A. J. and myself combine our ministries, I believe there will be a blessing poured out that can't be contained. Are you open to that?"

"Of course, Pastor. As much as I can be."

"As much as you can be? Because of your little coffee stand?"

"I believe God has a purpose for the coffee stand in my life, Pastor. It may not seem like much but it has been paying the bills and given me a way to meet people."

Evan chuckled. "Forgive me, Peter, I didn't mean to sound condescending. I think it's a wonderful outlet. You may, however, find it to be an unnecessary burden in the days to come. We can discuss that at a more convenient time. For now, what is a reasonable ministry schedule you can commit to?"

Peter leaned forward on the table. "I thought we were talking about weekends."

"True. But if churches are hungry, Peter, what can we do to feed them? Can you see yourself reaching the masses throughout the week as well?"

"Pastor, I can't just leave the stand. I don't have the staff and I've got to be honorable to Brad who's backed me financially."

"Alright, Peter, alright, I respect that, son."

Peter gathered his thoughts. "But I think I can get Nell to come in on Fridays for me occasionally. If so, then I can be available Thursday through Sunday. But I'd have to be back in time to open Monday morning."

Pastor Seager pursed his lips and nodded. "Not the full week I was hoping for, but we'll make do. I'd like to pencil us in for at least twice a month on that schedule, and perhaps a local church appearance when we're not on a revival tour. Agreed?"

"Agreed."

The two ministers shook hands. "You'll be making an eternal impact while being handsomely compensated." Evan picked up his binder then paused. "I'm reluctant to share this, so please keep it just between us."

Peter moved in closer.

"Now that the college is established, and the budget has been met thanks in large part to your efforts, I may be moving on to take a larger leadership role at Great Assemblies headquarters. Pastor Struthers will be taking over Great Faith College of Ministry."

"Congratulations."

"Thank you. Nothing is final, but everything appears to be moving in that direction. If so, Peter, I'd like to take you with me. You're a gifted minister with an exceptionally bright future. Your light shouldn't be hidden under a bushel. We'll talk more when everything is confirmed. I'll be in touch about this weekend. Please let me know as soon as possible, today even, if you can travel out of town this coming Thursday through Sunday night."

"Thank you for the vote of confidence, Pastor. I'll call you later today, tomorrow at the latest."

Nell was unavailable Fridays, but Stephen's school schedule changed a bit and he jumped at the opportunity to have more hours at the coffee stand. Peter called Pastor Seager to let him know he'd be available to travel later in the week. In turn, Evan had a round trip ticket waiting for him at the Southwest Airlines counter in the Sky Harbor International Airport Thursday morning. His first revival meeting would be in Colorado.

Peter arrived at 1:35 PM in Denver where a local pastor met him holding a sign reading *Pastor Bishop*. He almost walked past the man having never seen his name in print like that. Fifty-five minutes later he was checked into his room on the sixth floor of the Sheraton Denver West Hotel on South Union Boulevard.

The king suite was well appointed with ornate hard wood furniture. Peter looked out the thick glass window and to the view of the city below. The world had a glossy finish to it. It was a feel Peter openly liked and secretly loved.

"When you're ready Pastor, I'll take you to the church," came the voice from the entry way.

Peter had forgotten about his escort. "Oh, that's right. Let's go."

There were six enormous Great Assemblies Churches in Denver. Once a year they rented Mile High Stadium for a grand worship rally. This revival meeting would take place only eight miles from downtown Denver in the Great Assemblies of Lakewood church building, The Lakewood congregation was the smallest of the six churches boasting thirty-nine hundred in regular attendance and a staff of sixteen pastors and assistants.

Advertising for the four-night revival meeting was primarily word-of-mouth, but all indications suggested a good turnout.

Peter was led into the minister's conference area where Senior Pastor Seager and Pastor A. J. Jorgan were seated with several other pastors. When Pastor Seager introduced Peter to the group, Peter noticed a brightening ripple across the unfamiliar faces. He wondered what Pastor Seagar had told the group of men prior to his arrival.

A. J. Jorgan was a thick man in his early thirties whose manner was an intriguing blend of nervousness and down home southern charm. His hair was cut short and gelled to stand straight up even in high winds. He was married with four young children and one more on the way.

After an enthusiastic hug, he asked Peter, "Have you done many revivals, brother?"

"First one," Peter said.

"Oh great, oh great! That's great brother! I'm so thankful to be here serving God with you in Denver. We're gonna bless God and wins souls for Christ."

Peter thought the man was going to explode. "Yes, amen."

"Shall we go over the layout of the evening, Pastors?" Evan asked steering the group back to the table.

Everyone found their places and Pastor Seager opened a binder. Peter thought he saw the words *Revival Handbook of the Great Assemblies* on the cover. Another handbook. The Senior Pastor passed out the schedules for each evening and made sure every detail was covered. From the parking attendants to the ushers to the offering, preaching, singing and snack bar, at least one pastor was assigned to each part of the services.

Two hours before the revival service was to begin, a catering company set up a dinner buffet for the ministry staff. Musicians began arriving an hour later, followed by a few dedicated saints who prayed for lost souls. The auditorium was nearly filled by quarter till. The choir began singing five minutes before the top of the hour. At precisely seven o'clock, the Senior Pastor of Great Assemblies of Lakewood addressed the crowd using the clearest sounding wireless microphone system Peter had ever heard. The revival was underway.

Evan Seager was a master planner and organizer. Every thread of the unfolding fabric of the night was a study in pacing, color, emotion and timing. Peter watched Pastor Seager move his head gently like a quiet metronome in synchronized harmony to the program.

I'll introduce you as before, Peter." he said. "Just be yourself like every time before."

Peter acknowledged his instructions with a simple nod.

A wave of applause accompanied Senior Pastor Evan Seager to the stage. Every word was well rehearsed and fitly spoken. The second applause was Peter's cue to speak. A dozen steps away from the spotlight that covered the polished rock pulpit, Peter was jolted. His mind went completely blank. A dark void. He tried to swallow but his mouth was dry. Eight steps away. His eyes darted from the pulpit to the floor to the audience and back to the floor. Four steps away. He clinched his fists. Two steps. A deep breath. The center stage light pierced his pupils. One hand grasped the marble. The applause began to slip away. Last step. His other hand landed on the marble. One second of silence. Two seconds of silence.

"I don't know how you came to the Lord. But God used a big blue Sunday school bus to reach me..."

Peter didn't know how he got back to his seat after the offering, but now a familiar stranger occupied the stage. The man eloquently wove scriptures into a spellbinding story of tragic personal experiences. The listeners were ushered down a flight of stairs that no longer exist, into a condemned building of years ago, and beside a sweaty heap of a man holding a loaded revolver.

"Every day I see that man in the mirror," A. J. said pointing to the side of his face above his ear. "Every day I thank God I couldn't get that gun to fire a bullet into my head."

Time skipped again, and now people were moving past Peter trying to get to the area in front of the stage. The preacher repeated his call and more people emptied their seats and streamed to the overcrowded front.

"Come and receive Jesus. Let him have control of your life. Give him your sins and failures...."

Peter watched as pastors gathered around people to pray with them and to help them make a decision for Christ.

Old men and children, the finely dressed and the smelly vagrant, mothers and daughters they came without any pride or thought of who might see them. They came believing whatever the preacher told them.

"Would you repeat after me," A. J. Jorgan said, "I have failed...I was lost...But I accept Jesus Christ...who paid the price...for my sins. By his blood...I'm am clean...because of his death...I am alive...According to my faith...I am saved...I am whole...And I will live with Christ...for ever more...."

Peter noticed that Pastor Seager wasn't close by him anymore. Perhaps praying for someone.

"Thank you for your testimony, Pastor."

Peter looked into the face of a grateful, grandmotherly woman and her husband.

"Oh, you're very welcome. I'm glad to be here with you," he said, shaking their hands.

Another man behind them expressed his thanks as well. Peter appreciated the encouragement. He was warmed by the thought of being a blessing.

Peter listened to the choir while a spirit of prayer hovered over a slowly ebbing crowd of tear streaked faces. Mixed in with the multitude of seekers were several pastors handing out small NIV New Testaments and brochures from the church. A group of college girls giggled passed him. They would go home feeling more peace in their hearts than any other day in their young lives. They talked of coming back every night of the revival.

A part in the curtains to the left of the stage revealed a man surveying the scene before him and communicating into a cell phone. A closer look revealed the serious countenance of Pastor Seager.

Peter saw A.J. only briefly after service. The orator of only minutes before had evaporated leaving the nervous family man from Louisiana. He asked to return to his hotel room so he could visit with his wife and children on the phone before they all retired for the night.

The next three nights in Denver were nearly identical to the first. Every service was a seamless orchestra of music, preaching, seekers, finders, prayers and tears. And money. The total offering amount was just north of half a million dollars, but Peter wasn't privy to those numbers. He was satisfied with the uplifting spiritual experiences, the exceptional accommodations, and a tour of the sights and flavors of Denver. A check for $2,000 handed to him before taking his 10:25 PM flight back to Phoenix didn't hurt either.

Chapter Twenty-Seven

The blurry-eyed coffee stand owner read the handwritten note from Nell on the counter the next morning. *We're all out of milk.* A quick check in the small refrigerator under the counter confirmed the unfortunate truth. Peter jumped into his truck and picked up four gallons of 2% milk from the only twenty-four hour shopette within three miles. Peter heard a car drive up to the window and he hurried to open up on time. He didn't quite make it and the impatient customer let him know that.

Audrey was fourth in line at ten after six. "How was Denver?"

"It was nice. The church was packed every night," he said. "Whatcha needing this morning?"

"The usual."

"You don't have a usual."

"Cinnamon Mocha, silly."

"Yes *ma'am*."

"You take that back!" she said over her glasses.

"No, you deserve that this morning."

Peter disappeared, then returned with a large instead of a medium.

"Whoa, I can't drink all that. And my butt doesn't need all the whipped cream."

"You wear it well."

Audrey smiled and handed him four ones. "Are you gone again this weekend?"

"I think so. The success of this revival is leading to a string of 4-day trips. I've got everything covered here so that's fine with me."

"No rafting trip down the Verde River for you then."

"What? Rafting?"

Audrey pulled away from the window. "Bye"

Peter was in Albuquerque Thursday afternoon and on the platform next to Evan Seager at six-forty-five that evening. The large sanctuary vibrated with anticipation and a hunger for God.

Unlike most of the other church leaders, Senior Pastor Hernandez encouraged open worship. Like a musical kite in the sky, every song was chased by a long tail of extended praise in the presence of Almighty God.

Twenty-nine minutes into the service, Peter spoke to the gathered church. They responded with open checkbooks. A two family praise team sang a reworked medley of songs that ushered A. J. Jorgan to the stage.

Peter listened again to the preacher's personal story of a life rescued from sin and destruction. The altar scene was identical to the nights in Denver.

"Won't you come?" A. J. pleaded as streams of perspiration rolled down his face. "Won't you let go of the wheel of you heart and let Jesus drive? He knows the way ahead, friend. Don't drive into the darkness without Christ to light the way."

Peter watched from the stage as row after row of men and women, young and old emptied into the middle aisle and down to the front. Pastors and assistants scurried to meet with anyone who wanted someone to pray with them.

"It's like magic, isn't it?" Pastor Seager said.

Peter kept his eyes on the flow of weeping souls to the front of the stage. *Magic?* That was the last word Peter would've used to describe the clear working of the Holy Ghost. He turned to ask a question, but Evan was gone.

The night concluded at a restaurant just a few miles from the church building. Peter joined a dozen pastors and their wives as well as A. J. for a selection of appetizers loaded with ample amounts of deep fried goodness. The presence of God rested lightly upon the late night diners. Evan joined the fellowship half an hour later. He pulled up a chair behind A. J. and Peter.

"Pastors, I've scheduled us to be in California every weekend in June," he said with an unusual brightness. "I hope that works for both of you."

Peter and A. J. looked at each other like kids trapped in a candy store.

"We'll somehow make it though, Pastor," Peter said.

A. J. nodded. "Amen to that!"

"Good, good. We'll take the first weekend off in July off, then resume the weekend following. It's not definite, but Seattle and Tacoma might be on the schedule next."

The second night of the Albuquerque revival was dedicated to prayer for the sick. It was standing room only. Saturday night was focused on the next generation. A. J. shared the stage with Senior Pastor Seager, who challenged young people interested in ministry to consider attending the Great Faith College of Ministry. The front rows were reserved for youth and college-age attendees. Sunday night was the grand finale with extended music.

Flight delays put Peter into Sky Harbor Airport at 1:15 AM and in his own bed for a two-hour nap before opening the coffee stand. Knowing that a $2,000 check waited to be deposited later in the day eased the early morning weariness.

Peter waited till Wednesday to tell Audrey he would be in California the next four weekends.

She was not happy with him.

Peter, A. J. and Senior Pastor Seager were in San Diego the first weekend. Peter was heartened to see a tribute given to the many Navy sailors in attendance. The next two revivals were in Los Angeles. Four nights in Bakersfield rounded out the last stop on the tour.

On the first class flight out of LAX Monday morning, Evan reviewed the numbers on a simple spreadsheet and was pleased to see that the Golden State still lived up to its name.

The world was still a buzz about the President's extra-curricular activities with an intern in the White House when Stephanie dropped off Katie for an overnight 4th of July weekend visit.

"You're a dear, Peter," she said. "I'm meeting Edward, a friend from work, in Prescott. Then we're going to the Grand Canyon." She pulled him aside and lowered her voice. "If we decide to stay a little longer, can I impose on you to keep Katie another day?"

"Sure, Steph. Katie's my girl. Take all the time you need," he said, watching his niece inspect his apartment. "If things get real slow, I'll put her to work at the stand."

Peter and Katie watched from the curb as Stephanie drove away.

"My mom's gonna marry that creepy guy-I just know it. Uugh."

"Edward?"

"Yes! You have to help me Uncle Peter. He's this strange man with sicko eyes and bumps on his face. Oh! I totally get sick thinking about him and my mom together."

"C'mon, I'm sure he's not that bad," Peter said putting his arm around her. "you need more time to get to know him."

"No way! You obviously haven't met him. He's come over a couple of times. Once he stayed the night. Totally gross! Like they think I don't know what's going on in the bedroom. He's creeps me out, Uncle Peter!"

"Katie, please don't talk about that, okay?

The moody young lady grumbled as they passed the pool area and climbed the stairs.

"Some people who don't know you and me might think we're creepy," Peter said. "and they don't even know us."

"I don't think so. You're hot, Uncle Peter. All my friends say so when they see your picture at school. They say you look like that guy from Wings."

"What's Wings?"

"You know, that show on TV. The pilots in the little airport."

Peter shook his head.

"I think his name is Joe Hacket or something. Mom and I watch it sometimes. And at least I don't have big ugly bumps on my face."

"I don't think Edward *wants* bumps on his face, honey."

"Well, you won't have to live with him if he does marry mom."

"True. But at least give him a chance won't you?"

She lowered her stiff shoulders. "Whatever."

"That's my girl. Now, what should we do about lunch? Split a huge burger again?"

Katie frowned and turned away from him. "I'm not really hungry and I don't want to get fat."

"Fat? You're thin as a rail, Katie. Where in the world did you get the idea you were fat?"

"Nowhere. It doesn't matter." She turned back brightening. "You could show me your coffee stand. I still haven't seen the inside yet."

"That's right, you haven't. So I'll show you the stand, then we'll grab a bite to eat. Even if you're not hungry, I am!"

Nell stepped over to the grocery store, giving Peter the opportunity to show her how everything worked. Then they toured Glennwood looking for lunch, VHS movies, and windows to shop through before heading back to the apartment.

Peter prepared a large bowl of extra buttered popcorn for their late night movie marathon. Katie waited next to a pile of blankets on the couch with the remote in her hands. "C'mon, Uncle Peter! You're taking forever!"

The next evening, they watched the 4th of July fireworks at the lake. Audrey joined them and finally got to meet Katie. The meeting didn't go as well as Peter had hoped.

Later, he walked Audrey to her car. "Men will never understand women, or young girls, so don't even try. You'll hurt our feelings if you do something, and make us mad if you don't. She's sweet, Peter. She's just possessive of your attention right now. If I were her, I probably wouldn't want some strange lady interrupting a visit with you either. This will pass. I'll see you next week. Just don't tell me you're going to California again."

Stephanie and Edward arrived shortly before noon on Sunday to pick up Katie. Peter carried her suitcase to the car. The slightly balding man with thick glasses opened the trunk of his brown Buick.

"Peter is it? Edward Jinks."

They shook hands. "Nice to meet you, Edward." The bumps weren't that big.

Stephanie hugged her daughter and thanked Peter for watching her.

"We kept each other busy," Peter said, as the passengers closed their car doors."

"You must have," Edward said. She looks like she's lost some weight already. See you later, Peter."

Katie looked back to Peter through the rear window as the car slipped way. He waved to the unhappy face staring back at him. An uneasy, creeping feeling climbed up his back.

Chapter Twenty-Eight

After closing the stand on Wednesday, July 8th, 1998, Peter drove to Gilbert. He entered the back of *Stellar Coffee Company* and said to Brad, "Start the one year clock my friend!"

Brad looked at the check Peter held in front of him for the remaining balance on the loan. "Look at you, Mr. Money Bags! You're paid in full. Way to go, buddy!"

"This is ministry offerings."

"So there's good money in religion, huh? Maybe I should build a stage in the corner of the place and have an open mic Sunday and split the take with the preacher."

Peter laughed. "I guess anything's possible."

The coffee partners talked for another hour, then Peter drove over to Michael and Daylene's for dinner and stayed the night. He would catch a flight to SEATAC at 6:05 the next morning and meet Senior Pastor Seager and A. J. Jorgan at the Great Assemblies of South Tacoma.

Senior Pastor Winslow was a former NFL quarterback and now leader of a five-thousand-member church. The man's size and his Super Bowl ring were the first things that caught Peter's attention. Though a humble man, he walked with a commanding presence. He was greatly admired and loved by the mega-sized congregation.

By the end of the third night of the northwest revival, Peter was wanting a larger role. He was grateful to have a part in each service, but itched to do more than testify about the college and ask people to give. He wanted to preach.

In the hallway behind the elaborate stage, Peter talked to Pastor Seager about preaching. Evan listened to the young minister.

"Ah, Peter, it does my heart good to hear that you want more," he began. "I've been actually thinking the same thing. Let me share with you where we're at right now. The three of us are booked up to Thanksgiving with our current program. I can't emphasize the importance of the impact you are having right now just by doing what you're doing." Evan put his hand on Peter's shoulder. "If you can bear with me for a while longer, Peter, I think there will be much bigger opportunities for you next year."

The three ministers were in Seattle the following weekend where it rained every day of the revival. Las Vegas was next followed by Portland, Oregon. Without warning, it was August. Peter had to cover for Stephen who went on vacation and couldn't make the first night of the Oklahoma City revival. The offering taken that night was half of the average that had been collected from all the other first nights. When Peter did arrive he received a cool greeting from Evan. But the next two nights went without flaw and many souls rededicated themselves to the Lord. The offering totals climbed dramatically with Peter there.

On Sunday evening just before the start of the last service, Pastor Evan received an emergency phone call and left abruptly. The local Senior Pastor filled in the holes left by Evan's absence and kept the program on schedule.

Peter waited until Wednesday to learn what had happened. The General Superintendent of Great Assemblies International had suffered a heart attack and passed away early Monday morning. Senior Pastor Evan J. Seager was named his successor. Senior Pastor Robert Gibbons would now coordinate the revival meetings.

The revival team visited churches in the Midwest up through the first weekend in November. Then the demand for outside evangelistic preaching subsided giving way to special holiday preparations. Churches called to get in line for the evangelistic team to come beginning the last weekend in January.

Peter looked forward to the holidays and being home for a few weekends. But the sudden drop in income was sobering. *Bishop's Coffee Company* was making money but nothing like what he made with Great Assemblies.

Evan J. Seager's name was everywhere beginning in early

December. His picture was on numerous magazines and he made multiple appearances on *Great Sunday Celebration*. Wherever he appeared on screen or in print, he hinted at exciting changes and a new church structure for the approaching new Millennium.

"So mocha man," Audrey said looking up over her glasses, "You should come to our annual Holiday Mixer on Friday as my guest. Lots of great business contacts for you. The Merrit brothers are famous for their shoulder rubbing events."

"Count me in! I need to drum up more business."

"Okay. It starts at 6:30 and ends whenever. Business casual and bring some giveaways. You never know who you'll meet."

Glennwood's Main Street glowed with the flickering of red and green Christmas lights and holiday decorations. True to Audrey's description, the Merrit Building was the most festive place to be on this particular December evening. Peter drove around the block twice before finding a decent parking spot.

Audrey took Peter by the arm at the door and introduced him to her staff, Rich and Dave Merrit, as well as other local power players as they arrived. He was surprised how quickly the room filled with jovial business people looking to have a good time while making some profitable contacts.

Peter traded his *Buy 9 Get the 10th free* coffee punch cards in exchange for other business cards. Then he saw an older woman with a plate of mini pastries. The lively grandmother wore a blue apron and lighted deer antlers on her head.

"Did you make these?" he asked, picking out a lightly frosted sample.

"Every one, dear. I'm Amy of Amy's Bakery on 5th."

"I'm Peter. Bishop's Coffee Company on 9th and Holler Road."

They exchanged cards and talked business. Peter looked around the room and noticed Audrey was laughing it up with a couple of tall gentlemen in dark sport jackets near the door.

"Amy, these pasties are really good. Are these featured in other places or just your bakery?"

"Just the bakery."

"We should change that. I think my customers would love these with their coffee. Mind if I have another one?"

"Help yourself, dear. And let's be sure to talk more soon."

Three hours later, Peter had gone through his supply of coffee cards and was ready to call it a night. He'd connected with Audrey off and on, but she always seemed to be talking with some other men by the half full punch bowl.

"You're leaving already?" asked a tipsy Audrey.

"I've been up since four sweetheart, and I'm exhausted. But I had a really great time and made a few good contacts, just like you said."

"Good, Peter. I knew you'd enjoy yourself," she said before hugging him. "I'm busy this weekend but I'll see you way too early Monday. Be careful driving home."

"I will. You too."

Peter worked Sunday for Nell and pondered how he could best offer Amy's amazing buttery pastries. Window space was at a premium. But he could build some shelves on the back wall in view of the drivers. In a box of dishware, he found a plate with a cover for free samples.

On Monday after closing the stand, he drove down 5th to Amy's Bakery. She showed him her whole operation and her famous, made from scratch breads, pies and other delicacies that would pair well with his coffee.

After several taste tests and serious number crunching, Amy and Peter reached an agreement. They would try three pastries out for the month of January and go from there. After Christmas, Peter built some shelves and created a sign to advertise the fresh baked offerings.

Chapter Twenty-Nine

The Y2K bug didn't end the world or help new year's sales either. Amy's pastry samples were a hit, but most people were still recovering from the usual holiday sugar overload. By the end of the second full week in January, customers were more open to adding something sweet and flaky to their hot beverages. Sales inched their way upward as the year progressed.

On Wednesday afternoon, Peter, A. J. and General Superintendent Seager were on a three-way conference call to plan out the first quarter of the new year.

"The churches are hungrier than ever for your ministries, gentlemen. Calls are coming in from all over."

"And we're ready to serve the churches, sir," A. J. chimed.

"That's good to hear. Now Peter, how much leeway can we get from you on your schedule?"

"Sir, my schedule is about the same. Thursdays through Sunday will work consistently, but nothing more now."

Evan mumbled something inaudible over the sound of shuffling papers.

"Well, I wish we didn't have to contend with that. "Pastor Jorgan, are you all free?"

"As free as can be, sir. My wife's ready to give birth just any day now."

"Congratulations, A. J., that's good to hear." Evan paused. "Looking at the lay of the land at a glance, it appears that you two will be in the great state of Texas the end of January through the end of February." He chuckled. "I think I offended some of the brethren by not including them on our schedule at all last year, so I need to mend some fences. It's possible you'll need to visit then revisit one of the congregations."

"Sounds wonderful, sir. Texas is a great state," said A. J.

"And Peter, I haven't forgotten our conversation. I'm working on something now that I think you'll really like. Let's keep the same lineup for now, shall we?"

"Will do, sir," Peter said.

"I won't be going with you for obvious reasons. I have other matters that require my attention and presence. But I'm with you in spirit. I've spoken directly with each of the Senior Pastors about your schedule, accommodations and so forth. They'll be in touch with you a week before your arrival. I'm sure all will run smoothly."

The junior ministers thanked the General Superintendent and hung up. Peter missed the exuberant crowds, the amazing worship music and A. J.'s preaching, but he had to admit that he also really missed the money.

Peter's only encounter with Texas up to now was a two-hour layover at the DFW. Within six weeks he would visit five different cities beginning and ending with Houston.

Senior Pastor Stover met Peter personally at the Houston Airport and took him to his hotel and the Texas-sized church facilities. Pastor Stover asked Peter to wait for him in his study while he took care of an important matter in the church office.

Peter strolled down the wide hallway lined with offices for the Assistant Pastors. He could hear the sound of dueling southern drawls coming from one office.

"I like red on red."

"Too common, son. Silver's got more class."

Peter stopped at the open door where two men in sport coats and ties leaned against a wall. The men stopped and looked to him.

"Is this Pastor Stover's study?"

"Yes it is. How can we help you?" asked the older of the two.

"I'm Pastor Bishop here for the revival."

An invisible switch electrified the two pastors. "Come on in here, brother Bishop. We were just leaving anyway."

"How was your trip? Are you comfortable where you're staying?"

Peter was startled at the immediate change. "Yes, all is well." Peter took a seat in the comfortable leather chair. "Glad to be in Houston with you all."

"Well isn't God good to send you to us? We're expecting great things from this revival, brother. So glad you and Pastor Jorgan could be with us." With that the two men stepped down the hall and into another office and shut the door.

Senior Pastor Stover arrived a few moments later. "Forgive me, brother Bishop. We have a private school here and I'm both Pastor and Principal. I had to get a message to one of our teachers."

"Not a problem at all, Pastor."

"Excellent. I believe we have all of our I's dotted and T's crossed for you and Pastor Jorgan. I'll start the revival, then hand it over to our talented worship team. They will announce you to come up, and I'll bring our evangelist – rather – the Pastor of Evangelism up. Is that how you've done it before?

"Right about the same."

"Fine then. If I may, brother Bishop, there are many needs that the ministry staff is facing right now. I won't go into any details, but perhaps you might be directed in a special way for us here."

"I'll do my best and get out of the way so God can bless. How's that?"

"Couldn't have said it any better. Thank you."

The first Houston visit was Saturday and Sunday night only. Then San Antonio, Austin, Dallas and Abilene followed in that order before returning to Houston. Each church seemed hungrier and more generous than the next. The congregations varied in size and had their own flavors and styles of worship. Each was a delight to visit.

Peter had seen many beautiful women in his travels, but couldn't get over the number of attractive ladies he saw in each church in Texas. More than one sweet southern girl expressed an interest in Peter beyond casual conversation, but he was able to resist with the help of another brother, a closing elevator door, or the return of a husband.

The second trip to Houston was a full four-night event with a portion of each night devoted to the value of Christian education and enrollment in the private school. Peter sat in Pastor Stover's study again while he finished a long-distance call in the main office. Peter could see the school campus, softball field and parking lot. He wondered if he would have done better academically if he'd attended a private school. Probably not. School was school.

Two cars sped into the lot and parked in front of the building. The drivers got out and Peter recognized them as the Assistant Pastors from the Church. They had been so helpful during the short stay before and obviously had superb taste in cars. Brand new Ford Mustangs. One was red with a red interior. The other, a metallic silver convertible.

The two traveling pastors were stranded together at the airport Sunday night as a series of severe thunderstorms ripped through the south Texas sky. It gave them a chance to do something they'd rarely done much of - talk and get to know each other.

"I met Pastor Seager through another pastor friend in Georgia," Jorgan started. "The timing couldn't have been better. My old church was shutting the doors. There were lots of problems. Pastor Seager sat me down and made me an offer to join up with Great Assemblies. I couldn't refuse, Peter. It just made sense."

"Do you mind if I ask how you go about preaching the gospel? I mean, how did you come up with the words that you use?"

"That's how I've always heard evangelists preach. They don't get deep with lots of verses. Most sinners don't know the Bible. It's usually stories and personal experiences. I knew one day that's what I was called to do. I got all messed up with drugs and stuff, but when I came back I knew that's what I was supposed to do... share my story."

Peter listened to A. J.'s childlike view of his world and couldn't help but admire his simplicity. "Have you read the Book of Acts much?"

"I have, but not often. And not recently. Is there something I'm missing?"

"I got into Acts when I was going through the apprentice phase of the College with Pastor Barnes. The apostles had an interesting way of presenting the gospel. I was just curious if you were familiar with how they preached it."

"Not off the top of my head," he said looking out at the rain assaulting the glass of the terminal. "I'll have to look that up again. I guess in some ways I'm a preacher for hire. Great Assemblies is paying my bills right now so I'll keep preaching it the way they like it." A. J. turned to look more directly at Peter. "And you're the Rainmaker."

"Rainman?"

"Yeah. Money falls from the sky around you. You should've heard Pastor Seager when you couldn't make the first night in Oklahoma. He was lit up, boy! The offering was nowhere near what comes in when you take it up."

Peter sank deeper into his chair. "Never heard that before."

A. J. chuckled and shook his head. "Speaking of never heard that before, where did *Pastor of Evangelism* come from? I've always just been called an evangelist."

"Yeah. Every denomination's got their own words and phrases."

"You're telling me, brother," A. J. said with an exaggerated roll of his eyes. "Words, phrases, rules, or snakes. Does Great Assemblies do snakes?"

"Not yet."

"That's good to hear. I can't handle no snakes!"

Chapter Thirty

Audrey arrived at straight up six for her cinnamon mocha the next morning with a smile that was brighter than normal.

"Either you have a secret or you've been naughty."

"None of the above, Texas traveler. I do have some interesting news though. Remember those two tall guys from the December mixer?

"The guys you stared at and talked to all night?"

"Whatever. One of them is a location scout for some independent movie company or something. Anyway, they're going to shoot a movie at the run down house on the north side of the lake."

"Wow, that's pretty cool!"

"Yeah, they used our real estate company to find the property they liked so I get to help! We'll have to go out and watch them shoot their movie."

"Sounds like a plan. Maybe you could help me find me a house. I'm making decent money with the ministry and the coffee business is coming along."

"How's your credit?"

"I don't know. Good I guess."

"You need to know what it is if you're serious about a house. Come by the office and I'll hook you up with a good mortgage broker."

After getting pre-qualified for a loan, Peter and Audrey drove out to the north side of Mirror Lake to see the run down house the production company planned to use. Peter parked in front and they walked around inspecting the two-story, four-bedroom house.

"Are they shooting a horror flick?"

"I don't think so," Audrey said. "They were pretty hush-hush on the details. Afraid I might steal their story."

Peter looked through the dirty windows and saw several unfinished rooms, broken tiles on the floors, and no appliances or carpet. What he did see was potential.

The house was built close to the water. The downstairs back door opened to a deck with steps to a dock in desperate need of repair.

Peter looked over the whole scene again. "I'll bet it *is* a horror flick."

Occasionally, Peter saw a familiar face at drive-up window a little sadder than usual. Sometimes people opened up to Peter and shared their stories of heartache or loss. More than once, Peter took their hands and prayed for them right there. Days afterward, he'd ask about their situations. Some told of surprising changes and answers to prayer. For others there was little change. But everyone was grateful for the coffee man who cared about them more as people than customers.

Peter was back in the air Thursday morning headed to a four-night revival in Michigan. He was alone with his thoughts about ministry for four hours at thirty-six thousand feet in the air. *Rainmaker. Higher calling. Priesthood of Pastors.*

Peter turned to window. "Lord," he whispered, "You're providing for my needs and wants. I'm not complaining. But I hope there's more to ministry for me than asking people for money."

General Superintendent Seager initiated many changes within the organization. *Great Assemblies of Christ* was simplified to just *Great Assemblies.* The New International Version Bible, strongly suggested before, now became the *official* Bible of the church. Evan Seager dropped the title of General Superintendent in favor of the *High Pastor of Great Assemblies.* This was too much for some. Forty-eight out of twelve hundred Senior Pastors resigned before the month was finished.

To maintain order with the ministry ranks, High Pastor Seager crafted a twelve point *Articles of Agreement* to be issued and signed by each and every current and future Pastor of Great Assemblies. He met with his inner circle of Regional Pastors for review first. After some minor changes, the letter was printed on special stationary. The Regionals would talk to each of their respective Senior Pastors to make sure there was complete compliance. They in turn, they would approach their pastors and assistants. If any pastor refused to sign, they were to be stripped of their title and authority immediately and without recourse. Evan wanted all signed letters returned before the Fall Gathering.

Peter missed the movie shoot, but didn't forget about the house. He spent several days getting paperwork and funds together, and made an offer that was accepted by the motivated, out of state sellers. He was officially the owner of a house that needed tremendous attention. He would miss being so close to the coffee stand, but wouldn't miss the rowdy kids at the apartment who clamored up and down the stairs all hours of the day and night. He outfitted his home with appliances and furniture from with a local home stores to make the main floor livable. He'd focus on the downstairs later. His apartment lease was up at the end of the month, and the next day, April 1st, he was in his new house.

Peter was in St. Louis with A. J. over the weekend and back in the coffee stand on Monday. On Wednesday his friend was back at the drive through window.

"Hey, what happened to you Monday?"

"I was busy all weekend and late getting out the door. For my transgression, I had to suffer through a cup of lousy office coffee."

"As long as you suffered."

"I did," she said leaning on the car window. "Are you gone again this weekend?"

"Atlanta."

"Then we need to do lunch tomorrow. Can you meet me at the deli across the street from work?"

"Lunch, deli across the street, one o'clock, right?"

"Perfect."

Peter was five minutes late meeting Audrey at the deli. She was seated at a table for two in a jet black sweater playing with the straw and lemon in her ice water.

"If I didn't know any better, I'd think you were dressed for a job interview."

Audrey smiled. "Always the charmer."

Peter sat unsure about his usually chipper friend. "Are you ordering anything?"

Audrey shook her head.

"So we're meeting for lunch...but you're not eating?"

Audrey's eyes were filled with affection and a gaze Peter had never seen before.

"I'm leaving Glennwood, Peter. Alan's asked me to marry him."

He sat in silence watching her eyes moisten.

"Alan is the movie production guy?"

Audrey nodded.

"That was quick."

"He has a place in Carmel. I'm finally going to the coast, Peter. Pacific Ocean out the back window."

"I'm happy for you, Audrey," Peter said trying to sound happy."

"You'd better be, you liar."

Peter took her hands in his and kissed them. "You deserve all the happiness in the world, my friend."

"Thank you."

They held hands for another moment. Peter was out of words already missing her.

"I have so much to do at the office. I should get back."

Audrey let go of Peter's hands and stood wiping her eyes.

"I'm really going to miss us."

Peter looked up and nodded. "Me too."

She leaned down and kissed him on the forehead. And with a final hug, she turned and walked out the front door.

Chapter Thirty-One

Peter studied the invoice again and compared it to last month's order. Coffee bean prices were going through the roof. Worse was that the grocery store, a stone's throw away, now offered coffee and hot chocolate for less than a dollar. Peter had seen some of his customers pass his stand and go over there to get their early morning fix. Pastry sales were also down with the warmer weather coming on.

He looked over to the window again. She wasn't there. The sultry voiced he'd loved from the beginning would no longer grace his early mornings. Audrey was probably listening to the waves roll up onto the white sand somewhere. Feeling the salty breeze lift and play with her long russet locks.

A call from Evan pulled Peter away from his thoughts of Audrey. A. J. had requested a weekend off to tend to some family matters, so Evan invited Peter to come to St. Louis for a tour of the Great Assemblies headquarters.

After breakfast on Saturday, Evan showed Peter the offices, printing facility, the audio recording studios and then through a back entrance into a large building concrete building. Peter's eyes adjusted to the darkness while following Evan around a corner. Evan flipped a series of switches that ignited powerful canister lights overhead. Instantly, the room illuminated, revealing a miniature stadium surrounding a massive stage that was flooded with light. High on the back wall was the unmistakable logo. *Great Sunday Celebration.*

Evan led Peter up the steps. "Isn't this an amazing view, Peter? Seating capacity is six-thousand. We broadcast to twenty-three countries, translated in fourteen languages, with a potential weekly audience of nearly half a billion people."

Peter was awestruck. "Unbelievable, Pastor!"

Evan walked over to the comfortable chairs where various hosts and countless guests, celebrities, politicians and preachers of every stripe had once sat.

Peter sat across from arguably the most powerful man in the most influential protestant church organization in the world.

"Feels good, doesn't it?"

Peter nodded enthusiastically. "Amazing."

"Peter, I told you I was working on something for you. And I think we're almost ready." Evan sat forward. "How would you like to be part of the ministry team here on Great Sunday Celebration?"

He couldn't believe it. "Great Sunday Celebration? Are you serious, Pastor?"

"Oh I'm serious. More importantly, I believe the world is ready for you and your gifts, Peter."

"But what would I do. I haven't done any preaching."

"You'll start from where you are, doing what you're already doing but on an international scale. Then grow into your own special place on the air. There are several media pastors here who can see you hosting your own show segments that are being developed as we speak. We're working to have our own channel on satellite and cable television. Imagine, Great Assemblies broadcasting worldwide twenty-four hours a day, seven days a week. You'll be part of that."

Peter became dizzy.

"Not to mention a significant increase in your income. What you've received up till now is a drop in a very large bucket ahead of you.

They left through the same back door they entered and took the elevator up to the third floor to Evan's office. The walls around his desk were adorned with paintings and hangings from all parts of the world. Beautifully finished hardwood furniture, carvings and decorative gifts paying homage to the High Pastor, filled in the spaces around the peaceful, circular room.

"I don't expect an answer right away since it would be big decision. You'd obviously have to set aside the coffee business and relocate here to St. Louis. This would become your very full-time vocation and ministry."

"I'm finding it very hard to turn this down, Pastor."

"In your shoes, I wouldn't turn this down. But I don't want you to feel pressured. Instead I want you to think about it. I'll be sending you home with two things to look over. One is the preliminary offer to become a Media Pastor. The other is our Articles of Agreement. It's a formality that every Great Assemblies pastor must adhere to. Everyone working here has already signed it and is in compliance. When you consider the enormity of Great Assemblies and the challenges that lay ahead of us, the need for such documentation is important."

Peter took the folder from Evan. "Thank you for considering me for such a position, Pastor."

"No, Peter, thank you. I believe you'll fit in perfectly here. I can't imagine the number of lives you'll touch on a global scale." Evan scanned the monthly calendar on his desk. "Pastor Jorgan may be out of the picture for a few more weekends. "Do you think you can have an answer for me by the beginning of next month?

"I will."

Peter read over the Media Pastor offer and the required duties on the flight back to Phoenix. He was still in a daze from actually being on the set of the famous Great Sunday Celebration stage, as he was driving up to Glennwood. How many times had he imagined himself there, preaching Christ to the live audience and to those by the pale blue glow of their televisions? He was imagining those scenes again just after midnight at the edge of much needed sleep.

Peter walked around the coffee stand after closing the next day. In fifty-nine days the stand would be completely his and his one-year obligation to Brad would be fulfilled. The timing of the offer was nearly perfect. After restocking the stand, Peter went home to review the rest of the materials Evan had for him. He wanted to get everything signed before the mail got picked up.

He sat down in his quiet, unfinished kitchen and looked out at the lake. "I just got this place," he said aloud. "I think I can keep it though."

He opened the folder and set the Articles of Agreement in front of him. Then he took the cap off the gold Cross pen he got from Brad for his birthday and began reading.

• The ordained High Pastor is the head and authority of the church.

• The New International Version of the holy scriptures is the only accepted text from which all Great Assemblies pastors will teach, preach or otherwise minister from.

• Pastors will only minister from approved Great Assemblies teaching and instructional materials.

• Pastors are forbidden to company with former Great Assemblies pastors or their families...

Pastor Bishop put the cap back on the pen.

Peter watched the sun set behind Glennwood at the opposite end of Mirror Lake atop Whiskey Ridge. Lights from the houses and streets fell onto the water and silently rode the ripples toward him. He could faintly make out the shadowy outline of his own house and the dock that extended over the water twenty feet or more.

Peter searched in vain for Greg and Nona's phone number earlier. The last one he tried had been disconnected. Tom and Valarie were traveling in the Carolinas out of reach. Michael and Daylene were never much for doctrinal conversations. He was alone and God seemed all too quiet again.

On Tuesday, Peter decided to fast and pray for an answer.

After work on Wednesday, he went home and got out the Bible studies Greg had given him. He went through most of them again feeling strength from the undiluted scriptures.

Thursday Peter covered for Stephen who went to a skateboard fest of some sort in Phoenix.

By Friday, he needed a change of scenery. The deli he said good bye to Audrey in was closed for remodeling. Another place he heard had great sandwiches was off Highway 89A toward Prescott.

Peter slipped into a booth facing the door inside Elmer's Roadside Cafe. After deciding on a French Dip sandwich and a salad, he opened the folder and re-read the Articles of Agreement. He remembered one of the Army officers in his unit say that he went from being enlisted man to an officer to help change things for the better for the enlisted soldier. Peter wondered if that could happen within Great Assemblies.

After finishing the last bite of au jus drenched beef and bread, Peter resumed reading the list. There was nothing he could agree to from his heart. Everything would be lip service.

A new customer walked through the door. A man who seemed to be known by some of the staff.

"I'll just seat myself then," he said, picking up a menu and walking to the booth next to Peter's.

"Coffee?" asked a dark haired waitress.

"You know me too well, darlin'," he answered back.

The man looked familiar to Peter, but he couldn't place from where. The December mixer, perhaps? Maybe even a regular at the coffeehouse back in Gilbert. He tried not to stare.

Peter read over the Media Pastor duties again after giving up guessing who the man was. When his check arrived, Peter finished his ice water and collected his folder and keys.

He looked at the man again who nodded at him and smiled. Pushing passed the embarrassment of forgetting who the man was, he stopped in front of his table.

"Excuse me," Peter said. "I think we've met before and it's been bugging me that I can't remember from where. I'm Peter Bishop from over in Glennwood. I own a drive through coffee stand."

"Nice to meet you Peter. Can't say that I've been that way or ordered coffee there. But for what it's worth, I'm Jay Hammond.

Two hours passed before the two men even thought about the time. Peter recounted the scene from the living room where they first met. Jay spoke of events since Great Sunday Celebration. Then he read the Articles of Agreement from Peter's folder.

"According to this," Jay said, "You're in big trouble for talking to me now."

"Yeah, I know. What's a guy to do?"

Jay closed the folder and took off his reading glasses. "I thought things were a mess when I was in. Man, this takes the cake."

"So where are you now, Brother Hammond? How can I connect with you?"

The graying man took a deep breath, and thoughtfully responded, "You know, Peter, I used to think if could get with that certain person or that elder, I'd learn and grow so much. But I don't think that way anymore. Sure, it's important to get the basics down from solid elders, but after that, you need to carve it out for yourself. You need to develop your own spiritual muscles and learn to hear the voice of God for yourself. No one can do that for you. From everything you've told me, I think God has you right where he wants you."

"Really?"

"You're in the low lands of Decision Valley. Where you go from here will be life changing, no matter what you choose. But just as important as you *what* you decide, is *how* you made your decision. Did you seek God and his word, or did you go elsewhere? Did you trust in him or trust in man? No one can serve two masters, Peter. For either he will hate the one, and love the other, or else he will hold to the one, and despise the other."

"I just always thought Great Assemblies was where God wanted me to be, but I can't agree with this. I can't agree with many of the teachings."

"God may have wanted you to be with Great Assemblies for a time and season. He can use almost anything to teach us, and grow us up. But like training wheels on a bike, some things are meant to be temporary. We'll always be letting go of the lessor to make way for the greater."

Jay looked past Peter as though looking back through time. "I don't regret leaving Great Assemblies. It was good for me to leave when I did. I was starting to like those bright lights." Jay looked at his watch. "Oh no, Peter you've made me late."

"I'm sorry," Peter said. "But I just had to talk with you."

"I'm glad we did. It's done my heart good to know that maybe I had a positive impact on someone out there."

"More than you know, Jay."

"Do me one favor then."

"Anything."

"Whatever you decide to do from here on out, be honorable to God. If you're going to do your own thing or follow after man's ways, then at least have the decency to call it your own. Don't do things your way and then attach God's name to it. He gets blamed for too much of our stuff. Deal?"

"Deal."

A. J. Jorgan was still sick when Evan wanted to hear back from Peter. The realities of the drastic reduction in income was hitting Peter hard and he held off calling the High Pastor with the hope of one more revival meeting. But none were scheduled.

"Hello Peter, good to hear from you."

"Yes sir I wanted let you know that I've prayed and thought about the offer there in St. Louis. And I think everything looks great except for the Articles of Agreement. I cannot sign it."

"Peter, the Articles of Agreement are non-negotiable. Every Pastor is required to be in agreement. It's for the best."

"But I'm not in agreement. And the more I think about it, the more I have a problem with any organization that would force people to sign such a document."

Evan cleared his throat. "Who have you been talking to, son?"

"Sir, I will not sign this document. If that is a requirement, then I'm declining the offer."

Silence embraced the phone line. "Peter you're making a big, irreversible mistake. Once you leave Great Assemblies, you are out for good. Have you thought that all the way through, son?"

"I have Pastor. Thank you for the offer. Good bye."

Peter was shaking when he set the cordless phone down on the table. He hadn't noticed the clouds rolling over the top of the house.

The sky was a murky gray.

"Dear God, what have I done?"

Peter was in Brad's office on the 7th of June to celebrate the end of the yearlong agreement. He was so relieved to have the coffee stand and that he hadn't given in to Evan's urges to sell the business and go full-time with Great Assemblies. He was with Michael and Daylene, and Stephanie and Katie for dinner before driving back to Glennwood.

Over the next few days, Peter talked with Nell and Stephan about a change in hours so Peter could work more himself and make the stand more profitable. They reluctantly agreed to the new schedule, but really didn't mind having more extra time to themselves.

Late Friday night, one week into the new schedule, Peter was startled awake by the phone.

"Sorry to call so late, sir. Is this Peter Bishop?"

Peter turned on the light next to the bed. "Yes, this is Peter. Who's this?"

"Mr. Bishop this is Deputy Sheriff Andrews. I'm here at 9th and Holler Road. Sir, it appears a big truck has just demolished your coffee stand."

Chapter Thirty-Two

Peter drove south on Holler and was greeted with flashing red and blue lights a quarter mile away from the 9th street intersection. A forest green, three quarter ton Chevy Silverado was half way into the tall hedge on the other side of a pile of rubble that was once *Bishop's Coffee Company.*

Peter parked on the street and walked over to where the Sheriff and another man stood. Nothing of the stand remained upright. Splintered sections of exterior siding partially covered the battered stainless steel espresso maker. Paper cups, lids, stir sticks and foil bags of beans littered the asphalt. Peter saw a few house lights on and people in bathrobes gawking from their front porches.

"You Bishop?"

Peter unglued his eyes from the nightmare and looked to the man in the uniform. "I'm Bishop."

"Deputy Andrews, Mr. Bishop. And this appears to be our freelance wrecking crew for the evening."

Peter looked up to the embarrassed driver. "Are you alright?"

"I am," said the stranger. "Keith Roman's the name, and I'm sure sorry for all this." Then he cursed himself while avoiding Peter's eyes.

"Peter Bishop, owner of the former coffee stand." Peter turned to the Sheriff, "Was anyone hurt?" Peter asked.

"Doesn't look like it." The Sheriff pointed to the destruction before them. "I think your stand and his truck are the casualties tonight. Mr. Roman here says he had a few beers earlier but he passed the sobriety test. I'm almost done with the accident report and a tow truck is on its way."

A few cars on Holler Road slowed to watch the scene. The female passenger in a small Honda Civic said to her driver, "No coffee for you tomorrow."

The largest truck of the *One For The Road Towing* fleet arrived moments later to pick up the totaled Chevy. The driver climbed down from his rig and shook his head at Keith. "So, you build them and tear them down?"

The two men wrestled the Chevy into position for loading while Peter sifted through the rubble to see what he could salvage and throw into the back of his truck. A few moments later, Peter and Keith were alone in the glow from a noisy street light.

"Again, Peter, I can't tell you how sorry I am about this. I just looked away for a moment and when looked back, there was a kid on a bicycle. All dark clothes. And when I swerved to miss him I stepped on the gas instead of the brakes. Just a tragedy of errors."

Peter's anger gave way to understanding and sympathy as he listened to the man explain the night's events. "Is all your insurance information current?"

"Yep, it's all there and current," Keith said. "But I'll make it worth your while if we can keep the insurance out of it."

"How's that?"

"You've heard of Roman Construction?"

"No."

"Are you new here?"

"Apparently new enough to not have heard of Roman Construction."

Keith laughed. "Well, if I can trouble you for a ride home, I'll explain what I mean."

They traveled through downtown Glennwood then through two subdivisions of modern designed homes with prestigious vehicles parked in the drive ways.

"This is one of ours," Keith said pointing to a two story home. "And the one across the street there. Two blocks over was Glennwood's *Avenue of Dreams*. We've won the competition three of the last five years."

Peter came to a stop in front of Keith's house two miles and a long gravel driveway later.

"I'll get a crew out to clean things up first thing in the morning. Then how about we work on the plans together to build you a new coffee place?"

"That sounds like a plan," Peter said. "And how about something for my employees?"

"Oh yeah. Write something up and I'll take care of them too. It's only right. See you on site about seven."

Daylight was kinder to the forty-something Keith Roman who appeared more ragged the night before. A Bobcat loader and a dump truck made quick work of the small debris field, while Peter sketched out a stand design. Later, he was on the phone to Brad recreating an equipment list. Before the work day was over, several phone orders had been placed for coffee brewing supplies and building materials courtesy of the Platinum credit card billed to Roman Construction. Local building permits were acquired the following day and a six-man construction team began work early Wednesday morning.

The new drive-through coffee stand would be six inches wider, ten inches taller and a foot longer. Keith assigned one of his best carpenters to work with Peter to design space saving shelves and cabinets. The drive through window would be large enough to accommodate a small, easy access pastry case with an awning overhead to shelter drivers from rain.

Peter was with Keith every day and they became friends during the construction process. The U.S. Navy veteran left life on a carrier to get into heavy equipment. After several up and down years behind back hoes and fork lifts, he went to work in building construction.

"There was never a shortage of work," Keith told Peter over a tailgate lunch of burgers and hand breaded onion rings. "I took the reins, got my general contractor's license, slapped up a Roman Construction sign and away we went! That's my story. But how in the world did you become an ex-pastor?"

"I couldn't agree with what was happening," Peter said. "But the more I look at it, the more I realize that I didn't leave the church. The church left me. I don't think I'm done for good. Maybe just on hold for a while."

Nell and Stephen stopped by a few times each to check on the progress of their new place of employment. They were relieved to see the improvements.

Fourteen days after the accident, Bishop's Coffee Company returned to life with a new sign to welcome customers back to the best coffee in Glennwood.

Peter slid the drive-through window open and smelled the cool, early morning air. He wished his friend could see his new stand. In her honor he turned and made himself a cinnamon mocha.

The spicy dark chocolate mix sent his mind wandering over the flickering images and emotions of the past few months. He leaned up against the wall and quietly played out the scenes. The bright lights in different cities. The congregations. The luxurious hotels. Trading a small apartment for a house in need of fixing up. The feel of Audrey's kiss good bye. The last phone conversation with Evan Seager. From pastor to ex-pastor. And the death, burial and resurrection of his coffee stand.

The approaching sounds of a diesel engine overtook the last of his thoughts. Peter watched headlights circle their way around to the front where a Roman Construction truck eased up to the window. Keith waved from the passenger seat.

"Looks like she's still standing for you?"

"Yes sir, she is. You and your crew did me proud."

"We had to," Keith said with a smile. "Small town. Word gets around like wildfire and I've got a reputation to uphold. Your customers coming back?"

"It's slow this morning. But I think they'll be back."

"Well, let's get five regular coffees, as many pastries, and some of those punch cards."

Peter nodded. "Coming up."

Peter closed the stand at two that afternoon. The day's numbers were down nearly thirty percent from previous Tuesdays. He approached his truck thinking about what part of town to visit with coffee punch cards next, when he noticed a couple waiving from a motor home with a compact SUV in tow in the shopette parking lot.

"Hey stranger," Tom said from the high driver's window. "They tell us you're all by yourself up here."

Peter smiled from ear to ear. "You heard about right."

Valarie leaned over her husband. "We came to change that."

Chapter Thirty-Three

Peter gave them a tour of the house and property, then ran a hose and an extension cord out to the motor home for water and electricity. By late afternoon, they'd retreated into the more comfortable surroundings of the motor home. Valarie sat across from Peter at the built in table. Tom adjusted the blinds to allow for the early evening light to filter into the living area before sitting in the recliner.

"That's too bad about Great Assemblies, Peter," Tom said, refilling his empty glass with ice water. "We've been out of the denominational church scene for several years really, except with you there in Apache Junction. I suppose every place is going to have its way of doing things that seems strange to outsiders, but normal to insiders."

Peter considered Tom's words. "May I ask you about that? You say you've been out of the denominational church for years. How does that work when the Bible says to not forsake the assembling of ourselves together in the book of Hebrews?"

That's a good question, Peter. We get that every now and again on our travels. People think because we're not rooted to one location we can't really be a part of a church. Let me answer you with a question. What makes a church?"

Peter took a deep breath. "Well, a pastor, a congregation, a set time and place to gather for starters."

"Since you mentioned Hebrews, is that what Hebrews tells you, Peter?" Valarie asked.

Peter couldn't form an answer.

Valarie smiled. "How many people does it take to make a church? What scripture tells us the number?"

Peter searched his memory. "I can't remember a number."

Valarie and Tom studied each other.

"I had a dream a few weeks ago," Valarie said carefully. "I saw a clipper ship coming into a harbor after what seemed a long voyage. Once it was near the docks it lowered the anchor. It was done sailing. I had it three nights, one after the other. I think that ship is us. And I feel that our new harbor is with you, Peter. I always awakened with your face before me."

"I hope that's the case. I'd love for you two to be here in Glennwood. But I'm not a pastor anymore, unless you know something else I don't."

"When I sought the Lord about the dreams and coming out here to Glennwood, the word I kept hearing was 'unconventional.' I sense it's as much for us as it is for you."

Peter waited for more. "Unconventional...how?"

"Not sure exactly, but sometimes to grow in God, we need to let go of what we think we know. We need to be open. New wine requires new wine skins. May I ask you a few questions, Peter?"

"Anything."

"Do you still feel God wants to use you?

"Yes."

"Are you committed to Glennwood? Do you feel this is where you should be?"

"Good question," Peter said, pondering. "My niece got me out here to visit during the holidays. A coffee stand up for sale and approval from Great Assemblies to start a church prompted me to move." He looked back to Valarie. "I believe this is where I'm supposed to be."

"Good. It's important for a man to know that he's where he's supposed to be. The other question is about the Bible college. How much practical, useable instruction on prayer did you get there?"

Peter chuckled. "Almost zero."

"Then if I may say so, Peter, perhaps that's where we should start. My first husband I started more than one church. I can tell you Glennwood is ready for the gospel. But if we don't prepare ourselves first, then what we do will be in our flesh."

Valarie's eyes sparkled. "Where we're going can't be taught in Bible schools. You know why?" She leaned closed. "Because most teachers have never been where we're headed."

Tom, Valarie and Peter agreed to meet Friday night at seven for prayer at Peter's house. On Wednesday, Tom and Valarie relocated their motor home to Mirror Lake RV Park and got acquainted with Glennwood. Peter spent most of Friday afternoon turning his bachelor pad into a house of prayer.

Tom and Valarie arrived in comfortably casual attire in contrast to Peter's dress shirt and slacks.

"We aren't keeping you from a date are we?" Tom asked.

"No," Peter said. "I wanted to look nice for my guests, though."

Valarie gave Peter a hug. "You look fine, dear. I'm really excited about our time together."

After catching up on the day in the kitchen, they moved into the living room.

"Sorry it's a little dark," Peter said. "Not all of the outlets work and I'm still getting the place furnished."

Instrumental praise escaped into the room overhead through wall mounted Bose 901 speakers. The trio of praying saints stood in the center of the room a few feet apart facing each other. Light from the single lamp highlighted their faces. Tom and Valarie's eyes were closed. Peter watched Valarie sway slightly to the music. Tom rolled up his light blue shirt sleeves and rubbed his hands together praising the Lord soft and low. Valarie joined her husband in worshipful harmony.

Peter closed his eyes and listened to the two elders lift up the name of Jesus. He heard them skillfully and lovingly offer sacrifices of praise unto the Lamb who sits upon the throne. Their whispers grew into stronger, more conversational tones. Valarie left English behind to speak mysteries as the Spirit gave her utterance.

Peter felt the warm, holy presence of God envelope him. Open praise came easier with each spoken word. A moment later, he opened his eyes and saw Valarie in front of the window facing the dark lake with arms stretched upward. Tom was kneeling down at the far side of the sofa with his face hidden in his hands.

Peter began to gently pace in front of the silent stone fireplace speaking scriptures from memory. He moved his hands about him as though wading in a waist deep pool of water.

Several minutes of uninterrupted praise later, Valarie's voiced raised sharply. Peter watched wide eyed as she spoke in tongues in bold authority. She pointed and called out to the unseen entities near and far. Tom groaned into the cushions then looked up and called upon the name of Jesus again and again. Peter watched wild eyed. Tingles of excitement and fear of the unknown raced through him. He sat down in the soft chair next to the fireplace and watched. They were still praying in the Spirit an hour later.

When a sobering peace took over the air in the living room, Tom was seated on the sofa where he'd been praying. Valarie sat at the opposite end fixing her hair. Peter smiled nervously at her gaze. She was looking through him again.

"Peter, have you received the Holy Ghost?" she asked.

Her eyes moistened when he shook his head.

"Have you asked the Lord for it?"

Peter couldn't remember if he'd ever sought for the baptism of the Holy Ghost.

"I don't think so."

The prophetess in faded jeans rose and stood over him. "Do you want to be filled?"

Peter nodded like a child being asked if he wanted a candy bar.

She glanced over to her husband. Tom pushed past the stiffness in his joints and stood on the other side of Peter. The two laid their hands on Peter and prayed, calling on God for an outpouring of his Spirit upon him. Peter sat waiting not knowing exactly what to do or what to expect.

The moon crested the distant hills when Valarie embraced Peter. "Soon," she said. "God wants to use you mightily."

Peter stood. "When? When will I receive it?"

"Want to meet tomorrow night and pray again?" Tom asked.

"Yeah, that works for me."

Peter looked into the scriptures throughout Saturday searching for clues of what to expect. He wondered if speaking in tongues would hurt.

Shortly after seven, they were praying again. They stopped shortly after nine, agreeing to meet again the next night.

At ten minutes after eight on Sunday evening, the Holy Ghost came on a sweaty Peter Bishop as he knelt worshiping at his coffee table. A warm sensation rested upon his head then coursed down his shoulders and through the center of him. He loudly spoke with tongues then jumped up and down unable to contain his joy. He grabbed Tom and Valarie and they jumped with him.

They didn't leave for their motor home until nearly eleven that night.

Chapter Thirty-Four

Monday morning arrived far too early and Peter felt almost hung over but with the deepest peace he'd ever known. The memories of the last three nights of prayer slipped in and out of his thoughts while preparing to open for business.

Bishop's Coffee Company was non-stop busy from six-thirty to nine. It appeared that Peter's regular customers had made their way back after the crash.

"Walking in the Spirit I see," came a voice at the window.

Peter turned to see part of Tom's face behind sunglasses in a blue Suzuki Sidekick. "Yes, sir! That would be me! What can I get you this morning?"

"How about one of those mocha things, and the name of a good realtor."

Peter handed Tom a sixteen-ounce cup and a business card. "Kelley took care of me. I'm sure she'll help you find the right house for you."

"Thank you. Val and I were looking at some places across the lake from you."

"Best place to be if you can deal with a mosquito or two."

"Been bit by worse."

"True enough. Say listen, thanks for prayer these last few nights. I can't believe I could have gone this long without having the Holy Ghost. It's never been taught as a priority, you know?"

Tom found a place for his hot beverage and the business card. "And that's it, isn't it? How we've been taught. Most preaching I've heard in churches or on the radio rarely – if ever - mention the importance of the Spirit. We've been coast to coast a few times now, Peter, and I can count on one hand the number of times I've heard a message about the Holy Ghost." He shook his head. "I just don't understand it. Then when I tell people about healings and miraculous answers to prayer we've witnessed and that my wife has the gift of prophesy, they just look at me like I've got three heads or something. I just don't bother anymore."

"Well, you can bother me with it," Peter said. "I'm your captive audience."

"I think it'll be good for Val and me to be dug in somewhere we can be actively involved regularly. We haven't felt led to call someplace home for quite a while. But we're ready to now. And I better git before someone wonders what trouble I've gotten myself into. Talk to you later, brother."

Stephen gave Peter his two weeks' notice over the phone the following day. An hour later, Peter placed a help wanted ad in the local paper, then met Keith Roman for fish and chips lunch at The Run Aground Restaurant.

"So, you're meeting for prayer on Fridays," Keith said, holding a piece of breaded cod," but are you preaching anywhere?"

"We're just seeking God at this point, Keith. Seeking him for direction, for souls and what to do next. Why do you ask?"

"I don't know. Maybe it bugs me that you're calling yourself an ex-pastor. It just doesn't sound right. Seems like you should always be pastoring until you're too old, can't see straight and start walking into walls, you know?"

"Things may be changing. I don't know what's up ahead."

Keith sat back in his hard wood chair and watched the bubbles rise in his tall glass of light gold brew. "There for a while, half a dozen guys were coming over to the house after work on Fridays. I'd fire up the grill, everyone brought their own drinks and things to eat. We'd think of ways to reinvent the wheel and carry on till whenever. But you know what happened most of the time? We'd talk about life and our families, marriages, what's working, what's not. It wasn't just fluff and filler. It was real world. In fact, I think it was old Ted who said if church was like this I'd go all the time."

Peter listened intently then asked, "So what are you saying?"

"I guess I'm saying that there's a lot of people living outside of the stained glass Sunday morning ritual. I was thinking about firing up that grill again. And where there's charcoal and beer, there will be men. If you brought your Bible without the pulpit, I believe you'll have plenty of opportunities to talk about God."

The ex-pastor could only blink. "Beer, Bible and barbeque. That's about as unconventional as it gets." He smiled and wiped his hands of French fry oil and salt. "I'm sure we can move our prayer night. When are you thinking to start?"

"How about this Friday?"

"Why not?"

Four trucks and two Harley Davidsons were parked outside Keith's two story house when Peter arrived at six-thirty. He could hear music and the baritone laughter of men coming from behind the house. He decided to leave his Bible on the passenger seat since this first meeting would probably be more of an ice breaker than a scripture study.

Keith greeted Peter with raised tongs from behind a rising curtain of gray smoke. Peter waved back to him and to the few faces he recognized from the construction of the coffee stand. Eight men in well-worn t-shirts milled in and out of a homemade sports bar that doubled as a garage. Rumor had it that a couple more guys might show if they could negotiate their release from home. John Cougar Mellencamp was on vocals from the CD player on a shelf near the bar.

Peter made his way over to the grill shaking a few hands along the way.

"You made it," Keith said. "I'll have to give you a proper introduction." Keith banged the handle of a spatula against the rusty, red barbeque. "Hear ye, hear ye! Everyone needs to be on their best behavior cause Peter here is not only our resident coffee expert, he's also a preacher."

Peter rolled his eyes, embarrassed.

"A preacher?" shouted a dark haired man in an orange work shirt. "What's a preacher doing here?"

"Drinking beer and eating steaks with the rest of us," Keith shouted back. "Inviting a man of God here is my way of celebrating diversity!"

"Amen!"

"Hallelujah!"

Peter was asked the usual questions.

"Where's your church?"

"How can you be a preacher if you're divorced?"

"Aren't you kind of young to be a pastor?"

But his favorite question of the evening came from a short fuzzy man named Wally. "My wife and I are almost divorced but not all the ways yet. So as her husband still, if I tell her to go to hell, she has to obey me, right?"

After the laughing died down, Peter replied, "Wally, I don't think going to hell is something God would require a wife to submit to. And the Bible has a few things for husbands to do for our wives."

"Like what?"

"To love them as Christ loved the church and gave himself for it."

Wally thought for a moment. "Well, I ain't Christ, she can still go to hell, and you can shove that Bible."

In between strips of steak, kielbasa sausage, pretzels and chips on flimsy paper plates, Peter traveled the spinning carousel of conversations, not as a minister of the gospel, but as an everyday man, business owner, Glennwood resident, and tax payer. He listened to the sound of red blooded American men who love and hate, work hard and play to win, who appreciate genuineness and despise hypocrisy. Men who carry a respect for the Almighty even if they don't really know him.

Wally avoided Peter for much of the night, but the others included him and made him feel welcome. He tried to remember everyone's name and wrote them down on a slip of paper when he got home that night. It was his prayer list.

He underlined Wally.

Chapter Thirty-Five

Tom and Valarie were all smiles listening to Peter recount his adventure the next evening when they gathered for prayer. He spread out his list of names upon which they laid their hands on and prayed.

Though still very much a novice in the workings of the Holy Ghost, Peter prayed in the Spirit with a new authority. His mind was at rest, his body was charged and his spirit was edified.

For more than two hours, they worshiped, lifted requests, wept and quietly waited on the Lord. After a long silence, Tom looked over to Peter and asked, "Why don't you come over to the motor home in the morning and bring those Bible studies you've talked about? I'd like to see them for myself."

Over crisp bacon and plenty of coffee Tom, Valarie and Peter went through the scriptures together, taking turns reading. Each one was reminded of the straightness of the pure Word of God. At the conclusion of the first study, Tom said, "That's some red meat right there."

"It sure is," Valarie agreed. "If you don't get that God's Word is not to be tampered with, there's something wrong with you." Valarie flipped through the binder looking at the studies to come. "What do you see up ahead Peter?"

"I think before we go much further we should be in agreement," he said. "As much as we know about each other, I don't know what you believe or where we might disagree. I can still hear sister Nona's voice about how she and Greg were going back to the foundation of their faith. It's my turn now."

Tom nodded. "That's a good point," he said, looking at his wife. "You know, I've never been asked what I believe in a church before, have you?

Valarie shook her head. "Nope."

"Nor have I asked anyone else what they believed, Tom continued. "I just assumed we all generally believed the same thing. But we've all heard some crazy things taught from the pulpit before and no one's challenged it. We don't ask questions."

"I think we *should* ask questions," Peter said. We can do that around a table with our Bibles open on Sundays if that's alright with you and Valarie. Let's search out what we believe and why."

Peter hired Shannon Murphy on the spot after a fifteen-minute interview. The recent high school graduate spoke of staying in Glennwood long enough to save money for college.

"I don't want to be one of those girls who falls for the guy at the lumber yard, gets married, pregnant and stuck here in Glennwood for the rest of her life. I want to work for a while and save up enough to move out comfortably."

"What do you plan to study?"

"Not sure yet. I was thinking of a degree in business."

"You've got plenty of time to figure it all out," Peter said. He thought upon her smile and remembered how the wide open the world seemed right after he graduated. "When are you available to start?"

"I already have my food handlers card. I could start tomorrow."

Peter trained Shannon on Friday, then scheduled her to work with Nell for the weekend.

Peter arrived at Keith's with a family pack of chuck steaks. The same crowd plus two more men were hydrating themselves with the finest brew on sale while the host poured lighter fluid over a pyramid of black briquettes.

"Get those steaks over here, Peter! I can only hold these guys off for so long," Keith said with bottle in his hand.

"Steaks? I thought you said tofu."

The men erupted in shouts.

"Tofu? Are you outta your head?"

"Them's fightin' words around here, coffee man. You want me to get out the Folgers?"

"Ouch!"

He'd been accepted into the mix.

While Peter forged friendships over grilled red meat, a woman stood in line at a grocery store. She reviewed the items in her basket making sure she picked up everything, then looked up to the young woman working at the register. The courteous clerk with straight, dark brown hair went through the motions of her work efficiently and greeting each new customer with a smile.

The woman moved her basket forward in line. When she stopped, the awareness began. Like the building anticipation when theater lights dim before a movie, she took a deep breath and relaxed her hold on the shopping cart. She looked toward the clerk without looking at her.

The scenes without words fluttered across her mind. She saw fractured images and the color of brokenness. Then brightness. Then peace. She stepped forward and began to place her items on the black grocery conveyor.

"Did you find everything alright today, ma'am?"

"I did thank you."

The clerk with a cardinal red store apron scanned items through the laser light briskly.

"You're total is "Thirty-nine, eighteen.""

The woman handed over two twenty dollar bills and smiled to the woman waiting in line behind her.

The clerk tore the receipt free from the register and placed it and the change in the shopper's hand, "And here's your change. Thank you for shopping with us today."

They made contact for an instant.

"Claire?"

"Yes?"

The woman leaned closer. Claire did the same.

"You have a son in the hospital."

Claire nodded cautiously. "Yes, yes I do. How did you know that?"

"He's going to be alright, honey. He'll be good as new soon. But you have some family matters to tend to soon."

"Who are you? How do you know about my family?"

"Claire, you're going to hear from the doctor very soon. He has good news. But you must make things right with your parents, especially your father."

Claire stared back at the stranger with reddening eyes.

"You know what I'm talking about don't you?"

The clerk glanced to the impatient customers then back and nodded.

The woman smiled and collected her bagged groceries and walked away.

Clair blinked away the tears and cleared her register for the next customer. "I'm sorry for the delay. Did you find everything okay?"

The first item didn't scan. She flipped it over and tried again. Then she noticed something wrong with her apron.

She wasn't wearing her name badge.

She walked through the door of her apartment a few hours later to change clothes then to visit her son. The answering machine light was blinking. It was from the hospital.

The single mother listened as her son's doctor described a miraculous change in his condition.

"We moved your lucky little man out of ICU and he's resting soundly now. He could be home again in just a few days."

Claire finished the call and leaned against the sliding glass door. Scattered on the dry grass of the back yard were toys waiting quietly for their boy to return to play. She began to cry again.

When the trembling ended, Claire looked down at the cordless phone and dialed another number. She closed her eyes when the ringing began.

"Hi daddy, it's Claire. Can we talk for a few minutes?"

Peter looked through the back door window of the drive-through about closing time. Nell was showing Shannon how to clean the grinder.

"How's our new girl?" he asked.

Shannon smiled at Peter. "I think I'm getting the hang of it."

"She is getting the hang of it," Nell said, watching. "A lot faster than Stephen."

"That's music to my ears."

Peter opened a cabinet and pulled out a bag of ground coffee. "Everything else going well?"

"I think someone's stealing our tips," Nell said. "We've been about ten bucks below average the last two weeks."

"Really?"

Peter went to the drive-through window and looked down at the clear tip catcher. He could see a cracks on the edge where it was fastened to the outside wall. He stepped outside and inspected the container more closely. It was still firmly attached but it appeared to have been hit by something. He went back inside.

"I've seen some teenagers on bikes riding out there, but I've never seen them take anything," Nell said. "They look like the type who'd cause trouble, but maybe it's just me."

"Okay. I'll keep an eye out." Peter made a note on the coffee chart on the wall. "And let's watch Shannon here. She looks like the type who'd cause trouble too."

Shannon crossed her eyes. "That's why you hired me, right?

Peter arrived at the motor home for prayer with Tom and Valarie at sunset Saturday evening. He brought a bag of fresh ground Sumatra in a plain brown bag as a surprise. Tom came to the door to meet Peter.

"I'll just be right outside the door here, honey," Tom said toward the bedroom in the back.

Tom turned on the outside light and stepped down and closed the door behind him. "Hey Peter, how you doing?"

"Good. I brought you something you might like."

Tom took the bag and smelled the top. "You are a class act. I supposed I have to share that with the missus?"

"It's your house, brother. I'm sure you know what battles you can win."

"Well put," Tom said, leading toward the outdoor chairs. "Say, let's have a seat over here."

Both men sat facing the tree lined edge of Mirror Lake. Tom seemed reluctant to talk about something.

"Is everything okay?" Peter asked.

Tom looked out at the water and nodded. "Oh yeah, everything's okay. It's just that, some things aren't always easy to explain to folks."

Peter quietly waited for Tom to get around to explaining himself.

"I don't need to tell you Peter that my Valarie's a special woman. Her gifts are unique to say the least. So is the price that comes with them."

A pair of ducks landed on the lake thirty yards in front of them. The calm reflection broke into countless glassy shards then melted into circular ripples. Peter looked back to Tom.

"Shortly after we were married, Valarie gave a word to a man after church. I don't know what she said. I just remember the look of the guy's face. Something like the look on your face the night we met at your folk's place. Well, I thought that was that, and we went home. Then later that night, Valarie went into this deep, deep depression. She hid away in the bedroom on the floor and wouldn't come out. She cried and begged me to be close by, but not in the same room. She was a mess, Peter. She was like that for a couple of days, day and night. She wouldn't eat and wouldn't get up from the floor. And there wasn't anything I could do for her. I held her, I prayed for her, you name it. Nothing. There's no more frustrating feeling than not being able to help the one you love."

"Does that happen a lot?"

"Now and then. I think she said she spoke to someone at the grocery store before she hid away last night. She'd be horribly embarrassed if you saw her like this, so that's why I wanted us to be out here. I hope you can understand."

"Of course, Tom. I wouldn't do anything to upset her or you."

"I appreciate that and so does she. You know, Paul talks about a thorn in the flesh. Calls it a 'messenger of Satan lest he should be exalted above measure.' That's all the detail we read about this thorn. That's how I'm looking at this. A crippling thorn of depression, anxiety, sorrow, whatever it is. It comes upon her and won't leave until it's done. And I'll be right here with her for however long it lasts. We should postpone our Bible study tomorrow too."

Peter admired the love Tom had for his beautiful wife. "Thank you for being there for her and for being an example for me."

"It's the least I can do. She's my wife."

Chapter Thirty-Six

"Iced mocha," Peter said out loud to himself when the gleaming red '64 Ford Falcon Sprint rounded the stand and came to the window. The driver was a regular customer with dirty blonde, all American good looks."

"Mr. Mick," Peter said. "Will it be the iced mocha today?"

Mick lowered his sunglasses. "It's just one of those iced mocha kind of days, isn't it?"

"Coming up."

Peter worked his magic then topped it off with whipped cream for his valued customer. When he handed out the drink, he could see that Mick wasn't just tired or fatigued. He wore the face of a man overrun by weighty cares.

"What's up my friend?" Peter asked. "Your car seems happier today than you are."

Mick looked at Peter then looked away. "You ever -" he paused. "You ever find yourself doing something you can't stand, but you're really good at it and you're making so much money you can't stop?"

"In a roundabout sort of way...yeah."

"Well, that's where I'm at."

"Anything I can pray about?"

"Prayer," Mick chuckled and shook his head. "I can't remember the last time I prayed. I used to be good at that too. Another lifetime ago."

"I've found some great direction in the Bible, Mick. If you're up for it, we could pray together and get into the Word sometime. You'll probably find some of the answers you're looking for."

"Probably, Peter. Let me get back to you on that. Unfortunately, I need to get to work. But I know where to find you."

Mick stuck out his hand to Peter and they shook on it. Exchanging waves, Mick pulled away from the stand and made a left out of the lot and sped down Holler Road.

Peter turned off the Open sign and the brewer. Then he began to pray for Mick Jackson while closing the stand for the day.

The group of men at Keith's house was smaller than normal when Friday came around. After nearly emptying a frozen tub of Neapolitan ice cream, they sat in a comfortable circle with their tired feet resting on a large blue cooler in the center.

"We used to go to a church near the bowling alley," Ted said. "But it seemed like the pastor was always trying out something new and wanted us all to pay for it. 'Seed offerings' I think is what he'd call it. About every three weeks it was some new outreach program or a ministry for this and that. And if we weren't excited, he'd get onto us about not being spiritual enough."

"Was that Boutan?" Keith asked.

"Pastor Stanley Boutan, yes it was," Ted said with a smile of remembrance. "New Plan Stan was his name around town. Just never seemed to be settled. I think that church had more turn over than any I'd ever seen. Then two or three years ago, they moved on. Got some other church moved in there before it became a bunch of offices."

"Are you going someplace now?" Peter asked.

"No place regular. Just haven't found anywhere Meg and me fit in."

Keith tapped the pair of boots next to his. "What about you, Wally? You go to church somewhere?"

"Don't talk to me about no church!" came the gruff response.

Keith led the chorus of laughter. "Oh Wally, don't get your hackles up. God probably doesn't want you in church anyway. He doesn't want to have to strike you with lightning!"

Wally folded his arms and hid his emotions behind his scruffy red beard.

"What about you Peter? Where's your church?" The question came from Brian Moore, a plumber by trade, with dark brown hair and an inquisitive, freckled face.

Peter sipped on a light roast coffee to chase the cold ice cream down the back of his throat. "Funny you ask that, Brian. Because the more time I've spent in the Bible, the more I realize that I don't have a church. Christ has a church and I work for him. My job is to preach the Word and point souls to him."

His words hung in the air with the remaining smells of smoldering charcoal and grilled red meat. The men took their time processing the thought of a church without a man in black behind a big pulpit calling the shots.

Ted squinted slightly at Peter. "So if you don't have a church...how or where are you going to point souls?"

"I share Bible studies with people, usually in their homes, over kitchen tables. Their time, their turf."

Another long silence filtered into the room. Brian adjusted his feet. Ted looked over to Keith as if to see if he was making sense of things. Wally's eyes ran along the cracked concrete floor.

"So you're teaching Bible studies in people's homes?" Keith asked.

"One motor home at the moment with Tom and Valarie Warner. But I'll meet anyone just about anytime and anywhere for a Bible study"

Ted looked up to Peter. "Meg and I might be interested in something like that."

The others nodded.

Wally belched.

Valarie was the ever gracious hostess Saturday evening when Peter arrived for a light dinner before prayer. She seemed completely herself and unaware of his conversation with her husband. She and Tom eagerly listened as Peter described the openness from the men about home Bible studies.

"They all seemed to want something from God they're not finding from the churches in town," Peter said. "I may not have what they're looking for either. But I've got the Word and I'll give them everything I've got."

"This is how it starts, Peter," Valarie said. "The Word is preached, and disciples are multiplied. Things are stirring in the Spirit my boy. We must prepare ourselves."

They stacked the dishes then knelt down on the carpeted floor of the motor home. They each called out the names of the men, praying in the Spirit and with their understanding. Hairline fractures appeared in the strong invisible foundations of apathy hanging over Glennwood as Valarie called for their displacement.

"Be bound, be ye cast down, be ye removed!" she cried with authority. "Ye shall fall back! Ye shall not prevail!"

They concluded an hour and a half later after a quiet state of listening. A light rain began to fall outside. Valarie smiled and said, "There are battles ahead, but great victories follow if we will not faint."

Peter was back the next morning just before ten. Over coffee and toast they went through the study of the gospel. Peter watched Tom's brow furrow more than once.

"What are your thoughts, Tom," Peter asked.

"I remember hearing about a huge rift in our church back some years ago about baptism. I think it split the church right down the middle. I wasn't in on the details." He stopped.

Peter looked at Valarie who seemed quiet. "Valarie?"

"We were Trinitarian Pentecostals who preached Matthew 28:19, Peter. I have to say, we only got into the book of Acts to preach the Holy Ghost."

"This is a tough one," Tom said. "I was baptized Father, Son and Holy Ghost and never really heard it preached any other way. Now I've got what, one...two...three...four...five places staring right at me to be baptized in Jesus name." He turned to his wife who wore an expression of concern. "How can a person argue with this?"

Valarie shook her head.

Tom looked back to Peter. "I don't know what to say, Peter. I've read the Bible from cover to cover and I feel like I'm reading about this for the first time. Have you been baptized in Jesus name?"

Peter nodded.

Tom looked out the window toward Mirror Lake. "I thought about fishing today not going for a swim. But if I hope for others to change when they hear the Word, I suppose I need to as well.

Tom and Valarie followed Peter back to his house where a more private baptism could take place. In t-shirts and shorts the three entered the cool water where Peter called on the name of Jesus and baptized them both.

Chapter Thirty-Seven

An angry Shannon pointed out the window to the shopette parking lot where three boys rode bikes.

"I saw one of them stick their hand in our tips container. Little thieves!"

Peter watched them jump over curbs. "I can't do anything about it now. Let's start emptying out the tips more often throughout the day."

"I'll start by bringing a baseball bat to work," Shannon said with clinched fists.

Peter laughed. "You're a little fireball when you're angry."

"Yes sir! That's our money!"

"We'll get them, sunshine. Just don't go and kill anyone."

Peter looked into the small fridge under the counter while Shannon tended to a customer. He started counting milk containers when Shannon interrupted.

"Peter, there's a guy asking for you.

He looked out the window and saw the immaculate red Falcon.

"Hey Mick? How goes it?"

"It's going, my friend. Hey, let's talk about this Bible thing."

"Sure. Where and when?

"Well, like how does it work?"

"We could meet over lunch or something first, then decide on a good place to meet after that?"

Mick rolled it over in his head. "Yeah I like that. How about pizza, tomorrow around noon?"

Peter looked at the calendar. "Can we swap days, Shannon?"

"No. I'm busy."

Peter stared at his feisty employee with a smile.

"Unlike you, I have a life outside of here."

He looked back at Mick. "Can we make it later, like two-thirty?"

"Two-thirty? Yep. Dino's Pizza?"

Peter nodded. "See you there."

Mick drove away as Peter turned back to Shannon.

"You're tough."

"Yes I am." She leaned against him with one raised eye brow. "And here's your grocery list. I added M&Ms. Gotta keep your employees happy."

Diño's Pizza was a local favorite and landmark that the town of Glennwood had grown around. Marcus "Dino" Barbour was the savvy restauranteur who offered over twenty pizza combinations and Italian sandwiches that made his mamma from the old country proud.

Mick Jackson wore his trademark Fedora hat atop wavy blonde hair while browsing the menu. Peter joined him at a large circular booth in the corner where a brick wall met dark wood paneling.

"What kind of pizza are you in to?"

"All kinds," Peter said. "Especially the meaty ones."

"Me too, my friend. It isn't pizza without meat."

They ordered the Classic Carnivore on a garlic deep pan crust and a pitcher of Coke. A muscular man in a black polo brought their mozzarella cheese laden lunch fifteen minutes later. He served up individual slices onto plates and left the customers to enjoy themselves.

"Is that drive-through yours or part of a chain?" Mick asked.

"It's all mine," Peter said. "I worked for a guy down south who owned a coffeehouse. Taught me everything I know about the coffee business. So what does Mick do to stay out of trouble?"

Mick tipped his hat and leaned back. "Mick is a freelance photographer and is always in trouble. I travel around and do photo shoots."

"Really? Like landscapes and wildlife?"

"Something like that. I shoot for a few magazines."

"Any I've heard of?"

"I doubt it. Mick watched the dark bubbles surround the ice in his glass. He leaned forward and said, "These magazines want photos of beautiful women minus their clothes."

Peter waited for a punchline that didn't come.

Mick wrestled another slice of pizza onto his plate and looked up to Peter. "Shocked?"

"I don't know. I've never met someone in your line of work before. Is that what you were referring to the other day about making so much money you couldn't quit?"

Mick nodded. "That would be my dilemma. Not only is the money good, I'm good at what I do. Plus, the guys I work for are really great guys. I know it doesn't make it right. It just makes it hard to quit."

"Just out of curiosity, how does someone get into that kind of photography?"

"Oh, I've had a camera in my hand since I was little kid. Practically had my own photo studio by the time I graduated high school. I was a photo journalist for a while. Then a few years ago a friend of a friend saw some of my portraits. He asked me if I might be interested in something a little racier. At the time I was open to anything that would pay to keep me behind the camera. The shoot was for a swimsuit calendar. It was a lot of fun really. Then there was the shoot after that where the girls wouldn't be needing their suits. I started to back out, but he kept telling me to think of the girls as art. They *were* works of art. Truly stunning with makeup and the right light. I got paid for that job which led to another then another. I did that for a few years and met some other people who wanted me to get into video. I much prefer the captured moment of a still image. It's more imaginative and romantic. I went with them to check out what kind of work they had in mind. For some reason I wasn't putting two and two together about the movement they wanted. Sexual movement. It's so very different when you're on location, surrounded by people off screen. Here we were staring at two people having sex like performing animals. I was sick to my stomach. But what was really crazy was after seeing that I didn't feel so bad about single frame porn."

Mick cleared his throat and shook his head. "Still wanna have a Bible study with me?"

"Of course. Why wouldn't I?"

"Never know when you cross the line of no return with people.

Beyond help, you know?"

Peter smiled. "Yeah, well that's not me. I won't be judging anybody in this lifetime."

Peter finished his first his plate and wrinkled his brow. "So, what kind of girls want to be photographed nude?"

"The girls come from all over and from every background. Street girls, country girls, whatever. Ordinary girls-next-door with extraordinary features. And don't forget the money. Cold, hard cash has a way of making buttons almost come undone by themselves. Seriously. Very few will be finalists on Jeopardy if you know what I mean. Their breast size usually exceeds their IQ. Except for one. Sharp as a razor and cold as ice. She'd make the most amazing transition from mean to mesmerizing right in front of the lens." Mick's voice trailed off in thought. "I asked her once why she was doing nudes being as smart as she was. I'll never forget her response. She stepped close and looked me dead in the eyes and said, 'I hate men. I want them all to writhe in pain. But since I can't have that, I want the mastery over them. I'll use my body to exploit their weak little minds and ruin as many as I can.' The venom in her eyes was chilling. She must have been abused. I think a lot of girls are. Anyway, her words and that sex video incident really got me to thinking about changing course while I still could. I'll miss the money but I miss being so far from God. I grew up in a church going family and I know I shouldn't be doing this."

"What else would you want to do?" Peter asked.

"Keep shooting pictures. What did you say earlier? Landscapes and wildlife? Maybe I can start a studio somewhere. Something that won't eat at my conscience."

Peter shared the story of his love for God and coffee and how he came to live in Glennwood. By the time the check had arrived, Mick and Peter were good friends. They agreed to meet Monday afternoons for Bible study and prayer.

They exchanged a handshake and a hug in the parking lot. Then Mick watched Peter drive away through watery eyes. He sat behind the steering wheel and wept in gratitude. He wasn't out of his personal wilderness, but for the first time in four years he was taking a step in the right direction.

Two hours later and twenty-six miles north, Mick was focusing his 24-70mm zoom lens on the sultry emerald eyes of a young woman reclining on a blood red couch.

She was nineteen. No tan lines.

Chapter Thirty-Eight

The following week, Peter was deeper in the Word than he'd ever been. On Sunday he was with Tom and Valarie. Monday, he met Mick at Dino's. Then two men from Friday nights at Keith Roman's invited him over to their house. Steve and Ted had talked with their wives about Bible studies and they were open to having Peter come over. Steve and Cheryl Steckler were set for Tuesday. Ted and Meg Sanders were available Thursday.

Every Bible study was its own unique experience. Mick knew his way around New Testament as well as Peter did. Steve's wife Cheryl was wide-eyed and filled with all kinds of questions. In contrast, it was a quiet and straight-forward scripture reading around Ted and Meg's kitchen table. They were both dying for a cigarette after a few verses but held out till the end.

Everyone wanted Peter to come back the following week.

He drove home Thursday evening feeling more confident and at peace with himself and ministry than he had in a long time. Through repetition of the scriptures, he was becoming a workman in the word. He now answered questions he once looked to elders for help with. A mile from his house on the lake he looked up and smiled.

He wasn't feeling like a dime store preacher anymore.

Peter felt the early edge of fall riding on the morning winds as he handed a drive-through customer a caramel latte. More folks were ordering hot drinks and with an average cost of $3.20 per sale, Bishop's Coffee was doing very well. Peter closed his eyes and whispered words of gratitude to his Heavenly Father. He was prospering spiritually and professionally and never wanted to take it for granted.

He reminisced about working with Brad and Lori when he heard something roll by out front. He looked out the window and saw the rear wheels of a motocross bicycle disappear from view. He watched the teenage rider with a black baseball hat through the other windows.

The boy raced back around toward the drive-through window. Peter position himself at the open window. As the young man reached his hand into the tip collector, Peter leaned out grabbed his wrist. The boy was snapped off his bike and fell backwards. Peter spun around and darted out the back door. He grabbed the boy's neck and arm just as he picked up his bike.

"You're not going anywhere, pal." Peter growled.

"Let me go!" His squirming only made Peter tighten his grip. "Ow! Let go!"

Peter directed him to the back steps and forced him to sit down. The red-faced thief cursed in anger. "I wasn't doing anything!"

Peter pulled out his cell phone as the boy stood up. "Stay down or I'll knock you down."

"You can't touch me! You'll go to jail."

Peter shoved the boy back down onto the steps. "Let's get the police here and make sure you're right.

Peter explained the details to the dispatcher while glaring at the youth who was visibly changing from angry to scared.

Fortunately, a patrol car pulled onto the lot at the same time a drive-through customer appeared. Peter was able to talk with the officer between making drinks. After the bike was loaded into the trunk, the repeat offender was directed into the car as well.

"I know the kid's family," said Officer Denton. "I'll take him home and have a talk with them. He shouldn't be any more trouble to you. At least for today."

Peter thanked him for responding so quickly and watched him get into his cruiser. His passenger wore the anxious expression of fear. It was the fear of not knowing what awaited at home.

Peter locked up shop and decided to take in a matinee at the single-screen theater that played second-run movies. It was a waste of two hours as it turned out. The forgettable story only made him hungry for a Wong's Garden Chinese take-out dinner with a side of spring rolls. afterward. The rest of the evening drifted on uneventfully. By eleven o'clock he was fighting to keep his eyes open.

Under a giant heat lamp in the sky, Peter wrestled a small dragon on a beach when he heard the beep the first time. He looked up. A white bi-plane flew overhead. A man's voice shouted something in German. The electronic beep interrupted the pilot. The dragon sighed and sat down in the shallow water. Then he pulled sunglasses down over his eyes and shook his head. Peter pushed the dragon and the covers way. The dream abruptly ended when the heat lamp went out. The cordless phone beeped for the third time next to his bed. Who would be calling so late he thought.

"Hello?"

"Peter, this is Shannon," the excited caller said. "Sorry to call you, but you better come see this."

"Wow, Shannon. Can't it wait till morning?"

"It is morning. It's five-thirty."

Peter's clock validated her claim.

"Okay. I'm coming."

He hung up wondering why the dragon just gave up.

Peter walked around the stand with Shannon. "Thank God nothing appears broken, he said. "How's the inside look?"

"Fine as far as I can tell," she said."

They stood under the street light looking at the vile words and symbols spray painted on every side of the stand.

Shannon shook her head. "I thought I had trouble spelling, but these guys are idiots."

Peter chuckled. "I don't think they were trying to impress us with their literary skills."

He put his arm around his shivering employee and walked her up the steps. All was well inside.

"Are we opening as usual?" she asked.

"Yep. I don't want them to get any more satisfaction than they already have."

Peter was on the phone with Keith Roman at seven. By eight-thirty, Keith brought over primer, the original exterior paint and rollers. The vulgar graffiti was a bad memory by noon.

"You are a life saver, Keith," Peter said gratefully. "What do I owe you?"

"I'll work on that later for you." he said putting the last of bucket of paint in the back of the truck. "Tell me, how's the coffee business treating you? You making a living?"

"I'm doing okay with it. I'd like to expand. Maybe open another drive-through down the road."

Keith's shirt pocket vibrated to life and he pulled out his cell phone. He glanced at the incoming caller's information then looked back to Peter. "You know where you want to put one?"

"Not yet. "It's just wishful thinking right now."

"Let's talk more about it," Keith said, getting into his truck. Then he answered his phone and drove away.

Shannon stood on the top step looking at Peter. "Another stand? Who's gonna run it?"

"Not you."

"Why not me?"

"Aren't you leaving? Something about not being stuck in Glennwood?"

She pursed her lips and nodded as though remembering her plans. She watched a car pull into the drive way and said, "Yeah. That's right." Then she went back inside.

Tom and Valarie fell in love with a rustic four-bedroom house with a full finished basement for sale on the north part of Glennwood. Peter helped the Warners move things in from the RV and get settled.

"This kitchen was all I needed to see," she explained. "The butcher block island and windows all around. I have light for my plants. It's like the Lord reserved this just for me, Peter!"

"It's huge," he said. "What other families are moving in with you?"

Her eyes enlarged. "You never know. We've got plenty of things in storage we can put downstairs."

"Speaking of family, I know Tom has a daughter in Flagstaff, but what about your children?"

Valarie ran her hands along the hard wood surface of the island

and sighed. "Suffice it to say that I wasn't able to have children."

"Oh, sorry to hear that, Valarie. You'd have made a wonderful mother. I'm sure you have many spiritual children."

"Perhaps. Though it's not quite the same as having your own."

Peter chuckled. "Well, I think I'm going to pass on having kids especially with the way the world is today."

"Oh Peter you don't mean that."

"I think I do."

"You might become more open to fatherhood with the right woman. Children are a blessing from the Lord."

"I haven't met too many *blessings* lately. My niece is a little sweetheart, but she seems like an exception. She's probably better behaved around me than normal." He shook his head. "Do you really miss not having your own children that much?"

Valarie looked directly at Peter with a steely, sorrowful gaze as Tom walked through the kitchen carrying a small box of things for the den.

"This is the last of it," he said continuing through to the living room.

Valarie leaned against the sink smiling at her husband until he was gone. Then she looked back to Peter.

"Not wanting children is very different than not being able to have them." She turned her attention to the view out the window. "There is nothing like the emptiness of a barren womb, Peter."

A heaviness settled into the otherwise bright kitchen. Peter hadn't seen Valarie become so serious.

"Let's change the subject, shall we?" Valarie said with a renewed countenance. "You have how many Bible studies going now?"

"With ours on Sundays, four."

"Excellent. I think I know of some ladies who might also be interested." She pulled up a wooden bar stool and sat next to Peter. Peter joined her, relieved to see the inviting warmth return to her deep brown eyes. "But we'll need more copies, she continued."

"I'll get more made up on Monday."

"I have a better idea. Why not let the church secretary handle it?"

"We have a church secretary?"

"Me. Unless you have someone else in mind who can do the job, Pastor."

Peter smiled. "I can think of no one better."

"Good. If a church is going to grow here, we should start acting like one. Have you already filed your 501 (c)(3) paperwork?"

"No, I've done nothing like that since leaving Great Assemblies."

"I can pick up those forms as well," she said, making notes on a note pad.

Tom walked back into the kitchen. "What are you two scheming now?"

"We're getting serious about a church, Tom. Peter has Bible studies going, I think I can start some too. Didn't you say you talked with a guy who sounded interested?"

Tom filled a glass of water and sat across the island. "He sort of sounded interested. I'll see if he really is or just being polite."

Valarie put her hand on Tom's arm and said in a teasing whisper, "I'm going to be the church secretary."

Tom rolled his eyes. "Lord help us! Watch out Peter, she's going to want a nice corner office next."

"We'll need a building first. Perhaps rent something for a while you think," she asked.

"Renting is our only option for a while," Peter replied. "I've been keeping my eyes open for places for when we're ready. It may be a while though."

Within two weeks, Valarie was leading a Bible study with three ladies participating and Tom talked his reluctant friend into one as well. That study was more about fishing than scriptures, but God was mentioned now and then.

The church was growing.

Thanksgiving that year was a holiday to remember with Tom and Valarie hosting a festive gathering at their new home. The comforting aroma of a twenty-two-pound turkey and a brown sugar glazed ham filled the air by the time Michael, Daylene, Stephanie and Katie arrived at eleven in the morning from Phoenix. Daylene brought her delicious homemade rolls and pies. Peter showed up at noon bringing Mick and a variety of beverages. The house was filled with life under gray skies and cool temperatures that made a crackling fire in the fireplace a must.

The last few moments before dining, Peter looked around the room at the gathering of souls. Mick and Michael talked of pictures and travel. Daylene and Valarie plated food and visited in the kitchen. Katie helped Tom with the fire while Stephanie set the table and actually appeared to be enjoy herself. Each one contributed something to be shared with others. Each was a participant. Individual members, yet knit together as one. It was a family of families.

Peter captured the moment and filed it away in his heart.

Chapter Thirty-Nine

Most of the home Bible studies were postponed during the weeks leading up to Christmas and the new year. With the extra time, Peter brewed up some creative holiday marketing ideas, especially when he received an invitation to the Merrit Brothers Holiday Mixer. Peter's very first customer and friend in Glennwood made sure his name made it onto the exclusive guest list before she left town for married life on the California coast.

For the occasion, Peter ordered two cases of travel mugs with the increasingly popular Bishop's Coffee Company logo embedded on the side. Then he teamed up with a gourmet chocolatier from Sedona for creative gift baskets of whole bean coffee, chocolates and nut clusters.

Shannon watched Peter bring in four large cardboard boxes at ten on Wednesday morning.

"What's all this?" she asked, watching her workspace becoming more cramped by the minute.

"It's for the mixer at the Merrit building this Friday."

Shannon perked up. "What time are we going?"

"We?" Peter asked, closing the back door. "What's this *we* stuff?"

"You can't go to a mixer by yourself, Peter," she said opening the top box. "Since it's a business mixer...you should take me. I'd be your helper."

Peter watched his helper inspect one of the new mugs while avoiding his eyes.

"You mean my little elf."

"Whatever you say Santa."

The Merrit brothers played gracious hosts to another banner evening in Glennwood. The crowd had grown again over the previous year. The room was filled with clever decorations, festive laughter and cheery smiles. Peter watched Rich Merrit sneak another bottle of rum into the large egg nog bowl. The enormous tub had a sign sticking out of it that read, "No Fishing." It was classic Merrit.

Parting Ways

Shannon wore a navy blue, V-neck sweater and a reindeer antler headband that kept her long blonde curls bouncing lightly on her shoulders. Peter was lightly smitten. The last time he saw her in regular clothes was the day he hired her. He paused frequently during the evening to just watch her. She was the perfect assistant, mingling with the crowd showing off gift baskets while he handed out mugs and punch cards. Together they sold several baskets and only had a few mugs remaining.

After making their rounds, Peter followed Shannon through the maze of executive decision makers and politicians back to their corner of the room. Shannon spun around letting Peter walk into her.

"Admit it," she said over the loud music. "You're glad you brought me."

He laughed. "I am glad," he yelled back. "You're the best elf ever."

She continued leaning against him as though wanting to hear more.

"I'm very blessed to have you working with me, Shannon."

Peter was enchanted by her radiant smile and flushed cheeks. Her gaze moved from his eyes to his lips before she turned and picked up two cups from the table.

"I got us some more," she said handing him one.

"You're sweet. Thanks for thinking of me."

"I almost didn't share. This is the best egg nog ever."

They left the party at about eleven-forty and drove to the stand to drop off the boxes of unsold baskets. They teased each other playfully while attempting to put things back on shelves. Shannon leaned on Peter tickling him until he lost his balance. They fell together onto the floor where they stayed until they could breathe normally again.

"I take it you had fun tonight?" Peter asked.

She lifted herself on to her hands and knees and hovered over him. "I did," she said staring into his eyes. "And tonight's not over."

Peter's face was shadowed by the curtain of her descending blonde hair. She lowered herself to him. A half smile skimmed across her lips.

"I'm legal you know."

Before he could respond, Shannon pressed her lips to his. Peter's mind blurred. He was instantly absorbed in a euphoric wave of sensations. The unexpected attention, the sensual feel of a beautiful young woman, the scent of her hair all overwhelmed him. She'd been the delight of the evening. She was now the delight in his arms.

His hands contoured up the gentle slope of her back leading to her shoulders. He felt a fiery heat rise up through the woven threads of blue. She moved her legs to rest comfortably between his setting off a raging conflict in his heart. A conflict he was losing. He was an autumn leaf letting go of the last reason to stay on the branch.

She left his lips and came to rest her cheek on the top of his head. His misty eyes fell into the inviting shadows just beyond the opening of her sweater. He breathed long, slow breaths savoring the moment.

Reaching through the lightly perfumed air for some shred of restraint Peter whispered, "I should get you home."

Her half smile returned. "You could take me home with you."

He saw the same desire on her face he must have had on his own. He blinked her hair out of his eyes trying to be strong. In a single move he rolled her over and rested on top of her.

"Now we're talking," she said keeping his face close to hers.

Peter looked away and sighed. "Shannon, I'd like nothing more than to take you home with me. I'm flattered beyond words for all this. Really. But I think we'd be making a big mistake if we go any further. I'd rather we stop now and end on a positive note. No regrets later."

Peter worked his way to his feet, then helped Shannon to hers. He held her in his arms and whispered, "I'm not rejecting you, Shannon. I'm trying to do the right thing."

He could feel her nodding.

Peter flattened the two cardboard boxes while Shannon straightened up the counter. After locking the door, they walked to the truck together. Then Peter drove Shannon home.

To her home.

Peter had to cover for Nell who had a sick child at home on

Sunday. On Monday, just four days before Christmas, Peter received another shipment from Sedona. The gift baskets were in high demand and he had a third of his shipment sold by the time he closed for the day.

An awkward twinge surged through Peter when he saw Shannon drive into the parking lot. She walked to the back door like a celebrity hiding behind sunglasses in public. She surveyed the mess covering the floor at the window before opening the door.

"More baskets?" she asked removing her shades.

"Yep. Selling like hotcakes," he said. "We're definitely doing this again next year."

Shannon looked at the boxes then back to Peter searching his face for something.

"What's up?"

Shannon looked out the window before looking back to her employer. "I hope you don't think I get around, Peter. I mean--"

"I don't, and never have, Shannon."

She exhaled and relaxed. "I was having such a good time all night and was just going with the flow."

"You didn't hear me complain, did you?"

"Well ...no"

"Shannon, I haven't had that much fun since I can remember. And as far as what happened here," Peter motioned to the floor, "Let's just blame it on the egg nog."

She smiled sheepishly. "The *best* egg nog."

"It *was* pretty good.

She unzipped her light jacket and sat down in the other bar stool watching Peter sort through the boxes. He stopped when he saw she had more to say.

"The next morning, I just laid in bed crying. Not because of this. I don't know why really." She paused thinking. "It's like I'm just now realizing that I really don't want to go to college and I don't want to leave Glennwood. I thought I did. I loved being with those people last night and recognized a bunch of them from the drive through window. I feel at home around them. I want to move out and get on my own place but --"

Her voice trailed off. Peter nodded watching her eyes slowly fill.

"My parents have always wanted me to go to college and get my degree in something. Anything. But whenever I think about what I want to study, I'm a blank."

"Something will come to you, Shannon."

"Or something's gonna hit the fan if it doesn't," she said leaning back against the closet door."

Peter closed the lid on the open box and sat down. "What do you enjoy doing?"

"Honestly? I don't know. I like coffee and working here. I can handle early mornings and I love having afternoons to myself. I can still do things."

"Customers seem to like you and your boss thinks you're a great kisser."

She smiled. "Feeling's mutual."

They were both quiet for a moment. Then Shannon asked, "Are you really going to open another drive-through here?"

"Someday I hope. Glennwood is definitely big enough for more drive-throughs.

"Would you consider me to run it?"

"Sure I would. I think you'd do a great job."

"Really?"

"C'mon, you know me well enough to know I don't say things I don't mean."

"Managers make a lot more money, huh?"

"Not at first, sweetheart. It costs money to make money. We'd need to build up to it. But I do plan to give you a raise now. You deserve that."

"Thank you," she said. "I'll go blow it all on shoes or something."

"Yeah, all fifty-five cents an hour of it."

She smiled gratefully. "My parents will take things a lot easier if I can tell them I'm going to be a manager."

"I'll keep you posted on future developments."

She stood and wiped her eyes. "I should get going," she said wrapping her arms around him in gratitude. Then she pulled away, but held to his arms.

"And thanks for being a gentleman and keeping us out of trouble."

He kissed her forehead and said, "No regrets?"

"None."

Chapter Forty

The remaining traces of the holidays were taken down from street light poles lining Main Street and life was returning to its regular tempo in Glennwood by mid-January. All the home Bible studies started before Christmas picked up where they left off except for the study Tom had with his friend in town.

"It was getting too *spiritual* for him," Tom said on Sunday when they met around the table at their new house. "I think I pushed him into it anyway. I have someone else in mind that might be interested."

"Valarie joined the two and said, "Well my lady friends want to know when we're starting services, Peter."

"And I'm sensing interest with my Bible study folks as well," Peter said. "Perhaps it's time to get serious about finding a place. That's how it usually works isn't it?"

Tom and Valarie nodded.

"More than likely you'll see people come in off the street just to see what's new. That's how my first wife and I got into church, Tom said. "There was some grand opening, with signs and free Bibles and what not. Meet the pastor and his staff. We went once, liked what we saw and just kept going."

"Then I'll get out there and see what's available and what we can afford." Peter said. "I'll let you know what I've found next week."

"So what was your interest in the coffee business the other day all about?" Peter asked from the passenger seat.

Keith Roman turned his work truck onto Briarwood Avenue. "I've been thinking."

Peter waited. "Thinking about what?"

"Let me rephrase that. My knees have been thinking and my lower back has been helping me to pay attention to my thinking knees. They're telling me to consider another line of work."

"Working in a coffee stand isn't going to make your knees or back any happier." Peter said with raised brows.

"Not in the stands," Keith said shaking his head. "Partnering with you to start other stands." He studied Peter's reaction. "What do you think?"

"I think I like it."

"Good. I think I need a beer."

They continued their conversation on bar stools around a raised table at Rifkin's, a sports bar with an inviting view of Mirror Lake.

"So, a coffee partnership sounds plausible. That's good," Keith said. "What other wheels can we reinvent?"

"Church buildings," Peter said. "Something we can rent for cheap and grown into."

Keith thought for a moment. "What kind of building?"

"Almost any kind really. Something open with bathrooms."

"Whatever you find make sure you get the plumbing checked. Half the places around here are a flood waiting to happen." Keith worked on his pale ale thinking. "How big?"

"Nothing specific. Maybe a thousand square feet."

"How often are you gonna use it?"

"Sundays for a few hours."

"Like a regular church."

Peter paused. "Yeah, like a regular church."

Keith tapped on the table then moved closer. "Okay, help me out with something. "Non-exclusive use of a thousand square feet with toilets is gonna run you north of $500.00 a month. Exclusive use is a grand – minimum, and that's bare bones. Maybe no carpet and utilities on top of that. And you're only gonna use it once a week for a couple of hours. Does that sound about right?"

A look of doubt crept over the young minister as he nodded.

"Peter, you're a business man. Does that sound like a wise use of money or space?"

He took in a deep breath. "I don't think I've ever thought about it like that."

"A few churches that got foreclosed on here didn't think like that either. Big churches with bigger mortgages." Keith shook his head and chuckled. "I never could put that together. Good pastors, big hearts and close to God, yet idiots with money. No offense, of course."

"None taken."

"Hey wait a minute," Keith said with a big smile. "There is a place available for you. It's got a bathroom and it's even furnished and you can get it for even less than $500.00 per month.

"Where?" Peter asked.

"My garage."

Ice lingered on the shaded parts of the dock where Peter stood watching the movement of the lake. The remaining rays of the sun skipped across tips of the small ripples dotting the near frozen water. He couldn't get Keith's analysis out of his head.

Most churches run in the red, then they preach about stewardship.

Peter watched his breath escape into the January air. Lights flickered on inside the kitchen windows of the houses across the chilly waters.

The words came back to him once more. *Doesn't the Bible say something about how to run a church successfully?*

He turned back toward the warmer temperatures within the walls of his house determined to find out.

Peter found the well-used leather binder in a box labeled "Great Faith Stuff" and began sifting through pages of notes, charts, and Bible verses. There were no specific references in the scriptures on running a church, setting up a church, or even what a church was. All of his school materials pointed to an organizational template of church so defined by Great Assemblies – not the scriptures.

He paced his kitchen holding a bowl of rocky road ice cream and talked out a list of topics he'd search out. Each word was written down onto a list next to his Bible on the table. He would search out every instance of: church, churches, pastor, pastors, money, stewardship, tithes, tithing, and how the early church conducted itself.

He pulled his exhaustive concordance from another box and set it on the table just as his phone rang.

"When's your next trip to the valley?" his former employer asked.

"When should it be," Peter asked.

"Make it Monday," Brad said. "I've got something to show you."

Brad wouldn't give up any details other than it would be a worthwhile trip. He realized how much he'd missed his friend and mentor when he hung up. Whatever the reason, he was sure it would be a memorable visit.

He resumed his homework starting with the first word on his list.

"Church appears seventy-nine times in the New Testament," he said to himself. "Beginning with Matthew 16:18."

He flipped through the pages of Matthew and found the verse.

"And I say also unto thee, that thou art Peter, and upon this rock I will build my church; and the gates of hell shall not prevail against it."

The words sank into his spirit as they rolled off his tongue.

"Jesus is going to build his church. Not me."

He worked his way through the list making interesting - if not shocking - discoveries along the way. But in all of his reading, there was no defined pattern on how to run a church successfully.

"Maybe," he said gazing off into the gradient shadows of his house, "church isn't something to *run.*"

The knock at the door pulled him from his personal epiphany. He looked up at the clock wondering who would be stopping to visit after eight in the evening. He got up muttering, "You open up the Bible, and the phone rings, or someone's at the door..."

She stood under the porch light staring at him with pleading eyes.

"What are you doing here?" he asked.

"Don't make me go back, uncle Peter."

Chapter Forty-One

Peter cooked a small frozen pizza for Katie who talked incessantly like a self-propelled pull string doll. Between pieces of marinara coated crust, she talked of how school was stupid, the other girls were lame and how her mother couldn't find a decent guy.

"So she dumped the bumpy faced guy – or he dumped her – and then, like, went to the pawn shop and met this other loser. Oh my gosh, uncle Peter! And this one total weirdo who came over once kept wanting to hug me! Hello? Are you kidding me?"

Seizing on an opening to make it a two-way conversation, Peter asked, "So if you had to rank which is worse, is it school or the guys your mom dates?"

"School, totally, but only by this much," she said using a small pizza bite for her visual aid.

Forty-five minutes after finishing her plate, Katie's day long adventure caught up to her and she couldn't keep her eyes open. Peter made up the sofa for his guest while she brushed her teeth and splashed water on her face.

"Promise you won't tell mom I'm here?" she said settling under the cover.

"Don't you think your mom would want to know where you're at?"

"Do you *have* to tell her?"

Instead of giving her an answer, Peter ran his fingers through her baby soft hair watching her eyelids fall until her lashes meshed together.

Leaving her side, he stole away to the phone by his bed upstairs and dialed a saved Phoenix number.

"Hello?" The frantic mother's voice leaped out of the receiver.

"A certain young lady doesn't want her mother to know that she hopped a bus to visit her uncle."

"Peter! Is Katie there with you?"

"Yes, she's fine and already asleep."

"Thank you God!" Stephanie said before sobbing. "She was

supposed to be staying the night at Jeanie's, but when I called over, Jeanie's mother didn't know what I was talking about."

"Do you mind if I ask what's going on between you two?"

"What do you mean?" She sounded offended. "We have our spats, but we're doing fine."

Peter listened through her sobs. "She seems to hate school and... your dating choices --"

"Hey, hold on here. You're over stepping, Peter. You don't know a thing about it." She blew her nose into the phone. "Last time I checked, you didn't have a daughter, so don't go giving me advice on raising mine!"

"You've got me there, Steph. But at the moment, your runaway daughter is crashed on my couch. That doesn't sound like everything is fine to me."

The receiver was quiet except for a muffled television in the background.

"Look, I'm sorry," he said. "It's not my place. I'm just a concerned uncle."

"For which we're both eternally grateful. So, what – how do we get her home?"

Peter sat on the edge of the bed. "It just so happens I'm coming down there Monday. I'll be at the coffeehouse. Can the three of us meet there and talk? I don't want her thinking she can just run off any old time things aren't going her way."

"Monday's fine.

"All right. See you then."

"Thanks for calling, Peter. And thanks for taking care of us."

Katie spent half the time with Peter and half the time visiting and cooking with Valarie. The reunion at the coffee house with Stephanie was smooth and Katie apologized for running off. Moments after mother and daughter left, Brad took Peter around to see the new developments.

They walked down a smoky aroma filled hallway joining two rooms where a wall once stood. In the center of a room that was previously a retail outlet for shoes, a man with long hair and glasses stood spreading beans out with a thin paddle. The metal container holding the beans was near the base of a giant steel machine. The man nodded when he saw Brad. Behind him and stacked along the back wall were a dozen hundred pound bags of coffee beans.

We're roastin' baby," Brad said with excitement.

"I see that," Peter said. "How long have you been doing this?"

"Still working at it."

Brad introduced Peter to Ty Reynolds, the official roaster. Ty lowered his paddle down and said, "Cool, man. Nice to meet you."

A barista walked up to Brad telling him of a caller on hold.

"I'll be right back," Brad said leaving Peter there to watch Ty focus on making the finest roast possible.

The sounds and smells ushered an awareness over Peter like the sudden understanding of a dream. He was standing in the room where raw coffee beans were roasted to their flavorful perfection. Then, through windows situated around him, Peter could see the rest of the operation. In one window, customers waited in line or sat visiting with friends while sipping their drink of choice. Through another, the coffeehouse staff waited on guests, brewed shots of espresso, or stocked shelves. In the last square window, Brad Stellar, the brains of the whole operation, was on the phone in his office. There was a place for everyone, and everyone was in their place. He felt like he was looking at the pieces of a mystery coming together like a puzzle.

Peter saw Brad motioning to him from the window, and he joined his old boss back in the office.

"Ty isn't much for conversation is he?" Peter asked.

"No. The sixties were really good to him," Brad said taking a seat. "Not much on people skills but he can make some of the best coffee you've ever had." Brad filled two samples cups from a French press. "Try this."

Peter took in the velvety aroma first, then sipped. It was liquid earth and smoke with notes of chocolate.

"That is amazing, Brad."

"Isn't it? Midnight Silk. It's Ty's latest blend."

They looked out the window to the man and his roasting machine.

"Whatever brain cells he kept after Woodstock I hope will benefit mankind for many years to come." Brad said raising his cup.

They sampled more coffee blends then schemed over lunch. When Peter finished his visit, he'd agreed to feature and market the rich, bold flavors of Stellar Roasters to the drive-through customers in Glennwood, Arizona.

Peter sold coffee, taught Bible studies, searched the scriptures and discussed drive-through locations with Keith for the remaining days of the week. Then on Sunday, he joined Tom and Valarie with their Bibles in their kitchen around a plate of freshly made walnut-chocolate chip cookies.

"I think you're trying to make me fat," Peter said, dunking a cookie into his coffee.

"Not fat," the house cook said. "Just putting a smile in your tummy."

After prayer, they discussed how the various Bible studies were progressing.

Tom said, "No luck this week."

"Going well with my ladies," Valarie said with a smile. "They asked me again about where services will be meeting and when they get to meet the pastor. Any news on a location?"

Peter took in a breath. "I do have news, but it might be a little different than what you're expecting."

Tom said, "Give us both barrels, Peter."

"Okay, let me ask you this, how have the finances been with the churches you either started or were a part of?"

"Feast or famine really. Mostly famine," Valarie said. "Some months things were so tight we were late on the church note. But we made it up soon and never went without."

"You never went without, but did Jesus tell his disciples to go into debt buying properties or renting spaces?"

"You need some place to meet, don't you?" Tom asked.

"Some place, sure. Didn't we talk once about how you answered people who asked about your regular church attendance?"

"Yes," Tom answered, "But we were traveling. We're not on the road anymore."

"So, was church on the road less real because you were traveling? Was God different?"

"No, no. God was the same."

Tom looked to his wife who had a glow of curiosity about her. The men waited.

"Is what you're asking just about a location to meet, Peter?" she asked.

"No it's not. I've actually been questioning everything I've been taught."

"You're on to something here," she said. "keep going."

"Well, it's like God has been whispering to me and showing me parts of things but I still don't know exactly what it is. I've spent the last few nights taking words like *church, pastor, tithes,* basic things, and looking at every instance in the New Testament, looking for how it's used, what it means and how the early church functioned."

"And...?" Valarie asked excitedly.

"Let's take the word pastor. According to Great Assemblies, or most any church, what is a pastor? Who is he? What's he supposed to do?"

"Isn't he the shepherd? The head cheese," Tom said.

"I'd say the backbone, the leader," Valarie added.

"That's what I've thought all my life," Peter said. "I went to Great Faith College of Ministry to become a pastor and run a church. The Bible should be full of references about the role of pastors, right? Do you know how many times the word *pastor* is mentioned in the New Testament?"

"I don't know, a dozen?" Tom answered.

Valarie shook her head. "I think it's less than that."

"Once," Peter said slapping his Bible. "The only reference is *pastors* and not as leaders of anything. They're simply listed with apostles, prophets, evangelists, teachers and so on."

"Are you sure about that?" Tom asked flipping through the back of his Bible. "That doesn't seem right."

"See for yourself."

Tom searched out verses while Valarie beheld Peter as though in a trance. She looked through him. Her pupils spilled open as she peered into another realm.

"This isn't your only discovery, is it?" She asked still looking beyond him.

"No. There's more," he said.

Tom read to himself as Valarie took hold of Peter's arm and said in a tender voice, "Lead gently, Peter. Small steps at a time."

"Unconventional?"

She nodded. "Some people won't be able to make this kind of transition."

"Transition to what?"

"We'll soon see, won't we?"

Tom sat comfortably reclined in the living room with Valarie. She crocheted quietly while he was somewhere between a television show and a boating magazine. Valarie peered over bifocals watching her husband fidget."

What's wrong, Tom?"

He didn't answer right away. Then he turned and looked at her momentarily. "Where's Peter going with all this? Right after we got here, he showed me where I've been wrong all these years about baptism. Now I've had it all wrong about pastors and whatever is next about church. Guess I have that all wrong too."

"Tom," Valarie said, surprised at his tone. "Peter has never put it like that. None of this is about who's right or wrong. He's excited about what God is showing him. We're all learning more."

"Well, I hate feeling like I don't know anything about what I believe." Tom angrily cleared his throat. "I hate feeling stupid!"

"Honey, what's the matter with you?

"I'm old enough to be his father and I've been going to church a lot longer. I've read the Bible cover to cover twice and..." His face reddened searching for another personal merit badge. "I should know those things, Val!"

"Tom Warner, you stop this right now! You quit comparing yourself to Peter or anyone else."

She put her yarns and needles aside and sat beside her stewing husband. She took his hands into hers and waited for him to calm down.

"God uses whoever he wants whenever he wants. How often has he used you to heal, Tom? Often, as I recall. Peter is the vessel he's using now here in Glennwood. He's cutting into new territory, but he can't do it alone. We've both been directed here to help. We still believe that don't we?"

Tom nodded reluctantly.

"Then let's be all that God wants *us* to be. He wouldn't have called us out here if he didn't have plans and purposes for us too, honey."

Tom's agitation yielded to peace. He nodded to Valarie who embraced him till his embarrassment was gone.

"I'm sorry," he said. "I guess it's easier to hear new things from an eloquent preacher who's behind a pulpit, then from a much younger man in your own kitchen."

He set his magazine aside and took hold of Valarie's hands and asked, "Do you believe the things he's saying?"

"What he's saying goes against traditions we're comfortable with. But if we're going to find our way in the Word as we have agreed, then we need to let go of that which is not in the Word. Nobody said it was going to be easy. We need to become like new wine skins if we're to hold new wine."

Chapter Forty-Two

Peter went with Mick on a day trip to get pictures of the scenic wonders of Central Arizona. They drove through Jerome, then headed southeast through Camp Verde and along the Mogollon Rim before turning around in Payson. Peter watched his friend strategically set up each shot on a tripod. He was impressed with Mick's eye for detail and his patience to wait for a cloud to change position to alter the mood of a scene.

"I got some awesome shots of the Dude Fire that ripped through here back in 1990," Mick said, heading back to the car. "That was unreal. It's slowly turning green again."

They were back in Glennwood an hour before sunset. Before parting company, Mick had one more thing on his mind. He pulled his car up to the antique shop known affectionately around town as The Country Store.

"I thought you might want to see what's happened since we prayed together about my occupation."

Peter looked up through the windshield to the sign on the building. "You're in the antique business?"

"In the antique business...that's a good way to put it. Let me show you."

They stepped inside the store and made their way past memories and souvenirs from another time till they came to a room near the counter. Mick opened the French doors and turned on the lights to reveal all the makings of a photo studio carefully stacked around the room.

"I came in a few weeks back looking at some old cameras. The owners said they get people coming in asking about those old time sepia portraits. So we talked about this and that, which led to more of this and that and next thing you know, I'm leasing this room for a photography studio."

Peter turned to Mick and asked, "No kidding? Are you done with your other gig?"

"All done. My final shoot was last week and I said goodbye to the old crew. From now on, all my subjects will be properly clothed."

"Praise God, Mick!"

"Yeah. Finally, I can stop living under a cloud."

"What I'm saying is that there are several references to churches meeting in homes," Peter said opening his Bible. "Romans 16; *Likewise greet the church that is in their house.* 1 Corinthians 16; *Aquila and Priscilla salute you much in the Lord, with the church that is in their house.* Colossians 4; *Salute the brethren which are in Laodicea, and Nymphas, and the church which is in his house.* Philemon 1; *And to our beloved Apphia, and Archippus our fellowsoldier, and to the church in thy house.*"

"I can see that as a way to start," Tom said. "But what about when the church grows – which it will quickly - then what? You can only fit so many in a living room."

Peter moved closer. "I'm glad you brought that up, because that's exactly what I asked the Lord. And you know what he said? More living rooms."

"More living rooms?"

Peter nodded excitedly. "Most of the training I got to become a pastor was about numbers. Build a church to support me and send ten percent from tithes to headquarters. The bigger the congregation, the more blessed I'd be personally and Great Assemblies as a whole. Bigger congregations, bigger buildings, bigger offerings. But what I'm seeing in the scriptures is not a single big location, but many smaller locations."

"Wouldn't have to come up with rent every month," Valarie said.

"Church in houses," Tom said. "I suppose it can't hurt to give it a go."

"How about meeting here next week? Valarie asked. "We could invite the people from our Bible studies."

"The first get together could be more of an ice breaker with snacks. Get to know each other," Peter added.

They waited for Tom's approval.

"More living rooms," he said in a low voice. "Might as well start with ours."

It was a crisp and sunny Sunday morning when Peter met the Warners an hour before the appointed time for prayer. They prayed to know the way ahead and for all who would enter their home that day. They prayed for the souls of Glennwood to turn to righteousness. The praying trio was filled with great expectation to see what God was going to do as they stepped out in faith.

Lana Chambers arrived just ahead of Candace Dupree. The two ladies were friends of Valarie's. Ted and Meg Sanders, each carrying small crock pots, were next. Steve and Cheryl Sanders pulled into the front yard next and Mick rolled to a stop right behind them.

For almost an hour, the ten visitors made introductions and got to know one another while sampling a wide assortment of finger foods ranging from meat balls to chips and dips. Then Tom stood up and asked for everyone's attention.

"Thank you for coming to our house," he said with nervous hesitation. "Valarie and I met Peter some time ago and felt even then that our futures would somehow be connected. After a few years of RV traveling, we felt the Lord leading us here to Glennwood to assist in whatever way we could."

Valarie beamed at her husband as he stepped out of his own comfort zone. She admired the shy man who was more comfortable in the shadows than anywhere near the spotlight.

"I can tell you that I never dreamed about church in a home, let alone *our* home. It's a new concept to me. But it's in the Bible, so we'll see how it goes. And before I put my foot in my mouth, let me turn it over to Peter."

Peter stood and looked at the nine souls seated around him in the kitchen and living room. He saw people with expectations and concerns. People who were looking for a reason to stay or go. He took another sip of water.

"Since I was a kid, I've had a tender heart toward God. I can't tell you why. I just did. I wanted to see souls saved, so while I learned the coffee business I went to Bible school to become a pastor. After graduation I came to Glennwood, bought a drive-through espresso stand and started to build a church. I think I've seen just about everyone here at my drive-through window and I want to thank you for that. You're here today because you're hungry for God in some way and I thank you for that as well."

Peter needed more water before continuing.

"I should tell you that I'm no longer with the church organization I was part of when I came to Glennwood. I couldn't agree with their teachings. What's interesting is that I've found a lot of people in the same situation. People going to church, whether they agree with the preaching or not, so they can mark church attendance off their weekly to do list so their conscience won't bother them. Week after week, they come to church, find their seat, sit and listen, then go home. They're like spectators watching a performance, rather than participants growing in faith. I don't think that's what Jesus Christ had in mind for his church."

Peter paused long enough for Steve Steckler to raise his hand and ask, "What do you think Jesus had in mind?"

"The church is the body of Christ, right? Let's think about our own bodies. We have hands, feet, eyes, noses, etc., Each member is joined together with different abilities. Our whole body functions together under the leadership of our brains, right?" Christ is head of the church, not a pastor. The church is the body of Christ and each one of us is a member in that body."

Peter moved his hands around the room for emphasis watching each face. He was relieved at the approving nods. Peter opened his Bible. "I read 1 Corinthians 14 this morning and verse 26 leaped off the page at me. It says, *How is it then, brethren? when ye come together, every one of you hath a psalm, hath a doctrine, hath a tongue, hath a revelation, hath an interpretation. Let all things be done unto edifying.*"

He set his Bible down and looked around the room. "What does that sound like to you?"

Several faces showed the outward signs of inner turning wheels turning.

"It sounds like everyone brings one of those things to church," Lana said.

"Exactly," Peter said. "The more I consider church, the more I see a spiritual potluck. At a potluck, no one person makes everything. Rather, everyone brings something to share with others. No one is a spectator. No one just sits and listens. Everybody participates.

The questions and answers flowed for more than two hours, and when the concluding prayer was finished, everyone agreed to be back the same time next week.

Keith and Peter went through the paperwork to form a partnership early in the week. Then on Thursday Peter drove up to the coffee stand window as it was closing.

"What do you want?" Shannon asked.

"I've come to have my way with you."

"Ha! You already blew your once in a lifetime shot at that mister."

Peter laughed. "I'm talking about coffee, my dear. Let's go for a ride."

They drove to a home improvement center near Main Street. Peter stopped the truck at the far corner of the parking lot near a tall light pole.

"This is one of two locations Keith and I are looking at," Peter said pointing to the edge of the asphalt. "They want a pretty penny for space, but the traffic this place gets is three times what we get now. We're trying to talk them down. Keith is an excellent negotiator."

"Really?" Shannon asked. "This is happening a lot faster than I thought. Would I be working for Keith Roman too?"

"Yep," Peter answered. "But never forget you're always working for yourself first. If you take this stand Shannon, I want you to run it like you own it. If it does well, you do well. If it sinks, you go down with it. Got it?"

"Got it," she said, looking at the possible stand location with a sober, yet excited expression. "When do think it could happen?"

Peter put the truck into gear and eased toward the road. "I'd say within the next ninety days. We've got permits, plumbing and electrical to get worked out yet."

"Bathroom?"

"That too."

"Better toilet paper?"

"Don't push it."

Chapter Forty-Three

Two of the three weekly Bible studies Peter led came to an end, but each person still wanted to meet. Peter encouraged the people to take the same studies and share them with others, but met with resistance.

"I don't know how to teach a Bible study," Meg confessed. "I'm not sure I want to either."

"But that's how you'll really grow, Meg," Peter said. "That's the pattern Jesus taught to his disciples. Someone taught these to me, I taught you, and you can teach others."

"I'm not ready," Ted said."

Peter looked at Ted and smiled. "Neither was I, but we'll all learn by doing."

"But you went to Bible school."

"Not for these. I learned about these Bible studies after Bible school."

For the next several Sundays, Tom and Valarie's house was a place of lively discussions, fellowship and prayer. Lana brought a friend from work who thought she'd joined a cult. Lana told her, "It's just church like in the Bible," she told her friend. "Come see for yourself." Her friend came and the atmosphere in the room turned from excitement to tension. The woman was horribly disruptive and argumentative. Lana cringed in embarrassment. The gathering ended on a sour, confusing note.

Afterward, Tom asked Peter, "How do we keep that from happening again?"

"I don't think there's a sure fire way," Peter said. "But we do need to do something."

Tom thought for a moment. "You've really centered everything on the Word and Bible studies. What if that's where the invitation process begins?"

Peter shook his head. "I'm not following."

"What if we try to take people through at least some of the Bible studies before we invite them to gather with us? If someone's going to argue or fuss, let it happen out there so it doesn't happen here."

Tom's reasoning stacked like level bricks. "Brother, that's the best thing I've heard in a long time. Thank you for your wisdom."

Peter stepped away just before Valarie came to her husband. She leaned closed and kissed his cheek.

"See?" she said with bright, loving eyes. "You are a wonderfully important and wise man of God here, Tom Warner. No more talk about feeling stupid."

The church in Tom and Valarie's house grew from ten to seventeen in four weeks as a result of new Bible studies being taught. Peter assisted different ones until they felt comfortable and stayed close to his cell phone to answer questions. Baptisms took place almost weekly and several were seeking to be filled with the Holy Ghost.

When reviewing the plans for the new coffee stand, Peter asked his friend, "When do you want to get a Bible study going?"

"About time you asked me," Keith said. "You asked everyone but me you dog!"

"I figured you knew what I was doing and if you wanted to join in you were always welcome."

"It's still nice to be asked. And there might be someone else joining in."

"Who's that," Peter asked.

"Wally. He's been staying with me since his wife threw him out. He'll never admit to being thrown out, but take my word, he was thrown out."

Peter met Keith after work on Thursdays. In the other room watching TV was Wally with a remote in one hand and a beer in the other.

The volume on the TV was lower than normal when Peter was there.

She was jumping up and down when Peter arrived at the back door with supplies from the store.

"I want my stand! I want my stand! I want my stand!"

"You'll get your stand when it's ready, Shannon. Just hold your horses!"

"Well hurry!" she said nudging him.

Peter's cell phone rang out from his jacket pocket. Shannon took it out while Peter's arms were full.

"Is this from your girlfriend?" she asked.

"Probably. Just don't know which one."

She handed it to him and he stepped out of the stand. Ted was on the other end.

"Say Peter, is there any way you could stop by tonight around seven? One of the deacons from our old church is coming and wants to talk about why Meg and I aren't coming any more. I told him we were doing church in a house now. He asked me what that was, and I'm still kind of new to this. You can explain it better than I can."

"Okay, Ted," Peter said. "I'll see you about seven."

The young deacon listened to Ted as he described the last few Sundays.

Intrigued, the man asked, "And you're doing this without seminary training?"

Ted looked at Peter, then back to the deacon and said, "Where does the Bible say anything about seminary?"

"But to understand the Bible, you need to go to seminary."

Ted took a deep breath and asked, "Have you gone to seminary?"

"Yes."

"Do you understand all of the Bible?"

"Of course not," he said indignantly. No one can understand all of the Word of God."

Tom looked confused. "Can you get your money back from seminary?"

The deacon returned the following evening to Ted's house for the first Bible study.

Bishop's Coffee Company opened its second stand on the second Saturday in April. Any drink, any size that day was only a dollar. Sales were through the roof. Peter helped to make drinks and trained a new employee while Shannon worked the window. The line remained at least ten cars deep from 7:00 AM to 12:50 PM. Then it dropped to five cars deep till 1:30.

Peter watched Shannon suddenly lose her animation when a familiar white Lexus SUV approached the window. The driver, an older man in a gray sweater paid for two beverages without expression. Shannon carefully handed the order to the customer who handed the drinks to the woman beside him. Shannon and the driver paused in a wordless exchanged. Then the driver side window went up and the vehicle pulled forward and drove away from the stand.

Shannon stepped from the window and sipped ice water through her red straw. Then she set the large cup down, wiped her eyes and went back to the window.

"Hey there! Got your two mochas coming right up..."

"Having thirty people in our house isn't our biggest problem," Tom said hanging up the phone. "Having twenty cars parked out front and along the street is. That was the second complaint this morning from the neighbors."

Peter panned the room. Every chair was taken. Some sat on the floor and others stood. After everyone quieted down, Valarie opened in prayer and Peter addressed the packed house.

"Folks, we need to make some changes to be honorable to the neighborhood and not make our presence unwelcome. We have about thirty people here which is more than plenty for any one church in a home. I think it might be good for us to find two more houses to meet in and spread out so that we're about eight to twelve in house. What do you say folks? Who out there can be the host of a church in their house?"

Husbands and wives exchanged glances and talked amongst themselves.

A man seated on the floor raised his hand and said, "We can probably have a church in our house. But who's gonna lead it?"

Peter's eyes remained fixed on the man as the full weight of the next challenge came to rest on Peter's shoulders: Leadership.

"That's a good point, but let's find two more locations first."

Another hand went up.

"Are Sundays the only days we can meet? 'Cause I normally work on Sundays and can't get to any church. If there was another day or time I know there's more people who'd come."

218

Valarie handed Peter a clip board with a new note pad and pen. Peter took it and asked everyone around the room about times, places and availability.

An hour later, there were two more houses to meet in. One church would meet on Monday evenings. The other church of families with young children, would meet near a park on Saturday mornings.

Once the new locations were established, Peter made a list of those interested in becoming leaders and met with them after everyone else was gone. He asked the five men to take the next week to pray and study Paul's writings to Timothy and Titus before meeting again on Sunday.

It had all happened so quickly.

Peter was running on fumes by mid-week. His phone seemed to ring non-stop between new hire questions, new manager dilemmas, and new church situations. His nightly rest was interrupted with fears of forgetting something at either drive-through, or worse, that someone would expose him as a crack pot fraud preacher somehow and God would strike him down with lightning.

The other concern was his new manager and the recurring image of her blinking back tears on grand opening day.

Peter met with the five prospective leaders and discovered that only two had opened their Bibles at all since Sunday. Of those two, neither had been baptized nor wanted to be. They did all share a common interest: The prevailing wage for an assistant pastor. After some consideration Peter said, "There's no need to rush into this. Let's wait on the Lord a bit more..."

Chapter Forty-Four

"That is the look of a worn out man," Valarie said to Peter in the living room shortly before others would arrive Sunday morning. "How are your helpers coming along?"

"I think my helpers are not helpful at the moment," he said taking in a sip of heavily creamed hot coffee. "Getting paid seems to be a higher priority than the Word of God or the remission of sins. I think my drive-through manager is a more qualified leader and she doesn't want to have anything to do with church."

Tom looked at Peter from across the room. "Peter, I have a confession to make," he said. "The Lord has been kicking me all week to help you shoulder some of this load. I didn't say anything because, well, I've never led anything in church besides prayer before."

"That's the best news I've heard all week, Tom. You'd be perfect. And with your wife with you, you can't fail."

Tom chuckled. "Let's ease into this okay?"

"I'll be right here."

Later that morning, Peter opened with prayer, then asked Tom to serve as a host of sorts inviting each one to share something that would encourage others. If someone had a song, they sang and the others joined in. If another asked a question, everyone participated in the answer. If someone had a teaching, they brought it forward, then everyone discussed it. Prayer requests were shared and in prayer they concluded and dismissed. The warm presence of God lingered about the room as different ones made their way to their cars.

After the meeting, Peter asked Tom, "I think there's a good reason why Jesus sent his disciples out two by two. Would you consider going with me to the other houses?"

"Sure. I'd be honored," Tom said.

Peter and Tom visited each scheduled gathering and felt the blessing of the Lord on their partnership. They agreed to stay together and became a traveling team leading each congregation through a loosely organized time of participatory fellowship. Peter's depth and clarity in the Word combined harmoniously with Tom's hard earned life experience and compassion. Together they helped to encourage many spiritual wanderers back to a place of peace with their Maker.

As the weeks continued, more people were teaching Bible studies and the gatherings in living rooms and back patios got bigger and more numerous. Peter and Tom were meeting with some group every day of the week. One Monday, Valarie picked up fifty copies of the Bible studies from the printers. By Friday, they were all passed out.

An entire church gathering was planned for first day of summer at a park on the east side of Glennwood. Under the welcome sunshine, families gathered and visited while children played. It was a much larger group than anyone expected. Many of the people were part of a Bible study and hadn't officially come to a house meeting yet.

Peter was working on a loaded chili dog when he was approached by some people who'd asked to speak with him. He'd seen them before but couldn't remember their names. The first couple introduced themselves as Jack and Wendy Smith, a well-dressed couple in their late thirties. On their heels were Dean & Samantha Greyson, a younger, more casual pair.

Jack started the conversation. "You probably won't remember us because we've been bouncing back and forth between our other church and the Foster's house. But Dean and I have been going through those Bible studies, and we've been blown away with what we've learned."

Dean nodded in agreement. "It seems like we've been just sitting and listening where we're at. If you're not part of the pastor's family or close friend, you're not going to be doing anything except holding a pew down."

"Maybe ushering or helping with the kid's church," Dean added.

"So, after seeing what you're doing, and how everyone participates, our families feel like this is where we need to be. None of us is looking for a position, we're looking to serve."

Peter was moved by their sincerity. "Have you met Tom and Valarie?"

Peter introduced the couples to the Warners and scheduled to meet with them at Jack and Wendy's house later in the week.

The outside event was so well received, another park day was scheduled before school began. While Peter picked up some trash around the coolers filled with melting ice, Tom and Valarie walked past him to their car.

"You want to know how many came today?" Valarie asked.

Peter stopped. "I don't know. Should I get hung up on numbers?"

"Just asking," she responded.

Peter put the lid on the metal garbage can and waved to his friends as they drove away.

He was home a half an hour later after a stop at the store. The house was quiet compared to the activities at the park. The blinking light on the phone beckoned him so he pressed the button to hear his missed message. It was a single sentence from Valarie Warner.

"A hundred and fifty-four."

Jack and Wendy, Dean and Sam, Tom and Valarie and Peter met for a couple of hours on Wednesday evening. The new couples were in agreement with all of the teachings from the Bible studies and looked forward to eventually hosting churches in their homes. The next step was a multiplication of leadership. Jack and Wendy would go with Tom and Valarie to some of the groups. Peter would take Dean and Sam to the others.

By the end of the summer, there were ten house groups and a weekly lunch group for business people that Keith had organized. Peter taught about the relevance of the scriptures to business people while they ate.

After much prayer and consultation with Tom and Valarie, it was decided to further multiply. The Smiths, the Greysons and the Warners would each lead three groups. Peter would lead the lunch group with Keith, then would visit the other groups where needed.

The blessings of God rested mightily on the growing church. People who had no working knowledge of the scriptures before were now answering questions with confidence directly from their Bible.

Young people and the elderly, long time believers and new babes in Christ were participating together in prayer, singing, studying and sharing the goodness of God.

Daylene called Peter on Wednesday just after getting home from a house meeting. "Got some news for you," she said. "Looks like Stephanie is getting married."

"Really?" he said trying to read her tone. "What's he like?"

"What is he like... He walks upright," Daylene joked. "I don't know Peter. How much can you know about a person over dinner?"

"Very little. What does Katie think?"

"Katie is just trying not to think about it. If that girl is a sane adult it'll be a miracle."

"When's the big date?" Peter asked, getting a pen.

"Would you believe two o'clock on Monday? At least it's going to be a simple Justice of the Peace wedding."

"Monday? Who gets married on a Monday?"

"I don't know. Something about a mid-week honeymoon deal in Hawaii."

"Two o'clock on Monday. How about I meet you at the house and ride with you?"

"Would love it," Daylene said. "Oh, they don't want any wedding gifts so don't worry about that. Which reminds me --"

"Mom, don't start."

"Are you at least dating anyone?"

The ceremony was over inside of fifteen minutes. Richard and Stephanie Kragenburger led their party of thirteen friends and family members to an Italian restaurant for the reception where the Chianti flowed like water.

Richard was a pleasant, though forgettable man. He was two inches shorter than Stephanie, and about as attractive. He'd been smart with money early in life and was heavily invested in the stock market. He called himself a day trader. People around him just nodded and smiled.

When all the food was eaten, Richard and Stephanie stumbled their way around the room one last time thanking everyone for coming. Then before stepping out the door, Stephanie spun around and walked up to Peter.

"I want you to remember this day, Peter," she said with wild, intoxicated eyes. "You think I'm such a screw up --"

"Stephanie! I've never said anything like that!"

"My daughter loves you more than me. She thinks I'm a screw up too. But today's a different day, and I'm a different girl. I married a great guy and I want you all to mark this day down." Stephanie pulled out a gold pen. "Mark it down in big letters on your hand so you'll never forget my anniversary. Everything's gonna be different. You'll see."

Peter took the pen from the tipsy bride. "Okay Stephanie, I'm writing it down."

September 10, 2001.

The newlyweds were over California when the world was becoming aware of the terrorist attacks in New York, at the Pentagon and the plane crash in Pennsylvania. Hundreds of aircraft were ordered to land at the nearest available airport inside of American airspace.

Richard and Stephanie spent their entire honeymoon in the LAX terminal. Over half of Richard's investment gains evaporated in less than a week after the NYSE reopened the following Monday.

Every church in Glennwood saw a spike in attendance after that horrific day. Hundreds of people rededicated their lives back to God and even political adversaries were united in a common purpose of bringing those responsible to justice. As the days and weeks went on without further incident however, the shades of partisan politics and ordinary life returned. More brightly colored American flags dotted the landscape, but much of the country fell back into old routines.

As different believers expressed interest in becoming more involved, Peter paired them with other leaders for hands on learning.

For the holidays that year, Peter went down to Phoenix to be with his family. But he joined the Warners and a few others New Year's Eve for prayer.

Peter stepped out onto the deck to enjoy the night sky just before midnight. Tom and Valarie came out a few minutes later.

"It's been an amazing year," Peter said.

"It has," was all Valarie said.

Peter looked to her waiting for more. She'd been unusually distant most of the evening.

"What do you see up ahead, Valarie?" He asked hoping for words of peace and perhaps some encouragement to refresh is weary mind.

She looked up as though measuring the wide expanse of the starry sky. Then she took his arm in hers and said in tones just above a whisper and said, "I hear the rage of kings mourning their kingdoms. I hear the sound of fury approaching from the air."

Chapter Forty-Five

Denny Cummings parked his aging Honda Civic in front of the impressive Glennwood Central Church building. The rust spot on the hood caught his eye again when he opened the driver side door. "C'mon champ," he muttered. "You can go another hundred and fifty thousand miles – easy."

He paced through his usual Tuesday morning routine. Lights. Coffee. Office heaters. Computer.

The front door opened followed by light steps on tile.

"Morning Irene."

"Morning to you as well, Denny."

The sounds of a church office coming to life echoed down the hall. Irene appeared at the door with her sandy brown hair up off her shoulders.

"How was your day off?" she asked, holding her favorite Mickey Mouse cup.

Denny looked up from his computer screen. "It was fun right up to the part where the dentist, I mean orthodontist, said Jeremy needs oral surgery and braces."

"Oh braces. Sorry to hear that Denny."

"You and me both. They should give out sedatives before they go over the price of their recommendations."

"It's painful for everyone at first, but your kids will thank you later." Irene placed a manila folder on the assistant pastor's desk then turned back toward her office.

"If it's not braces, it's cars breaking down. If it's not cars breaking down, it's hot water heaters going out," he said to himself.

Denny opened the folder and reviewed the neatly displayed church attendance statistics.

The trend was continuing.

The heavy doors of the private entrance leading to the back hallway opened at 9:45. Denny and Irene listened. The steps were heavy and fast paced. The sound of a closet door opened then closed. Then the corner office door closed. Pastor Roland Blackwell had arrived.

Denny finished returning phone calls and was half way through emails when Pastor Blackwell opened his office door and abruptly called out, "Denny!"

Pastor Roland Blackwell sat in a black leather chair adjusting his sapphire tie pin. His hair looked aflame from a single shaft of morning light piercing the window. Even without an oversized hat and beard he was the human version of Yosemite Sam.

Denny entered and sat across from the church leader.

"I need you to get one of those mobile oil change services over here," Roland said. "Make sure they know the difference between a Lincoln and a Ford. I need my car ready to go by noon. Take it out of the general fund."

Denny started writing.

"I'm meeting with a guy from the radio station later today. You hear that? Radio! I think that would do us right, don't you?"

The assistant pastor nodded. "Radio could be good."

"You bet your antenna it would be! People tuning in ready to hear this preacher telling 'em like it is." Roland looked off into the mists of time. "I've always wanted to have my own show on the radio. TV might be more glamorous, but radio was king when I was a kid." He pulled himself back into the present. "Anyway, how we looking, Denny?"

Denny took in a deep breath and opened his folder. "There's no way to sugar coat this Pastor Blackwell. Attendance is down again. Nine weeks in a row."

Roland took out a brush and started to put a shine on his wing tips. "Are you counting children in that attendance count?"

"We always count children."

"Well, you know how kids are when they get back in school. Attendance fluctuates sometimes."

"Tithes and offerings are down significantly as well."

Pastor Blackwell stopped brushing.

"How far down?"

Denny placed the details in front of the pastor. Roland's detailed eyes followed the falling lines of a graph in the center of the page.

"Well, something needs fixing here, Denny. Better find out what's broke."

Assistant Pastor Denny Cummings spent Tuesday and Wednesday calling the families who'd been absent. He either spoke to a family member on the phone or visited the family in person. He compiled notes and on Friday, Denny was back in Pastor Blackwell's office.

"Glennwood Central has been handed a gift from heaven, Denny," Pastor Blackwell said in his boisterous manner. "I'm going to host a thirty-minute radio show that will be broadcast in Glennwood and over to Prescott."

"That's amazing, Pastor. They're just giving the church half an hour on the radio?"

Roland sat down behind his desk. "Not giving. More like auctioning. But we'll raise the winning bid with a special faith offering from all the folks coming back to church, right?"

Denny squirmed in his chair. "I'm not so sure, Pastor."

"Get some faith in you, son!" Roland slapped Denny's leg. "What's the hold up here? Do I need to go out and visit the flock? Bring home some wayward sheep?"

"It might not hurt if you did that because most of the ones I talked to seemed content going elsewhere for church."

Pastor Blackwell looked stunned. "Going elsewhere for church?"

Denny waited for the next explosion.

Roland stomped past Denny and closed his office door. Then he stomped back to his leather chair and stared intently at his assistant. "What do you mean, going elsewhere for church?"

Denny looked over his legal pad. "Nineteen families have left. Two families are moving out of Glennwood. Three more families aren't going anywhere but don't plan on coming back. That leaves fourteen families and every one of them say they're home churching or

228

something."

"Home churching?" Roland said laughing. "Lying in bed saying 'Oh God' isn't church, Denny."

"They're not laying bed, Pastor Blackwell," Denny said. "They're telling me it's right out of the Bible. They meet in someone's house every week for prayer and some Bible teaching. Everyone participates in some way and everyone is encouraged to teach Bible studies."

Pastor Blackwell rose from his chair and began to pace. He listened to Denny as though trying to decipher a foreign language. "Well, who's the pastor?"

"Depends on who you talk to. The way they described things, it sounds like they've got a team of pastors."

Pastor Blackwell's face reddened. "This is not right, Denny. Not right at all. Before you do anything else, find out who's in charge. Someone's got to be calling the shots and get me a meeting with him as soon as possible." Then he sat back down with a smoldering anger hanging about him like lingering smoke around a pot belly stove.

"This is sheep stealing, Denny. And no one steals my sheep!"

Chapter Forty-Six

Peter closed Keith's front door after their Bible study Thursday evening and walked toward his truck. Keith had been a sponge, soaking up all he could but they had come to the end of the series. "You need to make more of these studies, Peter," Keith said.

Peter hadn't thought about adding to the studies before. He considered possible topics when he noticed some standing next to his truck in in the dim porch light.

"Hey Wally," Peter said, surprised to see him.

Wally sucked in another breath through his filtered Marlboro. He let out a plume of smoke and struggled for words. He was a broken man with no more fight in him.

"Is it really true what you say about God answering prayers an all?"

"Every bit, Wally," Peter said. "If we do our part, God will do his part."

He only glanced at Peter before looking away into evening darkness.

"Like with marriages too?"

"Marriages too."

Wally worked into his cigarette a bit more. "So, how does that work?"

"Prayer is a two-way conversation with God, Wally. If we ask God for help, we should be willing to listen to his answer and follow through with is instructions. God knows all about marriage and how difficult it can be."

"Marta won't give me a chance. She won't answer the phone or the door when I try to talk with her. Maybe if someone else were there she'd listen to me. Will you help me?"

"Sure, Wally."

Peter followed the taillights of Wally's beat up Dodge into town and to the old row houses off Keller Avenue. Once there, Wally watched from his truck as Peter went up the walk way to the house in the center. A woman pulled back the drapes and looked to see who was at the door. Peter talked to the woman through the narrowly opened door for a moment. Then motioned to Wally to come.

"What do you want?" she said throwing her words at her husband.

Wally stumbled over a broken apology that was mixed with rare falling tears. Marta leaned against the door motionless, watching him through unblinking eyes.

"I don't know, Wally," she said. "You can't treat me like you do. You gotta promise me something better than what we got."

Wally glanced at Peter then back to the cement steps. "I know I do, Marta, I know. Peter here tells me I need to treat you the way I want to be treated and I haven't been. I was wrong and you deserve better. I'm sorry about that."

Peter's cell phone rang out from his jacket. He left the two of them and walked toward his truck. He didn't recognize the number.

"This is Assistant Pastor Denny Cummings from Glennwood Central Church, Mr. Bishop."

"How can I help you, Mr. Cummings?"

"I'm calling on behalf of Pastor Blackwell. We'd like to meet with you if possible to discuss some church related business. Are you available tomorrow afternoon about four?"

"I can make that work. Where are we meeting?"

"How about Andy's downtown."

"See you then."

Peter closed his cell phone and watched as Marta let Wally into the house. A toddler in light blue pajamas jumped up and down in the living room behind his parents.

Wally waved to Peter and closed the door.

Denny and Peter small talked until Roland Blackwell arrived at the table at 4:15. Peter sensed an odd tension in the air and watched Denny's manner chill a bit. After official introductions Peter waited to hear what the meeting was all about.

"I hear you have quite an operation going," Roland said with a curious smirk. "This home church deal. Living room fellowship."

"I wouldn't call it my deal, Mr. Blackwell," Peter said. "I'm just trying to be obedient to what God's put on my heart to do."

"Obedient to what God's put on your heart to do," Roland said in light mocking voice. "You know what I think you're doing? I think maybe you couldn't cut it as a real pastor and now you're moving in on another man's labor."

"And how would I do that?"

"Luring sheep away from an established fold to build your own, that's how."

"I've done nothing remotely close to that."

"Haven't you? How many families have left to follow this snake oil salesman, Denny?"

Denny was caught off guard. "Um...fourteen."

"Fourteen families. Children of God under my watchful eye and care."

Peter studied the red face preacher and asked calmly, "How have I lured someone away?"

"You beguiled them. Tricked them!" Roland pounded the table and rose to his feet. "You're a sheep stealer! If you have any decency in you, or claim to be a man of God, you'll return what's mine back to me. They're my sheep. My flock!"

Roland stomped his way out the front door leaving a wake of anger behind him.

Denny and Peter looked on till the glass front door closed.

"I should go," Denny said with uncertainty.

Peter watched Denny walk outside and out of view before noticing a bus boy at the counter.

"That guy's a Pastor?" he asked.

Peter nodded as the man rolled his eyes and carried a tub of dishes into the kitchen.

Valarie slid a piece of after dinner chocolate cheese cake onto the white porcelain dishes for her two favorite men.

"Sheep stealer," she said sitting back down on her chair. "I haven't heard that term in a while, but some preachers do that, you know.

Grow their church by going after saints in other churches."

"That's not what we're doing," Peter said.

"I'm well aware of that, but from his perspective we're attacking his livelihood. Families who regularly tithe are more rare than you'd think and preachers will do almost anything to keep them."

"It's as much about the dough as it is the soul," Tom said.

Peter indulged in his dessert. "I used to think we were all on the same team."

"Oh honey, far from it," Valarie said. "Some of the most bitter feuds weren't between the Hatfields and McCoys. It was between First Assembly and Greater Methodist. It'd be comical if it weren't true."

"So what do we do?"

"Jesus didn't change the Pharisees of his day, Peter, and we aren't going to change the Blackwells of ours. The road ahead might start getting bumpy, but I say we should keep doing what we're doing with perhaps one change."

"Which is..."

"We haven't been meeting for prayer like we used to. I know we've all been busy. But that which begins in prayer, must be maintained by prayer. Otherwise, we'll be trying to do spiritual things with carnal minds. I don't think that's wise."

There was a rift in the heavens high above Central Arizona. The number of people seeking God had reached a tipping point that tore into the unseen net of darkness that hung over Glennwood. The piercing prayers of the saints interceding for loved ones weakened the twisted fibers of apathy. On the ground, people became hungry to reestablish their relationship with the Lord. Neighbors once closed to anything about Jesus were now open to hear the truth from the scriptures. A fissure of light shot through the high places over the town, weakening the grip of principalities and powers that had been established for generations. Their screams sounded in the thunder of a violent overnight storm that yielded to a joyous sunrise the following morning.

Dark reinforcements were on their way.

Denny waited in line wondering how he would bring up the subject of a raise to Pastor Blackwell. He placed his order and moved forward watching the vibrating dots of rain water dance on the hood. The car was idling rough again.

He thought he'd try some place new for his one weekly indulgence. He hoped he made a good choice as he approached the window.

"Morning Denny," Peter said. "One double shot mocha, whip cream and an espresso bean"

Completely surprised Denny said, "Oh, you're *that* Bishop. I had no idea."

"I hope that's okay," Peter said, handing out a sixteen-ounce cup.

Denny paid for his drink remembering their meeting at the deli.

"Sorry for the other day with Pastor Blackwell," Denny said. "Even I was embarrassed. He's as well known for his antics as much as his oratory."

Peter looked to see if anyone else was in line. Then he wiped his hands and rested his arms on the counter.

"He didn't sound like he wanted to hear my side of things. Truth is, I taught a Bible study to some friends. They taught it to their friends and on and on. I've never even suggested that someone quit their church. As a matter of fact, I've discouraged some because they sounded angry and bitter. That's not right. If they're going to leave, fine, but do it right. Try to work things out the way Jesus taught us."

Denny set his cup in the broken but useable cup holder.

"I appreciate hearing that. Pastor Blackwell might be tougher to convince. It's hard on him to see so many supporters just leave. Must be nice for you and your staff, though."

"What do you mean?"

"You know, tithes and offerings."

Peter shook his head. "I don't collect tithes or offerings."

"You don't?" Denny looked confused. "Aren't you and your pastors supported from tithes?"

"Nope. You're looking at my livelihood right here. Coffee."

A van appeared in Denny's rear view mirror and he worked the car into gear.

"You've piqued my curiosity, Peter. I'd like to talk more – off the record of course."

Peter nodded. "Of course."

The Assistant Pastor stood in the silent foyer of the sanctuary contemplating Peter's attitude toward church. It seemed too simple, even naïve.

Denny looked up at the cathedral ceilings and to the eight-foot silk banner that hung from one of the beams. Roland's picture was on top with the words, "Pastor Blackwell Cares For You!" in bold italics underneath. Denny wondered if the good pastor was in a caring mood this morning.

"Denny!"

The voice seemed to come from the banner. Startled, Denny answered, "Coming Pastor," then quickly turned on his heels and marched down the hall.

"I'm sorry, I didn't know you were here."

"Sit down. We've got some intense planning to do here."

Denny sat in his usual meeting chair and turned over a long yellow page on his notepad. He watched his clean shaven boss as he paced.

"This radio deal is our top priority at the moment, Denny."

"You said they were auctioning off air time...?"

"Nathan Shay, the station owner, thinks a local, half hour church and community show would go over well here. He wants to try it out for six months and he's offering the host position to the church with the winning bid. It would mean weekly exposure and advertising for that church for at least six months."

Denny listened and scribbled notes as Pastor Blackwell continued.

"A little bird told me that at least two other churches have raised over three thousand dollars." Roland slammed his fist onto his desk, "That should be us, Denny!"

Pastor Blackwell sat down behind his desk and pulled some personal items out of the bottom drawer.

"I have to go to Flagstaff to take care of some things. While I'm gone I want you on the phone talking to every single member of this congregation about contributing to this radio ministry. If they don't have the cash, tell them we'll take a credit card payment."

Denny looked up wide eyed. "Credit cards, Pastor? You just finished a series on the stewardship telling people to cut up their credit cards."

"This is different! And don't question me or my methods, Denny," he said shooting out his finger. "I'm the pastor. I make the decisions here!"

Denny dropped his head and continued writing.

"When I get back, I want a report on how much we've raised. You probably won't be able to talk to some before they get home from work, but just keep trying."

Pastor Roland paused, looking over his desk. "Do you have anything else?"

Denny tried to say something but stopped.

"What man? Spit it out!"

"You said after a year that I could expect a raise," Denny said stammering. "It was a year three weeks ago and my family could really use the money. Jeremy needs braces."

"Who's Jeremy?" Roland asked.

"My son."

Roland got up and put on his sport coat.

"You want a raise, Denny? You get those lost families back here and get me on the radio. That's where your raise is!"

"Yes, Pastor."

Chapter Forty-Seven

Roland met with an old friend for lunch then finished his last errand at two-thirty. Another storm brewed overhead unleashing fat drops of rain over the sporty, silver frost exterior of his Lincoln LS. East bound traffic nearly stopped on Highway 40 as visibility dropped to a few feet under micro bursts of rain and hail. Once on I-17 headed south, Roland set the cruise control to 74 miles per hour and turned up the volume to savor the rich voice of Waylon Jennings as he sang about the love between a good hearted woman and a good timing man.

The minutes clicked by almost as fast as the miles did. Every mile was an elevation drop that reveled itself in fewer tall pines and warmer temperatures. Four lane highway became dotted on either side with shorter green brush and further away to the west were the red rocks near Sedona. He loved Arizona and only wished he were born in an era where men settled things on dusty streets with drawn pistols.

He turned the wipers on again noticing a pair of red emergency lights up ahead in the gray distance. He was glad his eight-cylinder horse was running in peak condition and pitied whoever was caught in this weather. He slowed as he neared the stranded motorist. Any fellow Lincoln driver was a worthy candidate for roadside assistance.

Roland pulled off the road ahead of the car, then back up to get close. The well-dressed driver ran to the passenger door holding his suit coat over his head. The man opened the door and dropped his brief case. Roland kept his chuckle to himself.

"Where you headed, friend," Roland asked.

"As close to the Phoenix airport as you'd care to go," the man said."

"Let's see how far that is. Hop in."

The man thanked him for stopping and seemed to relax more once he was settled.

"What do you plan to do about your car?" Roland asked.

"It's a rental," the man said. "The Diamond Club membership covers situations like this."

Roland remembered applying for a Diamond Club membership a

year earlier. He was declined.

"I take it you travel a lot."

"All the time," he said, watching the rain beat against the windshield. "Lately, I've been in the air more than on the ground." The man turned. "I truly don't mean to impose, but if I could somehow make it worth your while, is there any way you could take me straight to the airport?"

Roland looked at the asphalt ahead and the nearly full fuel gauge. Denny would still be making calls. He could call his wife and let her know he was being a good Samaritan. The ring on the stranger's hand was probably equal in value to his car...

"Think nothing of it. I'll have you at the terminal in no time."

"Thank you so much for training the new guy in your stand before sending him my way," Shannon said. "We've been so busy, there would've been no way."

"I'm glad the stands have identical equipment," Peter said. "How is he doing so far?"

Shannon kept her eyes on the ledger sheet in front of her. "He's doing really good. Funny too."

Peter saw a lightness to his manager. "Everything else going well?"

"Yep."

"Got your eye on one of the handy men working around here?"

She pursed her lips and looked up.

"That's it! Shannon's sweet on a handy man."

"I don't think that has anything to do with you or coffee," she said grinning.

"No, probably not," he said.

Then she looked off toward the home improvement warehouse.

"He is pretty handy though."

Roland maneuvered close to the sidewalk for departing flights. His passenger checked his watch. "You're a life saver, Roland."

"Just glad I could help a brother in need," Roland answered with genuine sincerity.

The man took his tickets out and closed his briefcase. After they exchanged business cards, he said, "I may be of some assistance with your radio ministry, Roland."

"Thank you."

"And let's keep in touch," he said handing him his business card. "I'll be curious to see how all this house church nonsense plays out. Unaccountable teachers like this Bishop fellow should be unmasked and put on public display as the phonies they are."

They shook hands before his passenger opened the door and walked through the traffic noise and slipped into the terminal.

Roland looked at his new friend's business card embossed with the unmistakable Great Assemblies logo and said to himself, "Thank you Evan."

On Monday, radio station owner Nathan Shay called Pastor Blackwell to inform him that a check had arrived from an anonymous contributor. Glennwood Central would be the host church for the new half hour program for the next six months.

Denny entered Peter's house late in the afternoon. "Thanks for letting me meet you here," he said. "The last thing I need is someone from the church seeing me talking with you, which would get back to Pastor Blackwell, and I don't need that kind of grief."

Peter served up a couple of Cokes in tall glasses with ice and the two ministers sat comfortably in the brightly lit, unfinished living room. They spoke openly of each of their pasts, how they arrived in Glennwood, family life and ministry. In mere minutes, Denny's perspective toward Peter changed from suspicion to admiration. Peter wasn't the devil Roland had venomously declared him to be. Rather, he was more like the brother he never had.

"I wish I were strong like you, Peter," Denny said. "I could never go out there on my own. Most everything you're doing and teaching is the exact opposite of how I've been taught. Speaking in tongues? That's complete taboo. We have baptisms when there's at least five people who want to get baptized since Pastor doesn't like to put on the robes and get wet. And he really doesn't want anyone teaching anything without his expressed permission. He's a bit of a micro-manager." Denny laughed.

"It's kind of funny really. My title is Assistant Pastor but I'm really more of a caddy or a janitor. I have about as much authority as the church secretary. Maybe less. Whenever Pastor Blackwell goes on vacation or is sick, he brings another pastor from out of town. I'll never be given the opportunity to preach or teach there."

"Does that seem right to you?" Peter asked.

"Right or not, it is what it is," Denny said. "This was the only open door in front of me, so I walked through it. It's how I serve the church, I guess. I'll keep at it until another door opens up."

Peter's respect for Denny grew by the minute as did an undercurrent of sadness. In his voice was the sound of a tender heart but his tone came from a broken spirit. He was a beaten man before even entering the ring.

Denny lifted up his glass and said, "Perhaps in another life we could have been friends."

Peter looked at the resigned man and replied, "What's wrong with this life?"

Denny pondered his words then shrugged.

"Why do we have to treat each other like enemies?" Peter asked. "Is God pleased with our imaginary fences and walls we've built up between each other?"

"I doubt it," Denny said.

"Jesus commanded us to preach the gospel, Denny. I've never once read where he commanded us to go build denominations to keep one group of believers separated from another group."

Denny stared into the air.

"Never looked at it that way before..."

The evening radio program was called *Afterglow* and aired for the first time on Sunday, March 17th. The live, thirty-minute show highlighted God in the local community and featured notable spiritual leaders and public figures from around central Arizona either in person or by phone. At times, listeners were invited to call in to the show as well.

Roland and the show's producer, Phil Dempsy, met on Friday's to review the list of topics and guests. Denny was present at the live shows to assist with anything from answering phones, to looking up scriptures to keeping Pastor Blackwell's coffee cup full.

From the beginning, *Afterglow* had a strong audience. The show was regularly advertised from the pulpit at Glennwood Central. Guest preachers would make announcements to their congregations when they would be featured as well.

Three weeks after the show began, Denny was glad to report that the decline in church attendance had leveled off and there had been an increase in visitors. Roland turned to his assistant and said, "Let's add a little more heat to the show, shall we?"

Later Sunday evening Roland approached the microphone toward the end of the next program and said, "Friends, we all hate to be duped don't we," he said with his signature elegance. "We think something is true blue, the real thing. Then later when it's too late, we realize we've been sold a counterfeit. It looked good. It sounded good. But it wasn't the tried and true. It wasn't the genuine article. Happens every day of the week, and in this case, twice on Sundays. Friends, as an ordained pastor with over twenty-five years of serving the children of God, I can tell you that there is a wayward movement taking hold here in Glennwood. A counterfeit church with no traceable roots, no stable location to, point to and no accountable leadership. Their past is questionable and their future is murky. I understand they conduct their secretive services in homes away from the light. Friends, be careful. Don't stray from the right way. Get on back to the fold where it's safe and under the watchful care of your pastor.

Thank you for listening. This is Pastor Roland Blackwell of Glennwood Central Church inviting you back next week to join us once more for Afterglow. Good night."

Church attendance was up the next Sunday.

Chapter Forty-Eight

Pastor Blackwell found inventive ways to steer conversations with guests and callers toward validating traditional church venues while undermining alternative gatherings.

"Even contractors have licenses," he railed, "If a minister isn't licensed by recognized church authorities is he really a minister of God?"

Roland found plenty of agreement within the pastoral community and frequently invited them to participate in the live discussions.

Afterglow provided long lasting fodder throughout Glennwood for days after each program. Pastor Roland Blackwell was becoming known as the "The Radio Preacher," a title he was most proud of.

"God is blessing my ministry," he said to Denny. "If we keep seeing more growth, you'll get your blessing too."

Denny was grateful to hear the words, but wondered exactly what "more growth" meant and how long it would take. The price of braces was about to increase and little Jeremy complained of discomfort in his gums.

Denny stopped by Peter's house again before going home. He asked Peter for prayer about his son's dental needs and let him know about the radio program in case he hadn't heard.

"He's got it in for you, Peter," he said. "I'm sorry to say he's like a bulldog that won't let go until someone wins. On the bright side, church attendance is up with new visitors. That's a good thing, I suppose."

They agreed in prayer together before Denny left. Then Peter turned his sofa into an altar and called upon his God.

The response from heaven was unmistakably clear.

"Have you listened to that Sunday radio show, Peter?" Tom asked during a meeting of the church leaders.

Peter shook his head. "I've heard of it, but haven't tuned in."

"It's not a bad show," Tom said, "They get some interesting guests on, but that Blackwell is one hundred and ten percent against anything out of mainstream religion. He's all but called us out by name as false prophets and devils."

Jack and Wendy nodded in agreement. "It's a popular show too," Jack said. "I hear people talking about it all the time at work."

"We should say something," Dean said with a determined look. "Call into the show or call the station. Put a muzzle on that guy."

"What do you think about that, Peter?" Valarie asked.

The group looked to Peter, who seemed lost in thought. The sudden silence pulled him back into the conversation.

"I prayed about this very thing the other night," Peter said. "And almost as loud as your voice or mine was the reply: *Be still. It's not your battle.* The Lord emphasized being still. Don't say anything. That's not easy. It's not what I want to do, but it's what I heard and what I'm asking all of us to do. Be still. Don't even say anything critical of Pastor Blackwell."

Peter adjusted in the chair and continued. "Then there was something else I felt in prayer. Pastor Blackwell's assistant, Denny Cummings, has a son who is experiencing pain in his mouth and needs braces. The family lives on a meager income and cannot afford anything dental right now even on a payment plan. I would like to share this need with the church and ask everyone to prayerfully consider helping this family."

"Why isn't their church helping the family?" Dean asked.

"I don't know why, Dean. I just know that Denny is a brother in the Lord and needs help. I would consider any financial help given to him as though it were helping a personal need of mine."

In every house the church gathered the coming week, the Cummings family was lifted up in prayer and offerings were collected. Later that week, Peter made some phone calls and got Denny's address and delivered a large, overstuffed envelope to the Cummings apartment.

Denny and his wife Leslie were still tearfully thanking God an hour after Peter left.

Afterglow was a local hit with the radio listeners. By the end of the third month, Pastor Blackwell "The Radio Preacher" was a household name. The radio staff hinted at extending the six-month agreement to Roland and Glennwood Central Church where even congregational losses had reversed. New visitors came every Sunday wanting to see the man behind the radio persona. Pastor Blackwell was only too eager to give them a show and a message they wouldn't forget.

Pastor Blackwell invested in another banner with his smiling face front and center before a golden microphone and the words, "The Radio Preacher Who Cares For Glennwood." The banner was placed in the sanctuary close to the front where everyone could be reminded about the broadcast. He regularly offered inside information on the show teasing the audience to tune in later that day.

Pastor Blackwell seized every opportunity to make biting remarks about those who'd left Glennwood Central in favor of less formal fellowship. "Meeting in homes?" he'd scoffed from the pulpit. "Would you want surgery performed in your house or in a hospital where it's sanitary? Surgery isn't for the do-it-yourselfer and neither is church, my friends! Sheep need shepherds who know how to properly feed and care for the flock. Not some rogue preacher with sweet sounding words who makes it up as he goes along!"

The growing crowds applauded, grateful to not be on the pointed end of the caring minister's barbs.

Tom and Valerie drove up to the window at nine Monday morning and ordered their usual beverages. Valarie leaned over her husband and said, "We're going down to Phoenix. Need us to pick up anything for you?"

"A woman," Peter said, handing out their drinks.

Tom asked, "One of those Victoria Secret women?"

"Tom!" Valarie said slapping his leg. "Peter, if I wasn't convinced God had a very special young lady picked out just for you, I'd look around for you."

"Okay," Peter said. "If you don't have a woman for me, how about an encouraging word?"

Valarie set her drink down. "You know, I did get a word this morning. I felt the Lord say, to 'pray for rain.' That's it. Nothing more or less, just 'pray for rain.'"

"Then I'll pray for rain and trust that the understanding will come later. On another note, has anyone asked you for copies of the Bible studies?"

"Not for a few weeks now," Valarie said. "Some folks might be making their own copies."

"Could be," Peter said. "I think some people are shaking in their faith because of Pastor Blackwell's weekly radio blasts. He's trying to make house church sound like a cult."

"Do you still feel to be quiet about it?" Tom asked.

"I do," Peter said. "In quietness and in confidence shall be your strength. Isaiah 30:15, or part of it anyway. So I'll be still and pray for rain."

Tom lowered his sunglasses and said, "And I'll keep an eye out for your woman."

Chapter Forty-Nine

"Friends, next week is going to be a show of shows. You must not miss next Sunday's program. Our guest is going to be a Christian filmmaker from Sedona whose mission is to create faith and family friendly movies. Remember stories with morals and Christian values? That's what he's working on and he'll be here to share his story with us. But this is the real reason why you must not miss next Sunday," The Radio Preacher moved closer to the microphone. "You've heard me talking about this underground, counterfeit church movement bouncing around from house to house like some fly-by-night operation. Some of you don't believe it. You think I'm making it up. But I'm not. I wouldn't conjure up something this diabolical. But you need proof. Next week, you'll get your proof. I'm going to name names. I'm going to expose the ring leader of this cult and some of you are going to flip your lid when you discover who it is. Thank you for listening. This is Pastor Roland Blackwell of Glennwood Central Church inviting you back next week to join us once more for an *Afterglow* you must not miss! Good night."

The answering machine had twenty-six messages on it when Peter arrived home late Sunday evening.

"Peter, what are you gonna do? Give us call."

"Peter are you home? Have you heard Pastor Blackwell's plans to destroy our church?"

"Hey Peter? Are you there? Peter?"

"Peter this is Keith. I know God's a big God and all, but this radio deal could really hurt business. Give me a call right away."

The only voice that carried an ounce of comfort came from Valarie. "We love you Peter. Keep praying for rain."

Peter took his tired body up the stairs and to a well-deserved hot shower. He could hear the phone ring. Another message left. Then another. The hot water rolled over his head and down his back.

"You tell me this isn't my battle Lord," He said. "But it sure feels like it. You said to be quiet and I have been. Valarie says to pray for rain, so I'm asking for rain. Lots and lots of wet rain, in Jesus name."

He tossed and turned all night until 4:30 in the morning when he got ready to open the stand. As the customers came to the window, he wondered how many listened to the radio on Sundays and how many might believe the distorted views of The Radio Preacher. He remembered Keith's words about reputations in small towns.

He wondered if there was life after bankruptcy.

Monday cartwheeled into Friday which turned into Sunday before Peter could comprehend. His stomach was bow tied into a singular knot and God seemed frustratingly quiet. If there was a glimmer of hope, it was that the beautiful July day would draw most of Glennwood out to the parks and surrounding forest for a day in the sunshine and away from the evening broadcast.

The morning gathering at the Warner's house turned into a prayer meeting.

Glennwood Central Church was near maximum capacity. Everyone sat on the edge of their seats hoping for some hint about who the soul-stealing villain in their midst might be. "Tune in later today church," he said with a wink. "I'll tell you all about this wolf in sheep's clothing..."

At 4:33 PM the radio station relayed a severe thunderstorm advisory for the entire the Yavapai County area including Prescott, Prescott Valley, Glennwood and Jerome. The recording from the National Weather Service had scarcely finished when sudden strong winds brought broiling charcoal clouds overhead. The angry darkness fought against the bright afternoon until day became night. Fierce bolts of lightning clawed through the air striking trees and buildings. In the drenched city limits driving joggers, bicyclers and families through the downpour and indoors where it was dry.

Doors slammed shut.

Windows closed tight.

Radio knobs turned.

At the station, a mile and a half from the violent storm center,

Phil Dempsy turned to Roland and said, "This is great!"

"Why's that?"

"The number of listeners just doubled."

Denny set a fresh cup of coffee and the show's outline in front of Pastor Blackwell. Then he knelt beside him and discreetly asked, "Is there any chance that we're being too hard on Bishop? We haven't really given him the opportunity to talk about what he's doing. Maybe's he not the bad guy you're making him out to be."

Roland turned abruptly. "What in God's name has gotten into you, Denny? Whose side are you on here?" Roland put on his headphones. "This is why you'll never pastor Denny. You haven't got a spine. Now have a seat. I've got a show to do."

The Christian filmmaker entered through the back door completely drenched. Denny took the man's soaked, black leather jacket and got him situated across from Roland. Then Denny moved to his side of the table and braced for the verbal lynching of his new friend Peter Bishop.

Most of Glennwood and the surrounding towns tuned in with great interest as The Radio Preacher interviewed John Petersen who, described his plans to start a movie community in Arizona starting with his current project. Roland enjoyed his guest's sense of humor and clever interaction so much, he invited him to stay for the whole show. John happily agreed.

A dozen people listened to the broadcast in Tom and Valarie's living room. Peter sat close to Valarie trying to keep the rumblings from his empty stomach to himself.

Roland looked at his guest. "John, I can tell you're a respectable young man. A professional with integrity, but I'll bet you've seen plenty of phonies in your line of work."

"Unfortunately, every day."

"Ever run into people who claim to be Christian, but really aren't?"

"All the time, Pastor."

"It's a shame isn't it?" Roland said shaking his head. "It's a shame to put your trust in someone who seems be the real deal, but isn't."

"That's probably why we should put our trust in the Lord and not in man."

Roland nodded. "Good point, John. But here in Glennwood we've had something going on that demands confrontation. Now, Lord knows I hate to be the one to have to do this, but I told the audience last week that I was going to expose a fraud. A man who purports to be a pastor is running some kind of underground church."

"Wow! Sounds like an interesting plot to a movie."

Roland nodded with glee. "Wait till you hear how this plot thickens. This man has used his trickery and false doctrines to lure good saints away from other churches to build his own church. And it's high time everyone knew who this deceiver is. His name is Peter Bishop. He runs a coffee drive-through by day, but he's something entirely different by night. He's the one who's been undermining our spiritual community."

Roland looked pleased with himself. Then he turned to his guest. "There probably is a movie in there somewhere, right John?"

"You bet there is, Pastor Blackwell," John said. "And a really great movie has plot twist no one saw coming. You ready for it?"

"Give it to me!"

"I know Peter Bishop. I went to Bible school with Peter Bishop. I got to graduate with my class because he loaned me the money for my license. Peter Bishop is probably the most Christ-like man I've ever met in my life."

Denny jumped up from his chair. He stood next to John, grabbed the microphone and said, "That is absolutely right, John. Folks, this is Denny Cummings from Glennwood Central Church, and I have to second everything John just said about Peter Bishop. I've only known Peter a few months but in that time he's shown me and my family more compassion than some pastors I know. Our son needed braces, but there was no way we could afford it. I only mentioned it to Peter as a prayer request in passing. But a few days later, Peter brought us a huge envelope full of money he raised from his church. It covered the entire bill and we even had some left over to put toward car repairs. If that isn't the way a church is supposed to work, I don't know what is."

Denny sat back down and looked at Roland. "Enough spine for you now Pastor?"

Roland sat in complete ashen faced astonishment.

John swung the microphone back toward him and said, "Pastor Blackwell, you were asking me if I run into phonies in my line of work. Yes, I do. I'm looking at one right now. I think it's disgraceful that you'd try to ruin a good man's reputation like this."

John looked over to Denny and asked, "You think Peter's listening?"

"He just might be," Denny said.

"If you're out there listening, Peter, it's J.T! Seems like God had other plans for both of us after Bible school, buddy. So call the station or something. We've got some catching up to do!"

Roland Blackwell threw his headphones down and stormed out of the building. Phil watched his departure from the other side of the glass and motioned to Denny to go a commercial break. After a brief announcement and the button push, the live portion of *Afterglow* was over for the day.

J.T. Peterson left the building after Peter called in to the station. Denny collected his notes and Pastor Blackwell's things and went in to the producer's booth.

"Now that was an interesting show." Phil said.

"You can say that again," Denny said, picking up his car keys. "Guess I'll be looking for a new job now."

"That's probably a safe bet from the looks of things. I've been watching how you operate, Denny, and I like what I've seen. How about starting that job search right here?"

Chapter Fifty

Both coffee stands were extra busy on Monday. Keith Roman pulled up to Peter's window and ordered half a dozen black coffees.

"I shouldn't have freaked out earlier, Peter. Sorry about that. My faith isn't all there when it should be."

"You weren't the only one freaking out, Keith," Peter said. "I'm just glad things worked out the way they did. I always wondered if I'd run in to J.T. again. Sounds like God had other plans for several us from my class."

Keith dug into a box in the passenger seat next to him. He held up a clear blue plastic candle toy and a rubber bicycle grip and said, "Not to change the subject, but could you use any of these? I've got a friend who pawned a bunch of these off on me."

Peter looked at the items. "Don't need any grips like that," he said. Then he picked up the blue candle and pressed the small button at the base. The light was piercing even in the morning sun.

"Wow that's bright for such a small light."

"Probably why they didn't sell around Christmas. Overpowering. Might be good in your car for roadside emergencies."

Peter handed the light back to Keith. "Other than that I can't think of any immediate use myself."

"No problem. But we do need to talk about our next drive-through. I have a couple of places in mind."

Peter waved his business partner on and reached for his buzzing cell phone.

"What did you do over the weekend," Shannon asked. "Every other customer is asking to talk with Peter Bishop. Did you save a baby from a burning building or something?"

"No, I think someone mentioned my name on the radio yesterday. Just some unexpected publicity."

"Keep it up. Got 'em lined up nice and deep here."

"Here too. Talk with you later."

Denny Cummings took over as host of *Afterglow* the following Sunday and continued the remaining two months allotted to Glennwood Central Church. Peter was a frequent guest who spoke of church beyond denominations and buildings. When a caller had a question, he did his best to answer from the open pages of his King James Version Bible in front of him. Some callers were encouraging and glad to hear of Peter's perspective on church. Others, mostly local pastors, were critical and argumentative. Peter challenged either type of caller to search the scriptures for themselves.

The number of home Bible studies being taught soared all over Glennwood. Some excited souls would even meet over the phone week after week with friends and family in different parts of the country. *House* or *home church* was a hot topic for months in Glennwood, Arizona as a direct result of the verbal attacks from The Radio Preacher whose air time was funded by a check from Great Assemblies.

The third coffee stand opened on the west side of Glennwood in early November. In the same month, Peter, Tom and Valarie met with four more couples who desired to host church groups in their homes. There were now twenty-two houses where people regularly met, facilitated by nine stable leaders. The average size per house group went from seven in mid-July to nine by Thanksgiving.

As the year drew to a close, Peter's thoughts were frequently caught away by the same familiar voice that spoke to him in his childhood apartment, on a dusty hill in Germany and while watching different ones carry out their duties in an expanding coffeehouse south in the valley. The voice, as light as a whisper simply said, "Let go."

Peter asked for all the church leaders to meet at Tom and Valarie's house on the first Sunday evening of the new year. The snow laden pines outside were darkening silhouettes when Peter stood next to the glowing fireplace and addressed the four couples who sat comfortably in the living room.

"This has been an incredible journey," he said, looking at his friends whose faces held the glow from the fire light."

"And it's only beginning," Jack said enthusiastically."

"Well put, Jack. It's only beginning. I believe it's time for more beginnings."

Peter looked carefully at Valarie who appeared as intrigued as everyone else. He wasn't sure if it that was a good sign or not. He'd often found her to be a comforting second witness on direction and decisions.

"After Jesus spent a few years with his disciples, he trusted them and turned them loose to preach his gospel. The Book of Acts tells us how and what they preached. Paul the apostle taught men like Titus and Timothy to not only preach but to teach others to teach. Then he instructed them to ordain worthy men to be elders in every city."

Peter stopped to make sure his spirit wasn't moving outside of the Word.

"For these many months, you have given me your trust, for which I am thankful. Now it's time for me to return that trust. As far as I'm concerned, you're all worthy elders. You're all able to lead others, teach sound doctrine and you're not doing any of this for money. Up to now you've been my assistants and small group leaders. I believe it's time for me to follow the Lord and ordain you all as elders. You'll no longer be my assistants; you'll be my peers."

The crackling of the fire was the only sound in the room as Peter's words sunk into his listeners. Dean's wife Samantha looked at her husband quizzically then asked, "Then if we're all peers, who's the pastor?"

Peter looked at Samantha and smiled. "Are you really asking who the leader is?"

Dean nodded as Samantha replied, "Yeah, I guess that is what I mean."

Peter saw the anticipation on each face. "Whose church is it? Mine? Yours?"

"Christ is head of the church," Tom said.

Peter smiled and nodded toward Tom. "That's right. Christ is the head. It's *his* church and all of us are members in his church.

253

Everything I've studied about biblical church leadership revolves around elders – plural not singular – and not pastors specifically. Everyone here in front of me is an elder, yet I see a prophet, a worker of miracles, at least one teacher, an evangelist or two and perhaps a pastor. Our spiritual gifts don't make us elders or leaders; our maturity and experience in the Word does."

Peter pulled a wooden chair over and sat down. "The Lord has been talking to me about the next step. Basically, it's time for me to step aside so you can grow. I wasn't sure how exactly that would take place until I got a phone call recently. You all might remember J.T. from the radio program sometime back. Well, he's asked me to come over to Sedona to show his group of filmmakers what we've been doing here. Keith Roman, my business partner, has family in Sedona and wants to go with me. So I'm proposing that we work together to raise up more elders who will take on more responsibility here. It's time to pass on to you the baton that was handed to me."

Chapter Fifty-One

For several days in a row, Peter worked with each couple to find others with a heart to serve. Then he worked with them individually to make sure they were sound in the Word. After three weeks and meetings almost every day, Peter felt it was time to start heading to Sedona.

"Let's plan for us all to get together again the first of March and see how things are going," Peter said to the wide eyed group of new elders. "I'm sure we'll have plenty to talk about, and I'll probably have as many questions and you will!"

The two local missionaries traveled to Sedona twice a week to preach the Word using the same Bible studies that were used in Glennwood. The results were the same as well. People who received the word were baptized in the name of Jesus, and many were filled with the Holy Ghost when Peter and Keith prayed for them.

The younger group seemed more open to churches meeting in houses then many in Glennwood were at first. One house meeting grew to three with J.T. taking the lead in the third house. Bible study groups regularly throughout the week in coffee houses and sandwich shops. Keith started a Bible study with his sister, Mary. She later hosted a church in her home.

In March, according to schedule, all the elders in Glennwood met together at the Warner's house. For four hours, Peter listened to each one tell of what was happening in each house meeting. The praises and problems, the situations, and more importantly, the solutions. Peter listened with joy as he heard how people were growing and how they were turning to the scriptures for answers. There was one interesting challenge that didn't have a chapter and verse answer, however.

"Because of a town ordinance we aren't allowed to put up any signs in front of our house telling people where to meet," Dean said. "Since we're trying to get people into Bible studies first, we may not want to do that anyway."

Different ones expressed running in to the same problem, though more people had cell phones and called if they got lost.

"I've got an idea," Keith said as he left the room and went outside. He returned from his truck with a box and set it on the table. He reached inside and pulled out the clear blue battery-operated candle lights he showed Peter at the drive-through.

He clicked the button and said, "How about that?"

Everyone looked away from the piercing light at first.

"Just stick that in your front window," he said with a smile. "It's so bright, if people can't find you, they shouldn't be driving!"

Peter laughed. "I think you finally found a use for those things."

"You're telling me!" he said. "They've been bouncing around in my truck since I showed you."

Everyone took a few lights and the box was empty.

The Peter stood up and said, "After hearing all the great reports from everyone, I think we're headed in the right direction. I also think it's time we call these small groups what they really are according to the Bible. These are churches. They're churches because believers purposely gather together in the name of the Lord to worship him and to edify one another. From here on out, let us love God and one another, preach the word, edify the church, and teach others to teach."

Keith lifted his coffee cup and said, "Here, here!"

Everyone else followed suit raising cups and glasses and shouts of praise to God.

Michael and Daylene drove up on a Thursday and spent most of the day with Tom and Valarie. Peter joined them for dinner at The Lariat restaurant after he was done resupplying all three coffee stands.

They left the restaurant shortly before eight and Peter followed the other car back to Tom and Valarie's house for dessert.

Immediately after crossing the Mirror Lake Bridge, Peter saw Tom's car pull sharply over to the side of the road. Peter pulled in behind wondering what was wrong. Daylene and Valarie got out of the car followed by their husbands.

Peter got out and approached Tom. "What's up?"

"You know these women, Peter," he said. "They'll stop for shoes or garage sales or no reason at all."

"Peter! Come quick!" Valarie called.

Peter walked briskly to where the women stood looking on as the soft twilight sky to the west yielded to the darkness to the north over Glennwood. Street lights and house lamps glowed brightly against the blackened backdrop of pine trees and rounded hills surrounding the peaceful town.

"Okay, what are we looking at?" Peter asked.

Valarie turned to Daylene. "Anything look familiar?"

Daylene started to shake her head when Tom said, "Boy those little candle lights Keith handed out are crazy bright."

Daylene's eyes widened. "The lights! Those are the same lights I saw floating around Peter when I was taking pictures at the house!"

Valarie nodded. "The same lights I saw when I first met him."

"What are they?" Daylene asked.

"Those are little candle lights showing where churches meet," Valarie said.

"We've seen a few lights on every evening when we cross the bridge. By my count, I see nine blue lights with that beautiful gold glow."

The prophetess turned to Peter. "You wanted to know what everything meant, but how could I explain what I couldn't see myself? It's more clear now."

"Thou art Peter. And from you will come many churches."

Epilogue

Katie Anna Rogers graduated from high school and spent the summer with Peter working in the original Bishop's Coffee Company drive-through. The evening before she left for Flagstaff to pursue a degree in graphic design, she presented him with a box covered with a light blue blanket.

"You need a friend, Uncle Peter," she said. "I think you're alone too much."

"I have friends," he protested.

"Not like this."

Peter lifted the blanket to see a sleeping ball of dark fur. He couldn't keep from smiling as he recounted the first time he met the little girl who became the lively brunette standing before him.

He gently lifted the snoozing feline out of the box and held him against his chest. "Did you name him or her?"

"It's a him, and no. You should name him," Katie said, running her fingers over his fuzzy back.

"Well, he's dark... So, In the tradition of other family pet names...how about Merlot?"

"Merlot the cat. Sounds good. I'll have to come down every once in a while to check up on you both."

"You'd better."

Katie's visits were sprinkled out over the holidays and summers. Peter always made time for her between four coffee stands, regular interaction with the church in Tom and Valarie's house and a new Bible study or two.

The next fall, Peter carved out time in his schedule to finally get his own house finished. He got new carpet for the living room and installed decorative light fixtures. Later, Mick and some others stopped by off and on to help with sheet rock or painting.

One evening, Mick brought a stunningly attractive young lady with him to help paint. Mick introduced her, then later pulled Peter aside and said, "You'll never guess who that is."

"You told me here name is Molly. Wouldn't 'Molly' be a good guess?"

"That's not what I meant," Mick chuckled. "Remember me telling you about a girl I used to shoot who hated men? That's her. Out of the blue she called me last week and we got together. She's made a total turn around. Says the Lord is in her life now and for some reason she seems sweet on me."

"She's gorgeous, Mick. If the Lord is in her life, then she's pretty on the inside too. I'm happy for you."

"Thanks, Bro."

After the living room was finished, Peter plotted the next sequence of updates that would include major work in the kitchen, dining room and the bedroom that Katie used when she stayed with him.

He was moving a box of clothes that was never unpacked when he heard something small and metallic hit the unfinished wood floor. The shiny object rolled to a stop against the wall. He set the box down and picked up the gold band along with all the memories attached to it. The house was quiet all around him as he considered his reflection looking back at him. He wondered if the young girl with bouncy chestnut hair married again. Audrey was still on the coast. Shannon married her handy man the summer before. Now Mick was dating a former calendar girl.

Love. Close enough to touch, but just out of reach.

The downstairs phone pulled Peter back into his currently unfinished world. He dropped the ring into a jar holding pens and picked up the receiver.

"Hello?"

"How's Merlot and my favorite uncle?"

"We're both missing our favorite niece," Peter said, leaning against the bar. "I've got the house almost livable for you. When you coming down again?"

"Funny you should ask," Katie said. "That's what I want to talk about."

"Let's do it! Come see me."

"Awesome!" Katie cheered. "Is it okay if I bring a friend?"

About the Author

Patrick Sipperly began writing after many years as a minister and video producer. He wrote *Snowed Inn*, a romantic comedy screenplay, and co-authored *Time Out On A Roller Coaster*, a book of short stories, with Linda Boulanger in 2009. *Parting Ways* is the beginning of a trilogy.

Patrick lives in beautiful Arizona with his lovely wife Charla.

Www.PatrickSipperly.com
www.ChristianHomeChurch.com
www.ArizonaVideoCompany.com

www.ingramcontent.com/pod-product-compliance
Lightning Source LLC
Chambersburg PA
CBHW070801200626
46811CB00023B/316